WAR OF THE DALEKS

JOHN PEEL

GW00536759

BBC BOOKS

Published by BBC Books,
an imprint of BBC Worldwide Publishing
BBC Worldwide Ltd, Woodlands, 80 Wood Lane,
London W12 0TT

First published 1997
ISBN 0 563 40571 6
Imaging by Black Sheep, copyright © BBC 1997

Printed and bound in Great Britain by Mackays of Chatham
Cover printed by Belmont Press Ltd, Northampton

For Terry Nation.
Thanks for everything

PROLOGUE: THAL SPACE

'Exterminate! Exterminate!'

Ayaka licked her lips, held her finger steady on the trigger and watched as her in-helmet display began to relay figures to her about the wave of Daleks moving across the plain towards the Thal encampment. She didn't really need to know that there were exactly six hundred and thirty-eight Daleks advancing, or that they were approaching at a rate of twelve units per minute. She could see them, feel the ground rumbling, and hear their mechanical war cry.

She could also feel the cold trickle of sweat down her spine. One thing that never changed in their war with the Daleks was the chill of fear that always kicked in when she first saw those ominous metallic war machines. She knew she should get over this instinctive fear; after all, she was a veteran of thirty-two battles now. She was twenty-six years old, and still alive. That made her a veteran. Most of her squad was at least four years younger, the only exception, of course, being Delani, their commander. She knew she should be over being terrified of the Daleks by now.

And she knew she never would be.

'Steady,' Delani's voice said in her ear, speaking to the whole squad. 'They're too far away for a good lock yet. Let them come closer.' He didn't sound afraid, he sounded eager, which he no doubt was. Killing Daleks was his sole purpose in life.

Let them get closer... Ayaka shuddered again, watching as the Daleks trundled over the uneven ground, still chanting. She shut off her external sound, not wanting to hear their voices any more. And there wouldn't be anything worth listening to out there once the battle began anyway. She licked her lips again, and wriggled inside her suit. Battle armour was necessary, of course, but never comfortable. There were always edges somewhere that wanted to worm their way under your skin.

Cathbad lay next to her, and he glanced at her. She could see his face through his helmet, and he gave her a nervous smile. This was only his fourth battle. He was all of twenty-two, and fourth in command of the unit. She managed a watery smile back. It probably didn't reassure him. It sure as hell didn't reassure her. She tried not to think that they were statistically bound to lose at least two-thirds of the squad in this fight. Since most of them were in their first fight, those were the likeliest casualties. Ayaka made it a habit never to get to know anyone in her squad until they'd been through three battles. It was too hard losing friends as it was.

And, of course, today could be the day when her own luck ran out...

She tried not to think about that. Dying here, on this barely surveyed world on the edge of Thal space... She hadn't even heard about the planet until two days ago, when the orders to defend it had come through. Terakis. Smallish world, near normal gravity. It wasn't until the ship was on the way down that Ayaka discovered there was a native race here. She had no idea what they were like, or how advanced they were. It didn't matter to the Daleks, of course. Whatever the natives were, they would be good only for slaves or target practice. The Daleks had no interest in anything else.

Then the Daleks opened fire. They were still out of range, but it didn't matter to them. A shimmering wall of electronic disruption sprang up before their advancing numbers. Ayaka didn't know whether this was meant to intimidate their foes, or whether the Daleks simply couldn't wait to begin their killing. Either way, it meant the battle was starting, and her fear faded away. Now she had to concentrate on survival.

'Steady,' Delani called again. 'Don't let them rattle you. Wait for the command to fire.'

Ayaka waited with all the patience she could muster. Several bushes about forty units away exploded into flames as they were raked by Dalek fire. That meant the Daleks would be in range in about three minutes...

Sweat trickled down her back, and she wished there was some way to scratch. She'd have to ignore it until the battle was over. Then she'd be able to scratch herself raw if she wanted to – or else she'd be dead. Either way, the problem would be solved.

The helmet display was starting to identify individual targets for her now. She could see the grey shapes clearly, their energy weapons humming as they moved forward. The worst thing about Daleks was that they had no external features to show you what they were thinking. Of course, since 'exterminate' pretty much summed up their entire philosophy, you didn't need to speculate too hard. But to see eyes, or a face, one that could show joy, hatred, or fear – that would help. The plain grey finish to their travel machines gave away nothing.

'On my word,' Delani said softly, excitedly. Ayaka's helmet told her the Daleks were sixteen units away, almost in range. Her rifle was powered, and she was primed. Her heart beat faster, and she could feel the adrenalin surge kicking in.

'Fire!'

She acquired her first target, and tapped her trigger. The rifle kicked, and the smart grenade whirled through the air.

It exploded about a unit from the Dalek, caught in the withering electronic fire laid down by their foes. Flashes along the line showed where similar efforts by her squad had also failed to penetrate. There were brief gouts of flame as Daleks were hit and erupted, but Ayaka ignored that, pumping further shots at the Dalek she'd sighted on. The third one penetrated the defensive fire, and the grenade sliced the top of the Dalek off. Green ooze flecked over the casing, which stopped dead, blazing.

Ayaka targeted her next victim, and fired again.

All around her, the squad was blazing at the line of advancing Daleks. She was dimly aware that Daleks were exploding, and then she heard the first scream of one of her own, as the Dalek line of fire reached the Thals.

Electronic death splashed harmlessly off her hardened armour. It was built so that it could withstand direct fire, but, if three or more Daleks concentrated their blasts on one target, even the armour couldn't withstand that kind of attack for very long. She pumped fresh shells into her rifle, and blew her attacker to hell and back.

Nothing was real for her now other than her rifle getting hot from the recoil, the blast of the shells as they launched, and watching for each Dalek to explode before moving on to her next victim. More Thals were dying about her. She could hear screams through her radio, before the victims' suits stopped transmitting. There was no way to tell how many had perished, or who they were. Cathbad was beside her still, firing away. His face was strained and pale as he concentrated on dealing death while cheating it himself.

The battle computer was having trouble tallying the death count of the Daleks. Smoke from blazing machines wafted across the battle line, making it hard to see physically.

Without the targeting radar in her suit, she'd hardly know where to fire. The radar locked on for her, giving her direction and range, and she fired and fired again. According to the display, over half the attackers were now destroyed.

And then a huge, silent explosion churned the ground about twenty units to her right. She felt the shockwave from the blast, but heard nothing with her external audio off.

'Special Weapons Daleks!' Delani called. 'They're moving in behind the survivors. Ayaka, Cathbad, Dyoni – flank right, to the ridge. Take them out with missiles.'

'Acknowledged,' Ayaka replied, hearing Cathbad and Dyoni echo her voice. She wondered for a second what had happened to the three men stationed there for precisely this eventuality, but dismissed the thought. She already knew.

Electronic fire blazed about the three of them as they leapt to their feet and sprinted towards the ridge. The Daleks were starting to lock in on them. Ayaka's helmet wasn't quite screaming at her that she was in trouble, but it was getting quite shrill about it. That meant at least two Daleks had a lock on her. She didn't dare pause to fire back, since that would make her a standing target, so she simply launched a few mines in the right direction, praying for luck.

And it held. The suit informed her that only one Dalek was now still shooting at her. She could afford to ignore that.

The missile launcher loomed through the smoke, and she saw that the three soldiers there were dead. Two had been killed by Dalek guns, the third decapitated by some blast. She avoided looking at his or her remains, pushing them aside to slip into the firing seat. Cathbad took targeting, and Dyoni loaded.

Ayaka could see nothing in the smoke and flames, but the computer-controlled radar could. Cathbad steered the cannon, and as soon as a target was acquired, Ayaka fired. The gun kicked back hard, rattling her around in her armour. And even she could see the great ball of fire that arose as the Special Weapons Dalek exploded.

But there was no time to rest or celebrate. Dyoni loaded, Cathbad aimed, and she fired. Again and again.

'Striders!' Delani called. 'Pull back, all units.'

Striders! Just how many troops had the Daleks committed to this fight, anyway? She hadn't seen Striders for the last three battles. This had to be a serious offensive, then, not just some simple backwater skirmish.

'Try to target them,' she ordered Cathbad.

'Negative!' Delani's voice cut in. 'Ayaka, your orders are to fall back immediately.'

'Damn,' she hissed, but knew better than to disobey. She jumped from the firing seat, Dyoni and Cathbad close behind her, and they moved back. As they did, the missile launcher exploded. The blast threw her, face down, into the mud, pressing her there with a fiery hand.

For a moment, she was stunned. The Special Weapons Daleks must have fired at the launcher and destroyed it. If she had still been in there... Fire rained down around her as she struggled back to her feet. Cathbad was already up and helping Dyoni. Ayaka could see a slight crack in Dyoni's armour.

'Dyoni,' she ordered, 'pull completely back. You've got a fracture.'

'I'm OK,' the other woman insisted.

'Pull back!' Ayaka snarled. If the Daleks targeted her now, her armour would split. 'Get repairs. Move!'

'Affirmative.' Dyoni's jets kicked in, and she flew towards the transports at low level.

6

Ayaka ignored her now. She and Cathbad scurried back to rejoin Delani and the others at the prearranged rendezvous. Dalek fire still burst all about them, but it was having very little effect at this range. On the other hand, once the Striders arrived, they would be in deep trouble.

'I've called for tactical support,' Delani told her on a secured channel. 'Air strike is on the way.'

'Why aren't they here already?' she demanded. 'They must have known the battle's begun.'

'They know.' He looked at her, his eyes bright. 'This is just one edge of the battle, Ayaka,' he explained. 'There are eighteen other squads down here, all under heavy fire.'

Eighteen others! Ayaka was astonished. She'd never been on an operation with more than three other squads before. 'Such a concentration of our forces...' she began. 'The Daleks are bound to realise...'

'That Terakis is a real prize,' he finished for her, with a nod. 'Yes. This could be one of the decisive battles for our people. Let's try to survive it, so we can join the celebrations, shall we?' He grinned. 'Here they come.'

Ayaka didn't know whether he was referring to the Daleks or air strike for a second, and then the smoke shifted slightly. Through the explosions that rocked the world, she could see the Striders.

These were at least ten times the size of a normal Dalek, but lacking the usual base. In its place were the eight long, flexible legs that carried them over the terrain. Around them, like smaller cousins, scurried the Spider Daleks. These were only slightly larger than the regular warriors, but with a similar eight-legged arrangement.

'What museum did they find them in?' Cathbad asked. 'I thought they'd abandoned the Spiders centuries ago!'

'On uneven terrain, they're more flexible than the regulars,' Ayaka replied. Even with their hover-capability, regular Daleks had trouble on less-than-even ground. The Spiders weren't so limited – they could clamber about. And the Striders could go almost anywhere they wanted to. Their bulbous bodies housed four cannons, firing ahead and below as they moved. There was no real way for the squads to take out a single Strider, let alone the ten that her helmet told her were here.

Then she saw trails of fire in the air, and realised that the promised air support had arrived. Eight fighters whipped overhead, streaking towards the Striders, and releasing their missiles. The Striders relocked their weapons, spitting fire and destruction at the Thal fighters.

Everything exploded then, and Ayaka's helmet filters darkened her visor. When it cleared, she saw that three of the fighters were down, blazing globules of wreckage on the shattered earth. And four of the Striders had been taken out. Two were locked in position where they stood, blazing away. The other two had collapsed, and exploded.

Six were still advancing.

The first of the Spider Daleks was in range now, and Delani gave the order to open fire. Ayaka raised her rifle, and targeted the closest Spider. Though they wore tougher armour than a regular Dalek, their joints made them more vulnerable. She pumped grenades, and took out two joints – causing her target to list – but it kept firing back at her. Then a third and finally a fourth leg all on the same side. The Dalek crashed down, scrabbling for a way to rise again. She finished it with a shot to the dome that spread metal, electronics and green fluid over the rocks.

Then she started over again with the next.

'Don't they ever stop?' Cathbad complained, as he kept up continual fire beside her.

'Not while there are any left,' she grunted, concentrating on her shots. She tried to avoid looking at the remaining Striders as they moved towards their position.

The fighters swung around for a second pass, their missiles blazing across the battlefield. Strider fire strobed across their sleek bodies, and two more exploded and crashed. Three more Striders stumbled, exploding into fireballs.

The final three Striders were now virtually upon them, their guns blazing, tearing up soldiers and ground indiscriminately.

'Fall back!' Delani called, rather belatedly to Ayaka's mind. Still, she took out one last Spider, enjoying seeing it stumble and burn, and then ran after Cathbad as the Striders approached. Fire scorched the ground about them as they dodged and twisted. She fired off two more mines, even though she knew they wouldn't be effective against their targets.

Was this the end?

Then two gravity tanks hurtled past, almost blowing Ayaka over in their wake. Their turrets opened continuous fire on the three Striders, hammering long and hard. The Striders ignored the foot soldiers now, concentrating on the more deadly tanks. Ayaka stumbled along, and saw that another tank was waiting for them. The remnants of the squad were hitching a ride on the outside.

'Transport,' Delani reported. 'We're falling back to the mountains. The Daleks won't have such a simple time of it there.'

'This was simple?' Ayaka growled, clamping her foot in a

restraint and her hand about a stanchion.

'Comparatively,' he answered. 'They're taking a beating.'

'In case you hadn't noticed,' she told him, 'so are we.'

'That's only to be expected.'

'Yes,' she agreed silently. 'But it doesn't mean I like it.' She and Cathbad had been the last, and the tank lifted off, shaking slightly with all their weight, and then set off away from the battle zone.

Ayaka looked back, her helmet doing its best to make sense of what she was seeing. One of the Striders erupted as a clean shot ripped open its belly. The fuel cells went up, turning it into a miniature sun. Then a tremendous explosion lit the ground as one of the tanks was finished. The second tank whirled, turret blazing continuously, and the penultimate Strider faltered and then fell, spouting fire and metal.

The final Strider was on top of the last tank, battering, pounding down with electronic fire. The tank surged forward, slamming into one of the great legs, and then mushroomed into a huge fireball that enveloped the Strider, too. The pilot had detonated the tank's remaining ammunition, taking the Strider with it.

Now only the warrior Daleks and Spider Daleks were left, following the transport. They seemed determined to allow no survivors. This was one of the longest and worst battles Ayaka had ever been in. Most lasted no more than fifteen minutes, and this had been playing for almost twice that. She was exhausted, emotionally drained. And there was no end in sight yet. She saw Cathbad's face through his helmet, just as tired as she must look. She wanted to give him an encouraging smile, but couldn't get the right muscles to work.

A few minutes later, the transport mounted a ridge of rocks, and drew up to a barricade that had been raised. There were other Thals there, survivors of some of the other squads. They helped Delani's troops to safety, handing out whatever grenades and mines they could spare. Ayaka glanced around, seeing that there were no more than about a hundred of them. One was Dyoni, her armour still cracked. She'd not been able to get restored.

Clearly, they were losing this battle.

'Any chance of a pull-out?' she asked Delani on their private channel.

'We're not finished yet,' he told her, grinning – almost cheerfully, it seemed to her. 'We've still got a trick or two to play. Let's just wait and see what happens, shall we?'

'What other choice do we have?' she grunted, and turned her attention back to the plains they had just left. The transport had vanished, probably going after some more survivors. There were pitifully few of them, but she'd weep later. If she survived.

Cathbad tapped her shoulder, and then gestured backward. Puzzled, she looked around, and gasped in shock.

She'd known the planet was inhabited, but she hadn't realised how close they had come to one of the native settlements. The ridge they were on backed towards a river, some twenty units below them. And on the other side of the river was an encampment. It looked pretty crude – wooden buildings, some canoes in the river, and large communal cooking fires. There were only a couple of the natives in view, and her helmet automatically focused on them.

They were tall, slender, and a rich brown in colour. They had large eyes, slits for mouths, and four arms. They were all carrying spears and some kind of bows. Hunter-gatherers, she realised. Barely on the first steps towards civilisation. But intelligent and aware. And undoubtedly very, very frightened. They could have no possible conception of what was happening to their planet.

Ayaka almost wept for them. If the Daleks wiped out the squads – and this looked very likely – then the settlement would be next.

'Poor wretches,' Cathbad muttered. 'The gods are making war, eh?'

'That's probably what they think, yes,' she agreed. 'It's world's end.'

'Here they come,' Dyoni called, levering herself into position on the barricade.

Ayaka ignored the natives, and turned back to the fight.

There should have been about a hundred Daleks, the ones who had been chasing the remnants of her squad. But they'd obviously joined up with the forces that had faced the other squads. There were probably a thousand of them on the plain, heading deliberately for the barrier. Spiders tapped their way forward. Warrior Daleks rumbled along. Many were damaged, but none were slowed.

Unless Delani had something very, very clever up his sleeve, they were doomed. She opened fire anyway, knowing she had no other option. All around her, the survivors joined in, strafing the oncoming horde with whatever they had left.

'Careful!' Delani called. 'Strike one is coming in. On my signal, down and harden your armour.'

What? Ayaka couldn't understand him for a second, and then his meaning hit her. 'You've ordered a nuke?' she exclaimed.

'Damned right,' Delani agreed. 'The electromagnetic pulse will fry their inboard computers.'

'Haven't you looked behind us?' she demanded. 'There's a native village there. And they don't have hardened armour.'

'Then they'll die,' Delani said, unconcerned. 'If the Daleks get past us, they'll die anyway. This way will be quicker and a hell of a lot less painful for them. And it'll give us a chance to live. Maybe you can avenge them.'

Ayaka didn't know what to say. To deliberately order a strike that would kill civilian targets... She couldn't think straight. All she could do was fire at the oncoming Daleks, blanking out her mind.

This is war, she reminded herself. They're dead whatever happens.

'Down!' Delani yelled.

She buried her face in the dirt, tightening her armour.

There was a shockwave so strong that it slammed her into the ground. She felt as if a rock the size of a tank had dropped on her. Pain lanced through her chest as one of her ribs broke. Then the ground shuddered as the aftershock kicked in. She groaned in pain as she was battered about inside her suit.

But she was alive. She struggled to right herself, discovering that the blast had pressed her almost a good thirty centimetres into the ground. Her helmet was crackling, and the picture was fuzzy. Her own sensors had nearly been fried in the EMP. But she had to know what had happened to the rest of her team and the Daleks.

Several other Thals were managing to struggle upright, Cathbad and Dyoni among them. The woman was lucky to be alive, given the crack in her armour. Then Ayaka saw she'd been lying on her side, the cracked portion shielded. She looked as if her arm was broken, but that was minor, all things considered.

Ayaka looked out over the plain. The Daleks had taken the brunt of the blast, in the open and unprepared. Most of them had simply been blown away. There were a few casings burning, and several squashed Spiders. But very little other evidence that the Dalek army had been there. The nuke had been effective on that score.

Then, terrified of what she would see, Ayaka looked back at the village.

The river had boiled away, and the far side of the gap was now sterile. The buildings had vanished. The watching warriors were shadows on the ground. Anyone else hiding there had been obliterated.

But they had won.

Her emotions refused to kick in. She stared numbly at the burnt ground, and was only dimly aware when Delani contacted them all again.

'Prepare for evacuation,' he said. 'We've a drop-ship coming in for us. Prepare to fall back in two minutes.'

'Fall back?' she echoed, dazed. 'What are you talking about? Didn't the blast finish them?'

'It finished the ones down there,' he answered.

With a feeling of dread, Ayaka began to understand what he meant.

The Daleks they had been facing had been only the edges of the force. In the sky, she could see the approach of the disc-shaped hoverbouts of the next wave. They would be here in a few minutes. Hopefully, not until the drop-ship had picked them up. She hated fighting hoverbouts, because the Daleks had full movement in the sky while she was stuck on the ground. The one-shot rocket pack she wore was fine for retreat, but nowhere near as manoeuvrable as a hoverbout.

'Don't they ever stop?' she complained.

'They've obviously decided that this is a priority target,' Dyoni answered her. 'They're committed to taking it.'

'Over our dead bodies,' Cathbad added glumly.

'Heads up,' Delani called. 'Here's transport.'

Ayaka looked up, and saw the drop-ship falling towards them. It had reached them first, but the delay while it landed and took them on wouldn't leave it time enough to jump before the hoverbouts arrived.

Delani obviously knew this, too. 'She's not landing,' he said. 'Prime your packs – we're going up to meet her on my mark.'

Ayaka's throat went dry. This was a risky step. The packs burned for only two minutes, and then failed. If they weren't in scoop range then, they'd fall back to the ground. And even in battle armour no one could stand up to a mile drop. Her stomach felt sick. And then she realised something else – Dyoni had already used her pack up to get back here. She couldn't go with them.

'Dyoni –' she began.

'I know,' her friend said. 'I guess I'm staying.'

'No,' Ayaka said grimly. 'I'll help you up. Hold on to me.'

'One pack can't lift two people,' Dyoni reminded her. 'We'll both die that way.'

Cathbad managed a weak grin. 'How about two packs for three people?' he asked. 'Hold on to both of us.'

Dyoni hesitated. She wanted to live, but not at the expense of her friends' lives.

'If you get too heavy, I promise I'll drop you,' Cathbad assured her.

'You'd better,' she growled, but she clamped her hands about Ayaka's and Cathbad's suits.

'Ten seconds,' Delani snapped. 'Ready for lift.'

The drop-ship was directly overhead now, its pulsers glowing as it started to hover. It looked close enough to jump to.

'Now!'

Ayaka and Cathbad triggered their packs simultaneously, and Ayaka fought back the pain from her rib as she tightened her grip on Dyoni. The three of them rose into the air, wobbling unsteadily, but rising. All about them, the remnant of the army rose, too.

The Daleks saw this, and notched up their speed a little. They'd obviously been expecting the ship to land, offering them a clear target. Even though the hoverbouts were too far away, they opened fire anyway as they raced towards their victims.

Ayaka concentrated on lifting. She, Cathbad, and Dyoni were falling behind the others, even as the drop-ship grew larger. Her helmet was still misbehaving, but it looked like she was down to thirty seconds of fuel. And there was no familiar grappling feeling from the ship's scoop.

Maybe Dyoni was right. Maybe they would all die together. She refused to think about it.

The hoverbouts finally found their range. Most of the shots missed, but one out of twenty locked on to a target. A Thal trooper some ten units above them arched in death spasm, and then folded. His or her pack shot the body off towards the ground. A blast exploded close by, shaking Ayaka in her suit, and making the helmet glitch again.

Eight seconds left.

She was going to die. Dyoni was struggling, knowing she was holding her friends back. She was determined to break free to give them a chance to live. Ayaka and Cathbad were equally determined that she wouldn't – and so far they were winning.

16

Then another shot from the hoverbouts exploded virtually in their faces. The shock slammed into Ayaka, sending her tumbling.

She lost her grip on Dyoni.

And the scoop kicked in at that second, hauling her towards the lock above, and out of range of the firing. Her pack died at the same second. Ayaka twisted, as far as her pain-racked side would allow, trying to see what had happened to Dyoni. Had she fallen to her death? Then she saw, with relief, her friend rising about five units away.

Hands dragged Ayaka into the lock, and then Dyoni and Cathbad followed her. They were the last. The crew members began the procedure to close the door when Dyoni gasped and pointed.

Descending from the clouds was a Dalek killcruiser.

'Oh, God,' Ayaka breathed. Was this never going to end?

'Ready for jump,' the officer at the lock called, as the door slid shut, sealing the ship. 'Get us the hell out of here.'

The ship lurched under her, and Ayaka gasped as her broken rib pressed into her side. Her vision faded for a second under the strain, and then they were in free space, above the planet. Relief washed over her like a drug, and she laughed, maniacally.

Around her, the crew were moving fast to their posts. There were several warriors slumped against the walls, all wounded and waiting for medical assistance. She knew she needed it herself. From the intercom, she could hear the reports coming in. 'Two killcruisers mark six seven zero. On descent path to Terakis.'

Two more? Ayaka was stunned. Three killcruisers, along with everything else? This was a major offensive. Their puny little ship couldn't hope to match the combined fire power down on the planet now.

There was a hand on her shoulder, and she turned to see Delani. His helmet was off, and he was grinning widely. Maybe he was enjoying this, but she couldn't see anything to smile about.

'They fell for it,' he breathed. 'I knew they would.'

'Fell for what?' she demanded. 'What's going on? What haven't you told us?'

'Operation Kill Zone,' he answered happily. 'We made the Daleks think that this planet was strategically important to us. They've committed half their Eighth Fleet to this battle. Three killcruisers, twenty destroyers and who knows how much else?'

'Well,' Ayaka said, not seeing why he was so happy, 'they've certainly won their objective, then. We can't go up against all that.'

'We never intended to,' Delani replied. 'We were bait in a trap.'

'Trap?' Ayaka realised she was being painfully slow here. 'What trap?'

'Come and see.' He led her, Cathbad, and Dyoni to one of the wall screens, and then punched in a code. A picture of the planet they were rapidly fleeing came up. He glanced at his chrono. 'You might want to shield your eyes,' he said. 'About… now.'

Ayaka was about to protest, but closed her eyes anyway, looking partly away.

The flash of light still almost blinded her. She heard Cathbad cry out in pain.

Opening her eyes, she stared at the screen. Terakis was gone – no more than rubble and vapour, expanding rapidly in space from where the planet once had been.

'What the hell happened?' she demanded, but she knew the answer already.

'Planet buster,' Delani said smugly. 'We planted it yesterday. Today's operation was merely to convince the Daleks there was something there we wanted badly enough to fight for. We lured down half their Eighth Fleet and destroyed it in one blow. Operation Kill Zone was a great success.' He looked at the three of them. 'God, you're a sight. See the medic, get patched up and then get some rest. We've a new mission coming up, and I want you all ready for it.' He turned on his heels and marched away, his head held high.

Ayaka slumped down against the wall, totally drained. Her emotions were so overloaded, she didn't know where to begin. She unfastened her helmet and threw it away down the corridor. It almost hit one of the crewmen. He looked as if he were about to yell at her, but when he saw her face, he wisely turned away.

She was not aware that she was crying until Dyoni brushed at her tears. She had her own helmet off, too, and her gloves. 'Ayaka, what's wrong?'

'Wrong?' She could hardly believe her friend could ask such a dumb question. 'Dyoni, that planet was inhabited! We killed them all!'

Cathbad bent down, his own helmet off now. 'Ayaka,' he said gently, 'they were dead the second the Daleks knew about them. Nobody could have saved them. But at least this way their deaths meant something. They took half the Eighth Fleet with them. You should be glad of that.'

'Glad?' Ayaka's heart felt as if it would burst. 'I know those aliens were dead; the Daleks were bound to kill them. And if they had, I would have hated them for it, for another senseless slaughter they'd performed. But they didn't kill those beings – we did.' She sighed deep within her soul. 'Now who can I hate for it?'

Cathbad didn't know what to say. He looked shaken and disturbed. Dyoni, however, shook her head.

'You have to look at the larger picture, Ayaka,' she said. 'The Daleks have been dealt a crippling blow. You heard Delani. The operation was a great success.'

Ayaka stared bleakly at the screen on the wall. The gas cloud that had been Terakis was now almost invisible. 'Yes,' she whispered. 'The operation was a complete success. But the patient died.'

PART 1
WAR ZONE

'He that is the author of a war lets loose the whole contagion of hell and opens a vein that bleeds a nation to death.'
Thomas Paine, *The American Crisis* (1776)

CHAPTER 1
BUSINESS AS USUAL

When Sam saw the new door, she knew that she would never, ever get used to the TARDIS. It was bad enough that the time machine was, according to the Doctor, almost infinite in size. She could at least cope with that by sticking to the small portion of the TARDIS that she had already explored. Or, of course, invest in a large ball of string or bag of bread crumbs and take a walk. But when she turned a corner to go to the food machine for breakfast and found a door that certainly had not been there when she went to sleep, she knew she was beaten.

She'd been tempted to try to draw a map of the TARDIS, but if it could grow a new door on a whim, then what was the point? Maps worked only when things stayed in one place. Feeling rather like Alice in a technological Wonderland, she opened the new door gingerly and peered through it.

It was a painter's study of some kind. On a large easel, a board had been set up. It was about two feet by four, laid horizontally. Someone had started a painting of what looked like St Mark's Square in Venice. At least, that's what it would have looked like had it not been for the head of some aquatic dinosaur rising from the water. The mixing palette had been discarded on a table, along with several tubes of oil paint that had been scattered with it. Several brushes stood soaking in a jamjar, filled with dirty purple water. Also on the table was a bowl of wax fruit. A smock hung on another easel, and the rest of the room was filled with empty canvases and various expensive-looking frames.

Had the Doctor just taken up painting, or was this somehow an old room that had been elsewhere in the TARDIS until today? Sam didn't have an answer, and she wondered if the Doctor himself did. Closing the door, she ran a hand through her short-cropped blonde hair, and decided that life was complicated enough without asking any further questions. She wandered over to the food machine and dialled up French toast and orange juice.

As always, she ended up with something that looked like a Mars bar and a glass of carrot juice. They had the correct taste, of course, when she bit or sipped, but she hated this. She could understand that it was impossible for the Doctor to stock all kinds of fresh foods in the TARDIS, but surely some wouldn't be too much to ask for. And, in all her wanderings, one thing she had never come across was a kitchen. Maybe there wasn't one. After all, when you had a machine that could synthesise almost anything you wanted, hot or cold, why bother with a kitchen?

She scowled at the food machine in disgust. Right! Time for action.

Sam marched down the corridor and into the console room, determined to let the Doctor know that she wasn't going to put up with this monotony any longer. 'Doctor,' she began, 'you really have to do something about...' Her voice trailed off as she stared about the room. There was no sign of the Time Lord at all.

The console in the centre was pulsing away, showing that the ship was still in flight, but it had an odd sound to it that Sam couldn't recall hearing before. It was hard to be sure, though, since there was an opera playing at full blast.

Naturally, she didn't recognise it, but it did mean that the Doctor had to be around here somewhere, even if he wasn't visible. The blue-and-gold infinity that was the ceiling of the TARDIS seemed to be static for once, instead of whirling about giddily. Was it possible that there was something wrong with the Ship?

'Doctor?' she yelled over the singing. 'Are you here?'

There was no reply. She sighed, and moved to the table beside the console. The pot of tea there was still warm, though the cup beside it was empty. The Doctor had been reading, and had left a bookmark about a third of the way through his autographed copy of War And Peace – in the original Russian, of course. He couldn't be far away, then.

She turned, and from this fresh angle she could see an open tool-kit beside the console, and a mass of wiring hanging down from a small flap. So she had been right – there was something wrong with the TARDIS. She mentally patted herself on the back.

'Doctor!' she yelled again, but she knew he could never hear her over the singing. 'Stupid fat cow,' she muttered. Crossing to the console, Sam tried to recall which switch controlled the CD, or tape, or whatever it was that was playing. She was pretty sure it was one of two rather ornamental brass levers. Praying that the other didn't control the artificial gravity or the air supply or something, she pushed them both back to zero.

The music stopped. Thankfully, nothing else of obvious importance did.

From the doorway that led to the outer doors, the Doctor appeared. He was frowning slightly. 'Why did you turn off *che soave zeffiretto?*' he asked. 'Don't you like *The Marriage Of Figaro?*' He had taken off his coat, and looked slightly dishevelled. In one hand he held a piece of some intricate mechanism, and in the other his ubiquitous sonic screwdriver. Despite the dab of dirt on his nose, he still looked like some disenfranchised nineteenth-century poet – a naive soul out loose in the cold hard world, and struggling to make some sense out of it. His fine features, curled hair, and turn-of-the-century costume all contributed to the feeling, but it was the Doctor's mannerisms themselves that made you realise there was a poetic heart – hearts! – and soul within the sensitive, attractive frame.

'Puccini's fine, Doctor,' Sam began.

'Mozart,' he corrected her. 'Really, what do they teach in English schools for music appreciation these days?'

'OK, Mozart.' Sam sighed. 'But you couldn't hear me over the fat lady.'

He raised one eyebrow. 'I don't mean to be rude, but I was listening to her first. And it's a duet between the Contessa and Susannah.'

Sam pointed to the mess on the TARDIS floor. 'What are you doing?' she demanded. 'Is the TARDIS acting up?'

The Doctor seemed puzzled. 'No, not really. I just thought this was a perfect time to do a few small repairs, that's all.' He gestured to the projected view on the TARDIS's infinitely high ceiling. 'Look at that nebula! Isn't it glorious?'

Sam examined it, and had to admit that he did have a point. It filled about a third of the sky, tendrils of coloured gases crawling away from several small, bright stars in its heart. Golds, greens, blues, crimsons all whirled together in some mad, creative dance. 'Very nice,' she agreed.

'Isn't it, isn't it…' he nodded, smiling.

'So, it's nothing serious, then?' Sam persisted. 'Just minor stuff?'

'Right.'

She eyed the mechanism he was holding suspiciously. 'And what's that?'

The Doctor looked down at it as if he'd never seen it before. 'The TARDIS lock. I've wanted to adjust it ever since the Master kept popping in and out of my TARDIS in San Francisco. It won't take long.'

'The lock?' Sam was aghast. 'You mean, anyone can just walk in while you're playing with that thing?'

'I am not playing,' the Doctor said, but his blue-green eyes were twinkling. 'And nobody can just walk in.' He gestured to the stellar expanse on the ceiling. 'We're parked around a nebula, after all, not in Piccadilly Circus.'

Sam sighed again. 'And what other essential systems have you taken off line?' she asked. Really, the Doctor could be very childish sometimes. Fancy conducting repairs on a whim in some interstellar backwater.

'None, really.' His nose twitched, and he scratched it with the sonic screwdriver. 'Of course, I had to disconnect the time rotor so I could take the lock apart. There are fail-safes to prevent me from doing it in flight. But we're not really going anywhere in a hurry, and it'll just take me ten minutes to reconnect it.'

'The TARDIS can't fly?' Sam asked, her bad feeling sinking lower and lower with every question. 'Couldn't you have just taken it into a shop somewhere for a quick overhaul and oil change?'

'Sam,' the Doctor said patiently, 'there aren't many petrol stations that can strip and service a TARDIS. And it's simple to do. It'll take me about an hour, and we can be on our way again. Just enjoy the peace and quiet while you have it.'

'I've seen all sorts of things on my travels with you,

Doctor,' Sam informed him. 'From vampires to shopping malls. The only thing I haven't seen is any peace and quiet.'

'Then enjoy it while you can,' he suggested. He gave her one of his incandescent smiles, and she couldn't help smiling back. His face was so... alive when he smiled. Then she frowned as he continued. 'Would you mind popping Mozart back on? I work better to music.'

There was absolutely no talking to him some days. Sam moved the ornamental levers back to the position she'd found them in, and the opera recital started up again. The Doctor vanished back into the vestibule to continue his repairs. Sam sighed, and poured herself a cup of the Doctor's tepid tea. Maybe he was right. It was possible that she was overreacting, and absolutely nothing bad would happen while he was at work.

But, given his track record, she strongly doubted it.

'Now, father, isn't that the most beautiful sight you ever laid eyes on?' Loran gestured at the nebula showing – slightly out of focus – on the small screen.

His father sniffed loudly, and shrugged. 'It's all right,' he replied.

'All right?' Loran gasped, offended. 'Where is the poetry in your soul?'

'There's no poetry,' Captain Balatan answered. 'Just a calculator. And you'd be better off if you had half my business sense. Now, stop mooning about and let's get down to the recovery bay and see what we've got.'

Loran rolled his eyes, and sighed loudly. But he followed his father down the corridors of the *Quetzel*. There was no point in talking to the old man some days. He didn't have an ounce of sensitivity within him. Everything with him boiled

28

down to just one priority: money. Naturally, they never had enough of it, which made him obsessive on the subject. A view of grandeur, such as the nebula, meant nothing people to Balatan unless he could figure out some way of charging to look at it. He couldn't grasp the aesthetics involved in truly appreciating the wonders of the universe – he just wanted to bottle them up and stick a price tag on them.

Several of the lights had died in the corridor again. Loran made a note on his comp to have them repaired. Of course, he had to hope that he had specs on the lighting system on his main comp, and that there were spare parts around close enough to being compatible to fix them. One of the wall hatches had come loose, and he kicked it back into place as he passed. He'd taken only two steps when he heard it clatter onto the deck behind him, having fallen off completely now.

The *Quetzel* was in dire need of repairs. As always. Well, maybe some of the stuff they'd swept up would be useful – if he could prise it from his father's greedy little fingers. Balatan would undoubtedly prefer to sell everything, every last nut and bolt, and expect the ship to hold together somehow out of a shared sense of pure greed.

They clambered down the ladder into storage bay eight, to discover that Harmon and Chayn were already there, cataloguing the latest acquisitions. Loran's interest in the room rose a notch. Chayn was definitely the most beautiful woman on the ship. Not that she had much competition, actually, since there were only three, but even on a pleasure cruiser she'd be something special. She was slender, dark-haired, dark-eyed and a genius at fixing almost anything. That the *Quetzel* still flew at all was testimony to her skills. She was very nearly perfect in Loran's eyes. However, she possessed just one tiny flaw.

She didn't find him at all attractive. She was always polite to him, but completely ignored any warm conversations he attempted, and all his attempts at flirting. Loran simply couldn't understand it. After all, she was beautiful and unattached – none of the other men on board had any better luck with her, either, and as far as he could tell she wasn't in the slightest bit interested in the other women. It didn't make any sense to him. He ran a quick hand through his full, wavy, dark hair and gave her a friendly smile.

'How's it going?' he asked.

She nodded. 'We've got some good stuff here,' she answered, gesturing. 'Dalek-made, definitely. Bits of a killcruiser, by the look of it. Plenty of circuits, some routine systems. There's not much of it left, though.'

Loran examined the scattered debris, and realised she was right. Normally, even if it had been destroyed in battle, there would be half to three-quarters of the ship salvageable. Here, though, there were only about twenty bulkheads, a dozen portions of walls and panels, and some scattered boards and circuitry. Less than five per cent of even a small ship.

'No signs of engines?' Balatan asked, his voice hopeful.

'Nothing,' Harmon answered. 'They're all gone. So is most of the weaponry. A lot of junk, some we can use, some we can sell.' He scratched at his bald head. 'Whatever took this one apart didn't leave much. Some new weapon, maybe.'

'Odd, too,' Chayn added. 'There's no non-Dalek debris. The other ship must have managed to destroy the killcruiser without getting a scratch itself. And I've never heard of anything that could do that kind of damage to the Daleks.'

'As long as it's not still around,' Balatan said nervously.

'The screens don't show any other ships at all in this

region,' Chayn informed him. 'We wouldn't be here if there were.' That was one of Balatan's prime rules: they only scavenged areas where the fighting had stopped. There was no profit to be made by being shot at.

'And how well are the screens working right now?' he demanded.

Chayn shrugged. 'About as well as ever.'

'Maybe we should overhaul them, just to be sure,' Balatan muttered.

'Couldn't hurt,' she agreed. 'As soon as I'm done inventorying all of this and seeing what's usable.' She bent back to her comp, recording and logging the items one by one.

Loran moved to her side. She seemed to be in a good mood, so maybe now might be the time to make a move. 'Are you doing anything when your shift's over?' he asked.

'Fixing the screens, by the sound of it,' Chayn answered, without looking up. 'I'm sure it'll be a thrilling evening.'

'I meant after that,' he persisted.

'After that I'll probably crawl into bed,' she replied. 'Alone.'

There was no answer to that line, Loran thought, his hopes dashed again. He wanted to say, 'Don't you like me?' but thought it would sound petulant.

Chayn gave him a thin smile. But it was a smile that said she liked him as a friend. Just that. Nothing more.

She'd managed to slip away from him again, Loran realised. There wasn't any way back to chatting her up after the finality of that line, of that meaningful smile. If only he could think a little faster, but just being this close to her overloaded his senses. Even though she dealt with mechanisms and repairs all day, she didn't smell of oil, but had a slight hint of fruit about her. It drove him crazy. And even the faded coveralls she wore only served to emphasise her trim form.

'That's interesting,' she said, studying the comp.

'What is?' Balatan scurried to join them, greed obvious in his voice. 'Something valuable?'

'I don't know,' Chayn answered. She threaded through several of the bulkheads, the three men in her wake. One of them was leaning against a teardrop-shaped ball of metal. 'Now what could that be?'

It was about ten feet tall, and eight across. The finish was pockmarked and scarred from debris. There were a couple of seams visible, but no hatches or access ports.

'Looks like some sort of a pod,' Loran said. He'd never seen anything quite like this. 'Storage container, maybe?'

'Or a survival pod?' Chayn suggested. She was clearly intrigued.

'Daleks don't need survival pods,' Balatan sneered. 'They can survive in space on their own.' He shook his head. 'No, it's some kind of a container.' He slapped it with his hand. 'And if it's sealed up well enough to survive whatever wrecked that ship, then *I* want whatever's in it. It's got to be *very* valuable.' He scowled at her. 'Can you get any readings on whatever's inside it?'

'Nothing,' she replied. 'It's well shielded. Some kind of power source, possibly stasis field. I can't be sure. We'd have to open it up to find out what's in it.'

'Is that safe?' Loran asked, worried.

Chayn gave a barking laugh. 'Opening a Dalek artefact? Of course it's not safe. It's most likely booby-trapped, and could contain something nasty and lethal. Even Varga plants, maybe. But there's no way to tell without taking a peek inside.' She shrugged. 'Or we could just leave it sealed, and try to sell it as is.'

Balatan shook his head. 'No way,' he decided. 'If we did that, we could lose out on the big money. I want to know just what we've got before we try to sell it. That way, we can ask for more.'

Chayn grinned, and Loran realised that was what she'd been expecting his father to say. He could see that she was dying to find out what was inside it. He only hoped that dying wasn't what she was going to do. But he had confidence in her. She was careful, and wouldn't do anything rash.

'We'd better seal off the bay, then,' he suggested. 'If it is Varga plants or some other biological nasty that the Daleks have developed, we don't want it running about the ship. We'll have to be prepared to destroy it.'

'Destroy it?' his father echoed. 'Are you out of your mind? If there's something living in there, I can think of at least three companies who'd pay a small fortune to examine some Dalek biotechnology. And they'd want it alive.' He turned to Chayn. 'Can you rig some sort of biological containment field in there, just in case?'

She shrugged. 'It'll take some time,' she said thoughtfully. 'Putting it together won't be easy, given our supplies right now.'

'Top priority,' he ordered her. 'You can scavenge from elsewhere if you need to, with my blessing.'

Chayn grinned. 'Then I can do it. It'll take me six, eight hours, though. I'll begin after I reboot the screens.'

'No, forget that,' Balatan decided. 'That can wait. Open this up first. This means money.'

And the screens might mean our lives, Loran thought. But he knew better than to contradict one of his father's orders.

Besides, he, too, was curious to know what was inside this can.

'Right.' Chayn scratched her ear absent-mindedly. 'There's no opening mechanism I can see. I'll need the heavy-duty equipment from bay ten for this.'

'Fine.' Balatan nodded at Harmon. 'Harmon can help you. Do you need anyone else?'

'I don't mind lending a hand,' Loran offered, trying not to sound too eager.

'I'll call you if I need you,' Chayn promised. 'But I think Harmon and I can handle it alone for now. We'll let you know how it goes.'

'Good.' Balatan turned back to his son. 'Come on, let's get back to the flight deck and get the rams up and running again. Where there's one wreck, there's almost bound to be more.' He rubbed his hands together. 'I can smell profits in this!'

With a last, hopeless look back at Chayn – who was already deciding which bulkheads she'd need to move to access the artefact and had probably forgotten all about him already – Loran followed his father back to the ladder.

Harmon rubbed his head, and then grunted at Chayn, 'Back in a moment. Got to take a personal break.'

'No problem,' she answered. 'I can handle this.'

He nodded, and hurried out of the bay. He found a com port on the wall, and removed a small handset from his work pack. He plugged it in, established a link, and then sent the prearranged signal. This wasn't one of the ship's links, which meant that it worked perfectly every time. The call went through in seconds, and the response came in.

'Report!'

'The artefact has been found,' he said quietly, glancing

34

around to make certain he wasn't being overheard. There should be nobody in this area, but it didn't pay to take chances. 'They're planning to open it in a few hours.'

'Negative,' came the reply. 'The artefact must not be opened. It is your duty to stop them.'

'Understood,' he confirmed. He had suspected as much.

'We will make rendezvous as soon as possible,' his contact stated. 'Delay all operations on the artefact.'

Harmon licked his lips. 'Fine. Uh... there won't be any casualties, right? I mean, you promised –'

'We will keep our word,' was the answer. 'Keep yours.' The line went dead.

Harmon removed the link and replaced it in his pack. He was sure he could trust them, but he hated all this cloak-and-dagger stuff. Still, they'd promised to reimburse the *Quetzel* for finding the artefact, whatever it was, so Balatan would be happy when all of this was over.

There would be no problems. None at all. He just had to prevent Chayn from opening the thing, and everything would be fine once his allies arrived.

Whistling, he headed back to the cargo bay.

As spectacular as the nebula was, Sam was bored with staring at it after her second cup of tea. At least this was real Darjeeling, and not some more of the food-machine liquid. It had a solid, healthy brownness to it, and the Doctor had real milk to add to it.

She jumped to her feet again and marched across the room. He was in the vestibule with even more mess around him. It looked as if he'd taken half of the door apart in no particular order. Panels and wiring were leaning against the wall, and Sam couldn't help feeling disturbed by this.

'Is that safe?' she asked.

'Safe?' The Doctor blinked, looking up from the circuit he was working on. 'Not if you touch it.'

She gestured at the denuded door. 'I mean that. There's not much between us and hard vacuum right now, is there?'

'There's plenty,' he replied, encouraging her with a smile. 'And there's the force field outside of that.' He frowned slightly. 'I'm almost certain I didn't turn that off.'

'Almost certain?' Sam repeated, wondering whether to panic or simply get mad. 'Don't you know?'

He looked pained. 'Not exactly,' he confessed. 'It depends what the default settings currently are.'

'What?' She stared at him in horror. 'Didn't you program them?'

'Yes and no,' he replied, rubbing at his mouth. 'It was me, but one of my former selves. It's hard to recall all the details after two or three regenerations, you know.'

Sam took a deep breath. 'Maybe it would be a good idea to check?' she suggested, with mock sweetness.

The Doctor laughed and bounded to his feet. 'What a good idea!' he said enthusiastically. He hurried past her, leaving her to follow in his wake. He stopped before he reached the console, staring up at the starscape. 'Hello! We've got company.'

Sam followed his gaze, and saw a small image of a starship of some kind. The USS Enterprise it wasn't. It looked like something a couple of model-makers might have assembled if they'd dropped a couple of kits together, scrunched them around and then decided they had to use every part while imbibing ferocious amounts of alcohol. It was basically a couple of elongated egg shapes, with dozens of engine nacelles, spikes, fins, and knobbly bits stuck to it. In short, it was an eyesore.

'Is that "company" as in "good company"" or as in "rape, plunder, and pillage"?' she asked politely.

'The former, I hope,' he replied. 'At least, it's no design I've seen before.' He frowned as he examined it. 'In fact, it's a bit of a hotchpotch, isn't it?'

'Beauty is in the eye of the beholder,' she told him with mock pomposity.

'Then I think someone's seriously overdue for their eye test.' The Doctor crossed to the console and started flicking switches. The opera cut off, which was blessed relief as far as Sam was concerned. 'Well, they're certainly heading this way. I wonder if they'd care for a spot of tea?'

'To drink or to swim in?' Sam asked him. She was starting to get a trifle blasé about meeting strange alien species.

'A good point,' he conceded. He bent to examine the controls. 'That's odd...' He was about to slam a fist down on the panel when he caught himself. 'That's right, I disengaged the drive, didn't I?'

Sam eyed the growing ship with concern. Maybe the visitors were friendly, but given her adventures so far, she wasn't willing to gamble her life on it. 'Maybe now would be a good time to re-engage it,' she suggested. 'I mean, I'm sure they're real party people, but it would be nice to have an escape option if we need it.'

'Always keep your escape options open!' the Doctor agreed enthusiastically, nodding furiously. 'Quite right.' He started working on the controls, with one eye still on the image above them. 'That's interesting. It's a Bussard ram jet. I haven't seen one of those in centuries.' He smiled at her. 'Do you know what they are?'

'Yup.' The Doctor's face fell just a fraction. 'I've been

doing some reading,' she informed him. '*Jane's Spaceships.*'
Sam had reckoned that knowing something about them
couldn't hurt. 'They're powered by drawing in interstellar
dust and junk.'

'That's right,' he told her. He pointed to two thick fins on
either side of the ungainly craft. 'Those are the intakes. They
suck up whatever's in their path, and use it for fuel. Very
efficient.'

'Doctor,' Sam said, trying not to panic quite yet, 'In case
you haven't noticed, we're in their path.'

Realisation dawned suddenly. 'Oh, good grief!' he
muttered, and returned to work feverishly at the controls. It
was starting to look like it might be a good time to panic.
'Don't panic,' he said, without looking up. 'It's just a few
minutes' work.'

'OK, fine,' Sam replied, her stomach starting to pitch. 'I'll
boil us an egg or something to pass the time.'

The Doctor looked at the controls in desperate hope. 'The
HADS! Maybe they're working still.'

'HADS?' she asked, running her fingers through her short
blonde hair.

'Hostile Action Displacement System,' he explained. 'Surely
I told you?'

'That's what made the TARDIS disappear when it was
attacked back in the 1890s!' cried Sam, remembering back
to an earlier adventure. 'So will it get us out of this?'

'Conceivably'.

'Try definitely!' she said. 'Set them now, to be on the safe
side. Then we can just hop out of the way.'

'I can't do that unless the drive's on line.'

'Oh…' Sam glanced up. The ship filled almost the entire
ceiling now. 'Please tell me you've fixed the drive,' she said,

quite pleased with her coolness.

The Doctor looked slightly bemused. 'I haven't. But if you think it would help, I could tell you anyway –'

The TARDIS gave a shudder, and Sam grabbed the edge of the console.

'Magnetic lock,' the Doctor said, worry in his voice. 'We're in the scoop. Hang on! This may be a bumpy ride!'

Sam locked her hands in place. 'The TARDIS is indestructible, right?' she asked, trying to fight the panic that was growing. 'We're not really in any trouble, are we? It's just going to be rough, right?'

'Rough, yes, yes,' he replied, still fiddling with the controls. 'But "indestructible" is such a relative term.'

'No it isn't!' she yelled, unable to stop herself now. 'It means we can't be hurt!'

'Usually, yes – but with so many systems off-line...' He stared at her. 'If we're sucked into the jet itself, that's going to be a very intense field.' The noise seemed to vibrate out of the very heart of the gutted ship. 'Atoms being ripped to shreds, that kind of thing. It's possible that it might be enough to scatter the TARDIS across half the galaxy. Not very likely, of course. But possible.'

'Marvellous,' Sam sighed. 'So glad I checked!'

The TARDIS shuddered again, and she could tell that they were now being sucked directly into the intake for the stellar drive. In seconds – if she'd done her homework correctly – they would be hurled into the mix chamber, where the forces of a miniature sun would converge upon the TARDIS.

Would they get through it?

Sam stared at the Doctor, torn between wanting to kick seven shades of Shoreditch out of him for messing with the

TARDIS systems and giving him a last, desperate kiss before utter annihilation. She was still trying to decide which she favoured when the whole ceiling suddenly went black, and the TARDIS tumbled end over end into the maw of the vessel.

CHAPTER 2
A PILE OF JUNK

Sam clung on for dear life as the ship tossed and crashed about her. The Doctor managed to look a shade more dignified, though hardly less panic-stricken. He was holding on to the console with one hand and frantically manipulating the controls with the other. The TARDIS was caught inside the collectors, she assumed, probably being sucked into the furnace that powered this starship. Sam's nerves were frayed almost clean through, but she managed to clamp her mouth shut. She was not going to die screaming.

Abruptly, the TARDIS was shaken again, and twisted, this time whirling about like a top. Sam was getting rather giddy when abruptly the TARDIS slammed into something very solid, and came to a sudden halt.

There was a long, heavy silence.

'We're alive,' Sam breathed, astonished. She glanced around the console room, shaking with relief. 'You did something brilliant at the last second!'

The Doctor's mouth twitched. 'Perceptive, but wrong.'

'You mean we're not alive?'

'I mean I didn't do anything brilliant at the last second.' He looked puzzled. 'The drive still isn't back on line yet. Whatever happened wasn't my doing.'

Sam scowled at him. 'So we were just lucky, then?'

'It would appear so.' As they were no longer in space, the holographic ceiling was of no use to them. He switched on the smaller scanner instead, and used it to survey their surroundings.

They were in some kind of a cavernous room, one that seemed to be filled with broken items. Parts of walls, small machines, pipes, girders and other mess littered the room beside them.

'Wherever we are, the owners aren't too tidy,' the Doctor eventually decided. 'Let's just pop out for a quick look, shall we?'

'Right,' Sam said enthusiastically, then, 'Er, Doctor… d'you think it might be a good idea if you got the TARDIS operational again? Just in case. We've almost been killed once already this morning.'

'Hmm. You may just have a point, Sam. I'll just fix the drive, and then we'll take a look around.' He looked hopeful, like a child bargaining to play with a favourite toy. 'Agreed?'

'Agreed,' she smiled.

Humming to himself, the Doctor worked on the controls for another few minutes, adjusting, fine-tuning, and correcting. Finally, he brushed his hands together and gave a satisfied smile. 'Right, there we are. Fully flight-capable again. If there's any trouble, we hare it back here and leave immediately.'

'Good.' Sam felt a lot better now, knowing that they had an escape route. She'd been surveying the room they were in using the monitor, but had seen no signs of life as yet. The Doctor collected his long dark-green frock coat from the hatstand as they passed it, and scooped up his sonic screwdriver from the small table beside the outer door. Sam eyed the pieces of the disassembled door. 'Will the TARDIS be safe like this?'

'Oh, I'm sure it will be,' the Doctor replied. 'We're only off for a quick look around, and maybe a cup of tea. Then I'll come back and fix that.' He opened the outer doors, and led the way into the room beyond.

Sam closed the door behind her, and stared around. The place was just as it had seemed on the screen – large, mostly empty, but with a pile of absolute junk in the centre of the room. The Doctor, naturally, found all of this terribly fascinating. He had wandered off to examine one of the shattered wall fragments close by. Wiring, tubes, and electronic parts showed at the shattered edges, and he peered at these with interest. And then with alarm.

'I recognise the workmanship,' he said softly. 'Daleks!'

Sam felt a thrill go through her at the word. The Doctor had talked about the Daleks so often Sam felt she'd actually met them herself. 'I'm old enough to dodge Daleks' was one of her favourite retorts to the Doctor's occasionally overbearing paternal streak.

'Something tore their ship apart rather severely,' he said. 'And, judging from the micrometeor punctures, I'd say several months ago at least. I think we're perfectly safe here for the time being.' He glanced upward. Sam followed his gaze and saw there was a huge funnel suspended from the ceiling on what looked like a shaky support system. Small machines were spaced evenly about the mouth.

The Doctor smiled. 'Now I know what saved us, Sam,' he announced. He gestured upward. 'This ship is a salvage vessel, flitting the space lanes, sweeping up anything of interest in its path. The intake devices scan the debris, and anything over, say, an inch or so is diverted to a storage hold to be examined. Only the really small stuff ends up as fuel.'

'Then I'm glad I never went on a diet,' Sam decided.

'You don't need to,' said the Doctor, smiling.

Sam almost gaped. Rare were the occasions when the Doctor gave any indication he actually noticed what she looked like.

'So instead of being fuel, we're now officially junk?' she asked.

'Something like that.' The Doctor wandered off absent-mindedly, examining another piece of broken bulkhead. 'Another bit of Dalek debris. And I don't think it's from the same ship, either.' He looked puzzled. 'There must have been a major battle here several months ago. Odd.'

'What's so odd about it?' Sam asked. She was just glad it was long over. Seeing a war from the inside had little appeal to her, and bits of wrecked spaceships weren't her idea of fun, either – even if the Doctor was fascinated.

'It's just that I –' He broke off as they rounded the bulkhead fragment and came face to face with a Dalek.

Sam didn't need to be told that this was what it was. She'd seen pictures, and there was absolutely no mistaking what they were faced with. The Doctor jumped in front of her, instinctively protecting her. Then he relaxed.

'It's all right, it's dead,' he announced.

'How can you be sure?'

'Because we aren't.' The Doctor gave her one of his chilling, penetrating stares. 'If it were alive, we'd be smoking corpses by now.'

Sam nodded, getting the point. He had been willing to die to buy her time to escape. She realised she was almost taking his self-sacrificial streak for granted. This isn't a game, she told herself. She would make it up to him.

They moved closer to the Dalek, and Sam could see that part of the back of its dome was missing. There were stains of something green at the edges of the gash.

It didn't seem to be quite so threatening close up. It was only about five feet tall, shorter than she was. It was a uniform grey all over – except the green stains – and didn't seem to be too formidable, considering the respect the Doctor seemed to have for them. It had three protuberances; the one at the top was clearly an eye of some kind, since she could see the lens. One of the lower sticks looked like some sort of gun, and the other looked not unlike a sink plunger.

'This is it?' she asked him. 'The most evil creature in the universe? It doesn't look like much.'

'Appearances can be deceptive,' the Doctor replied. 'The Daleks are the most single-minded and efficient killing creatures ever to exist.'

Sam snorted. 'Look at that silly plunger!' she mocked. 'How can they rule the universe if they can't even open a door?'

The Doctor glowered at her. 'They use their guns. Frequently.'

Sam sobered up slightly. 'I bet I can guess the punchline to all Dalek knock-knock jokes, then.'

'Yes.' The Doctor tapped the dome, studying the sound in some way. 'And they climb stairs through telekinetic force. They can withstand total vacuum, shots from most artillery weapons, and many other things that would reduce you or me to our molecules in seconds. They can fire their guns about a thousand times without recharging. They have solar collectors to repower their units automatically, and inbuilt computers to provide tactical and sensory data.' He gave her a very bleak smile. 'They never sleep, and they never deviate from their orders. They have no mercy, and no interests in anything other than domination – through total destruction if necessary. And it usually is.'

Sam sighed. 'Talk about needing to get a life.'

'To *take* life,' he snapped back. 'The need is inbred. They're cloned and grown in vats. They are then implanted into the travel machines like this one, and form an instant bond. Daleks come out of the nursery armed and ready to fight. Their nutritional needs are met by a biological solution inside the casing, and the only desire that they have is to kill. They have no culture, no arts.' The Doctor thought back. 'Not any more…'

'No cordon bleu cookery, obviously,' Sam joked weakly.

'No.' The Doctor smiled abruptly. 'And they began as humanoids. They lost everything: love, fear, their consciences. They might know deep inside that they're lacking something. But instead of trying to improve themselves, they've elected to annihilate anything and anyone different to themselves. They want to remake the universe in their twisted image, so that the only living creatures within it are Daleks.'

Sam shuddered. The Doctor was really getting himself worked up. 'There's no appealing to their better nature, then?'

'I tried that, once,' he admitted. 'I don't think it worked.'

There was the sound of a door opening, and the Doctor shook himself out of his introspective mood. He flashed her a smile. 'Company!'

Sam followed him automatically, still deep in her own reverie. She might have a curious nature, but she'd gladly give the Daleks a pass after that little speech! It was quite obvious that they scared the Doctor. And anything that scared the Doctor terrified her. She just hoped that whoever owned this ship was friendly.

Rounding the pieces of bulkhead, the Doctor waved

cheerfully. 'Halloo!' he called.

Two men were climbing down a ladder set near the door, and both looked around as they were greeted. One was older than the other, but both wore the same expression of surprise on their faces. They also both wore slightly ratty suits. They might have been trim and white once, but the colour had faded in patches to a brownish cream. The younger man's elbows were patched, and there was a small tear in the legs of his trousers. The older man looked even worse, since he'd not bothered to even try to repair his clothing.

'Where did you come from?' the older man asked.

The Doctor gestured back towards the TARDIS. 'My ship,' he replied. He and Sam met them halfway across the deck. 'I'm the Doctor, and I'm very pleased to meet you. This is my good friend, Sam.'

'Captain Balatan,' the older man said. 'My son and first officer, Loran.' He stared at the TARDIS. 'That's your ship?'

'Yes.' The Doctor bent forward and said quietly, 'Your capture field just sort of swept us in by accident.'

'It looks a bit small for a starship.' Loran said. Then he looked at Sam. His eyes gleamed, and he straightened up. 'Oh, sorry. Pleasure to meet you.' He held out a hand.

Sam didn't know whether she was expected to shake it or kiss it, so she settled for the former. 'Hi.' She could see his eyes looking her over and sighed mentally. When he spoke again it confirmed her worst fears.

'It's not very often that we have such charming company aboard the *Quetzel*,' he informed her. 'Actually, it isn't very often that we see anyone else at all. Months, in fact.'

'Stop trying to chat her up,' Captain Balatan snapped. 'We're here to work, not fool around.' Loran flushed, but didn't say anything. Balatan walked over to the TARDIS then turned to face the Doctor. 'This is your starship, then?'

The Doctor joined Balatan by the TARDIS. 'Oh, it's not a starship,' said the Doctor, humbly, and paused before continuing. 'It's not that limited. And it may be small, but we call it home.'

The old man examined it with a critical eye. 'Past its prime, but I'll give you two hundred credits for it. It'll make nice scrap.'

'Two hundred credits!' The Doctor was shocked.

'Three hundred, then,' Balatan answered. 'And that's my final offer. And that's good for scrap.'

The Doctor drew himself up and glared at the man. 'Sir, this is not scrap! It's a Type 40 TT Capsule, and you're never likely to see another in your lifetime.'

'Oh, so that's it, is it?' Balatan scratched his nose. 'Trying to make out that it's an antique to raise the price, eh? Well, it won't work.'

'Doctor,' Loran said hastily, squeezing in next to his father. 'You'll have to excuse my father. He can't help it. He's never had an eye for the finer things in life. Not like you and me, though, eh?' He gave a conspiratorial chuckle. 'I can see that this craft of yours is a sleek, unique model.'

'Thank you,' the Doctor said, levelly.

'Four hundred credits.'

The Doctor rolled his eyes. 'It's not for sale, I'm afraid.' He held up a hand. 'And please don't make any more offers. I wouldn't want to offend you by having to turn them down.'

'You drive a tough bargain, Doctor,' Loran began, obviously not put off. Sam could see that neither man was getting the message. Thankfully, there was a timely interruption.

'Captain Balatan! Over here!'

Sam hadn't realised there was anyone else in the hold with them, but she felt a sense of relief. It had been a woman's voice, so that meant she wasn't likely to be latched on to by the rest of the crew. Maybe she'd misinterpreted Loran's interest in her, and he *had* only been trying to be polite after all.

The Doctor was the first to move, obviously glad of the respite from the unwelcome bidding. He hurried in the direction of the voice. Balatan and Loran followed, and Sam found herself bringing up the rear.

The woman was examining what looked like a fork-lift truck that had attempted to mate with a crane and become stuck. She slapped it in disgust and turned around. 'The power grid's been shorted out and the lifting gear's...' Her voice trailed off as she caught sight of the Doctor and Sam. 'What the blazes?'

'Hello,' the Doctor said quickly. 'I'm the Doctor and this is Sam. And you must be...?'

'Chayn,' the woman replied. She was tall and slender, with short-cropped dark hair and a stunned expression on her face that made her look like an overgrown elf. Sam had seen that kind of look on women's faces before. The Doctor sometimes had that effect upon them. It was up to Sam to discourage it.

'What are you talking about, woman?' Balatan demanded, glaring at her. 'Something's wrong with the equipment?'

Chayn dragged herself back to the subject at hand with a lingering glance at the Doctor. 'Um, yes.' She concentrated, and went on, 'It's inoperable.'

'It was fine this morning,' Loran protested.

'This morning, yes,' Chayn agreed. 'But it's been deliberately damaged.'

The Doctor leaned forward to Sam and said in a stage whisper, 'This is usually the part where we get accused of breaking it for some inexplicable reason and then get thrown in the brig.'

Balatan obviously heard this, as he had been meant to do, and he scowled hard at the Doctor. 'Did you do this? You two were in here on your own when we arrived, so you had the opportunity.'

'What did I tell you?' the Doctor asked sorrowfully. He smiled at Chayn. 'Do you mind if I take a look?'

'Go ahead.' Chayn moved out of the way, but not too far, Sam noticed. The Doctor moved past her to examine the interior of the lifter. Sam pushed her way past Chayn to join him, not knowing what she was even looking at.

'Did you do that?' Balatan repeated.

'No,' the Doctor answered. 'Chayn's right, though. That machine's inoperable without some major repairs, and it has been done deliberately.'

'*You* could have done it,' Loran insisted. Sam could see that he wasn't blind to the effect the Doctor's presence seemed to have on Chayn, and he was clearly jealous. Was Chayn his woman?

'Not really,' the Doctor replied. 'If I'd sabotaged it, I'd have done the job a little more elegantly. This was a typical bull-in-a-china-shop sort of sabotage. Not my kind of thing at all.'

Balatan scowled again. It seemed to be his favourite expression. 'Well, Chayn wouldn't have done it, and I know I didn't. Nor did my son. So who *did* do it?'

'I don't know,' the Doctor said. 'How large a crew do you have?'

'Forty-eight,' the captain replied.

'And do you know where they all are?'

'Not a chance,' said Chayn drily. 'Even if the internal scanners were all working – which they never are – they're easy to fool if you want to.' She turned to Balatan. 'I believe him, Captain. If he *had* sabotaged the unit, he must be stupid to stick around and greet us.'

'Or very, very sure of himself,' Loran added.

'Oh, I'm never very sure of myself,' the Doctor assured him. 'I'm quite undependable.' He turned back to Chayn. 'Thank you for believing me, though.' He went on, thoughtfully, 'Why would anyone want to sabotage a lifter, though? Don't you have more?'

Chayn snorted. 'You really haven't been on the *Quetzel* very long, have you?' she asked. 'We don't have spares for most of the equipment on board.'

'Ah.' The Doctor nodded sagely. 'Jerry-built, eh?'

'I'm sorry?'

The Doctor raised an eyebrow. 'And you're the one who keeps it going, I assume? You must be very inventive.'

'That's enough of that,' Balatan snapped, before Sam could say pretty much the same thing. The Doctor and Chayn were obviously starting to admire each other. 'Do you think you can repair this, Chayn?'

The engineer sighed. 'Before or after the other repairs?' she growled. 'Captain, I can't fix everything.'

'I can,' the Doctor offered. 'If the two of us pitch in together, I think we could get this up and running in a couple of hours.'

The thought of the Doctor and Chayn together for a couple of hours, repairing stuff and getting friendly, was not particularly appealing. 'Doctor,' hissed Sam, 'this isn't our problem. A quick cup of tea, and goodbye, remember?'

'But that would be so rude,' the Doctor protested. He

lowered his voice. 'Besides, we didn't sabotage this equipment, but somebody clearly did. Aren't you at all curious as to who or why?'

'Not really.'

'Splendid. So am I.' The Doctor smiled and turned back to Chayn. 'What do you say?'

Chayn grinned back at him. 'I'm game.'

I thought you might be, Sam thought. 'So, what am I supposed to do? Stand around and pass you both left-handed screwdrivers?'

'No,' the Doctor answered. He lowered his voice so that only Sam would hear. 'Stick with the captain and his son. Be nice to them. Find out what you can.' There was an oddly distant look in his eyes. 'I need to know what's going on.'

Sam was about to protest when Loran moved in. 'What about a spot of dinner?' he offered.

It seemed more like lunchtime to Sam, but the TARDIS's time and local time rarely matched. Her stomach was reminding her of the Mars bar she'd only half finished. 'Reconstituted muck?' she sniffed.

'Certainly not,' Loran answered, appalled. 'We may not be the smartest ship in known space, but we don't skimp on the food.'

'Real food?' Sam asked hopefully.

'I think tonight's the Breccan turkey,' Loran said, temptingly.

Real food… Sam was torn for a second between staying and keeping an eye on the Doctor and eating something that wasn't made by a machine. The food was very appealing – and the Doctor did need information. 'OK,' she finally agreed. She gave the Doctor one last, doubtful look, but he was already deep in discussion with Chayn about the repairs. Fighting back her irrational surge of jealousy,

Sam smiled at Loran. 'Let's go.'

Harmon had watched most of this exchange from the doorway. He hadn't been able to overhear much of the conversation, but he caught enough to realise that the strange man was going to help Chayn with the repairs. That could cause a problem. Chayn alone couldn't fix the lifting gear in less than ten hours, but if this man knew what he was doing, then the time could be halved. Would his allies be here by then?

Maybe another diversion was called for… As Loran, Balatan, and the girl moved to leave the cargo bay, Harmon slipped off, heading back to storage bay eight.

Chayn smiled at this Doctor as they worked side by side. He was good-looking, intelligent, and polite, she thought – just about everything she liked in a man. And his delicate hands were quick at making repairs. 'Just passing through?' she asked him, as she worked.

'Generally,' he agreed, reworking a circuit board.

'Will you be here long?'

'Hard to say.' He gave her a smile. 'It depends if anything catches my interest.'

Was that a come-on line? With any other man aboard the *Quetzel*, especially that simpering fool Loran, Chayn would have been certain. But with the Doctor, she realised, you couldn't be absolutely sure of anything. That was what made him intriguing. That and the fact that, unlike the rest of the crew, he didn't seem to be a loser in a dead-end job. She'd only signed on to get experience, and had no intention of re-signing when this flight was over. She'd take her money and run, fast and hard. And then… could the Doctor have a use for a good engineer?

'So,' he asked, in a seemingly casual fashion, 'what do you need this lifting equipment for?'

'Lifting,' she replied. 'The *Quetzel*'s a garbage scow. We ply the areas of space where wars have been fought, picking up whatever junk we can find. You'd be surprised how much can survive even a battle intact. What we can use, we salvage, either to repair the ship or to sell. What we can't feeds the engines.' She gestured at the bulkheads on the floor. 'A lot of the technology's salvageable.'

'And reused,' he observed, gesturing at the circuit board he was fixing. 'This is Draconian, the manifold's Terran and the power source is Dalek. Yet you've got them all working in harmony. You're quite an engineer, Chayn.'

'Thanks.' She found herself blushing, something she thought she'd forgotten how to do. 'And if you can differentiate between the types, you're no slouch yourself.'

'I've picked up a trifle here and there.' He replaced the board and began testing it. 'So, what is it specifically that you're trying to lift?'

'Some kind of a storage pod we picked up,' she answered. 'An unknown type. It was in the wreckage of a Dalek killcruiser, but obviously it doesn't contain a Dalek. We're not sure what might be in it.'

'If it's of Dalek manufacture, it's not likely to be a birthday cake,' he pointed out.

'We know that.' Chayn gave him a smile and inched a little closer. 'I've set up a containment field about bay eight already. Just in case.'

'Smart move,' he said approvingly. He finished testing the board, and moved on to the next, a few inches closer. Chayn liked that. 'Do you think it's possible that the lifter was sabotaged to prevent you from opening the pod?'

Chayn frowned. 'That's possible,' she admitted. 'But only four of us knew that was the plan.'

'Let me guess,' the Doctor said, his eyes sparkling. 'You, the captain, Loran… and…?'

'Harmon,' she replied. 'Our communications specialist.'

'Who isn't here,' the Doctor finished for her. 'Interesting. You wouldn't happen to know if he's been here, would you?'

'No,' Chayn answered, seeing what the Doctor was thinking. She pulled her palm comp from her pocket, and keyed it for communications. 'Faylen? What are you doing there? Where's Harmon?'

Her friend's voice came back, puzzled. 'I'm not sure,' she answered. 'I haven't seen him since he asked me to sub for him. You want me to find him?'

'Please. And Faylen – don't let him know, OK?'

There was a pause. 'What is this, some kind of surprise?'

'Something like that. Humour me.' She signed off, and then looked at the Doctor. 'OK, let's assume that it was Harmon who sabotaged the lifter. Why would he do that?'

'Offhand,' the Doctor answered, 'I'd say it's possible that he might know what's in that pod of yours. And that for some reason, he doesn't want it open.' He gave her a cheerful smile. 'Do you think that, once we're finished here, I could take a quick peek in bay eight?'

'After we're done here,' she told him, 'I'll take you anywhere.' God, was that too forward?

'Splendid,' the Doctor replied. 'Bay eight it is.'

The turkey was left at the side of the plate, but the vegetables were heavenly. Sam had been intending only to have a quick lunch, and then get back to the Doctor, but eating real food again proved too much of a temptation. Even having to listen to Loran didn't ruin her appetite.

'It's a lonely life out here in space,' he said, for the third time.

'Then why do you do it?' she asked him, not really caring.

'It's the family business,' he explained. 'All this will be mine one day.' He gestured around the galley.

A broken-down spaceship kept together only because Chayn knows what she's doing? thought Sam. What a thing to look forward to. 'It's very tempting,' she said, pretending to empathise. 'Owning your own business and all.'

'Oh, it can be very lucrative,' Loran assured her. 'Lots of money to be made when you find the right stuff. Anything technological sells for good money these days. Biologics are even better, of course.' He lowered his voice confidentially, so the three other crewmen also eating their dinners couldn't hear him. 'Like the artefact in bay eight.'

That sounded interesting. Maybe even what the Doctor wanted to know about. 'What artefact is that?' she asked, trying to sound casual.

'Don't know really,' he confessed. 'It's what we need the lifter for.'

Sam could put two and two together without much help. 'Maybe that's why the lifter was sabotaged,' she suggested. 'To stop you opening your little treasure.'

'You could be right!' Loran exclaimed, grasping her hand. 'You're smart as well as beautiful.'

Too smart for you, mate, she thought. 'Can I have my hand back?' she asked. 'I'm still eating.'

'Oh. Sorry.' Loran released her. 'It's just that it gets so –'

'So lonely in space without a woman, I know,' Sam sighed. 'Well what about Chayn? She certainly looks like a woman to me.'

He had the grace to blush at least. 'Oh, she's a woman,' he admitted. 'But, well, she's just not on my intellectual plane, you see. I need more than physical stimulation.'

'I can see that,' she told him sincerely. Electro-shock, probably, she thought. 'And I might be the woman you need... only...'

'Oh.' Loran almost groaned. 'You and the Doctor...?'

'Certainly not!' Sam exclaimed. 'It's just that I'm...' She lowered her voice. 'Under-aged. Just a child, really. I know, I'm very mature for my age, but, sad to say...' She let her voice die out, as if regretfully.

Loran withdrew his hand instantly. 'I had no idea!'

'I know.' Sam sighed theatrically. 'It's a curse, being so young and looking so...' She paused, as if seeking the right word.

'Desirable?' Loran suggested.

'Quite.' She patted his hand, and he almost cringed. Too smart for you, mate, she repeated mentally. 'Thank you for understanding.' She smiled brightly. 'Maybe you could show me some more of the ship.'

'Oh, yes,' he enthused. 'Wonderful idea. Let's take a look at the bridge, shall we? It's quite impressive.'

Sam had been hoping for cargo bay eight, but she didn't want to be too obvious. The bridge first, then she'd ask to see the bay.

They were finished in less than an hour, which amazed Chayn. She was good with machinery she'd always known that. But the Doctor was a magician. He seemed to have perfect affinity with whatever he touched, and it was primarily due to him that the repairs were completed so swiftly.

He was getting more and more interesting all of the time. Chayn was feeling almost intoxicated in his presence. He was like a little boy in a man's body, his enthusiasm contagious and real.

'Now,' he said, when the lifter checked out perfectly, 'which way is it to bay eight?'

Chayn sighed, and followed him out. 'This way, Doctor.'

In the corridor, he stopped and looked at one of the conduits. 'Your work?' he asked her, indicating the spliced power flows. She nodded, suddenly embarrassed. 'It's very elegant,' he said, and she blushed at the praise.

'Just a patch job,' she mumbled.

'You're too modest,' he told her. 'You have a real skill for this.' He grinned. 'I'll bet you could take apart a Dalek killcruiser without the Daleks knowing you were doing it. This way, is it?' He moved on before she could think of anything to say.

They reached the bay a few minutes later. Her face was still warm, and she couldn't think what to say to him. Usually she had the man eating out of her hand. But this Doctor…

'It appears to be locked,' he said, gesturing to the access panel.

Chayn frowned. 'Why would anybody lock it?' she asked rhetorically. There was nothing in there worth stealing – or small enough to walk off with. Only crew cabins normally had locks on them. Why bother anywhere else?

'To keep us out,' the Doctor suggested. He stared at the panel. 'Can we see what's going on in there?'

Chayn brushed him aside, hormones forgotten for the moment. 'Yes.' She tapped in her control code for the screen. It stayed dead. 'I'm locked out,' she muttered.

'That's a problem.'

'Not really.' Chayn tapped in Balatan's code next; she wasn't supposed to know it, of course, but there was precious little about the *Quetzel* that was a secret to her. This overrode the lockout, and the door hissed open.

The Doctor pushed her aside as a staser bolt zapped through the air where she had been standing seconds before. She crouched behind the bulkhead, stunned.

'I think we've found our saboteur,' he murmured.

'It's very... impressive,' Sam said, looking around the bridge.

'I knew you'd like it,' Loran beamed. 'This is my seat. Try it.'

Sam could hardly refuse. She sat in the chair and surveyed the bridge. It was about twenty feet deep and the same wide. The ceiling was about twelve feet high. She'd been expecting *Star Trek* and had ended up with early BBC. It looked like a set from some Fifties TV serial – tiny, cramped, and claustrophobic. There were five work stations, all manned, and the main viewscreen was about the size of the big-screen TV back home. The room was dimmed, probably because some of the bulbs had died and not been replaced, rather than for technical reasons. It was the sort of bridge a couple of computer nerds might build, and not the kind of thing you'd expect to see on a real starship. Sam felt definitely let down.

'It's very... comfortable,' she said.

'From here, I can survey the whole bridge,' Loran told her proudly. 'That's navigation, that's power, that's comm, and that's scanners.'

Sam nodded as he gestured to the various stations, wishing desperately she were somewhere else.

'Loran!' That was the woman at... what was it? Oh, yes, communications. A slightly overweight, pleasant-looking blonde. 'I'm getting a signal. Another ship. No,' she corrected herself. 'Two ships. Approaching fast.'

'What?' Loran looked puzzled, and then out of his depth. 'But there's not supposed to be anyone here, Faylen. This area was abandoned as strategically useless. We wouldn't be here otherwise.'

'I think someone's found a use for it,' Sam said, starting to worry.

'What am I going to do?' Loran asked her, fidgeting nervously.

'Maybe they're nice guys,' Sam suggested. She jumped out of his chair. 'Sit down, and calm yourself. Try opening hailing frequencies.'

'What?'

'Contact them,' she snapped, exasperated. 'Find out what they want. Arm all weapons. Raise shields. The usual stuff.'

'Weapons?' he echoed. 'Shields? What are you talking about?'

Oh, wonderful! 'Thank you, Doctor,' Sam muttered. Trust him to strand them on a ship with no weapons, no defensive shields... and nobody home in the captain's seat. Where was Captain Kirk when you needed him? 'Maybe you should call your father?' she suggested.

'Right!'

Since he didn't seem to be giving any commands, Sam called out, 'Put them on the main screen!' She hoped that made some sort of sense to these idiots.

It evidently did. Faylen tapped something into her console, and the screen sprang to life.

Two heavily armed ships were approaching, obviously quite swiftly.

Loran went pale.

'Doctor,' Sam muttered, 'I'm going to kill you. If either of us live that long.'

CHAPTER 3
REVELATIONS

Chayn and the Doctor stood with their backs to the bulkhead, the door to storage bay eight open. 'At least he's stopped shooting,' she said.

'I don't think whoever that is wants to kill us,' the Doctor mused. 'Just to stop us.' His eyes lit up. 'I'm dying to get a look at whatever it is he's guarding.'

'I wonder if it's Harmon,' Chayn said. She pulled out her palm comp and tapped in Harmon's access code. 'I'm sending a call signal to him,' she explained.

The call signal – two fast, one slow – sounded from the bay.

'It's him,' she said, feeling both satisfaction and irritation. 'He's always been a bit moody, but this is downright antisocial.' She moved to turn off the comp, but the Doctor stopped her. It felt rather nice to have him touch her, but this was neither the time nor the place to explore that.

'Maybe he'll talk,' the Doctor suggested.

To her surprise, Harmon answered the call. 'Chayn, stay back,' he said. 'I don't want to hurt you, but it's important that you don't open this artefact.'

'Why?' Chayn asked.

'I'm saving it intact for a client,' he replied. 'It's just business, nothing personal. They should be arriving any time now.'

'Who should?' asked the Doctor gently.

The comp link switched off.

'I suppose it's a trade secret,' the Doctor decided. 'We need another way in.' He glanced at the roof. 'Can we get into the collection tubes?'

'I don't see why not,' Chayn answered, grinning. 'He'll be watching the doors, but he may not have thought about the tubes. It's this way.' She started to lead him off when her palm comp chimed. She opened the link, expecting to hear Harmon again, and was surprised when she heard from Faylen.

'You'd better get to the bridge immediately,' Faylen said, clearly agitated. 'We've got two battle cruisers closing in on us.'

'Dear God!' Chayn signed off. 'This could be trouble. We're not armed.'

'I don't think they'll open fire,' the Doctor replied. 'I believe Harmon's customers have arrived. I wonder if they'll want their purchase gift-wrapped.'

'I'd still better get to the bridge,' Chayn decided.

The Doctor nodded, and accompanied her as she ran along the corridors. What had Harmon done now? Maybe the owners of the battle cruisers weren't going to open fire, but just having them close by made Chayn very nervous. She'd never trusted the military mind, of any race. She tended to hate all violence but especially when it took the form of weapons being pointed in her general direction.

She burst in on the bridge just behind Balatan, who glared at the image of the closing ships. The Doctor slipped over to join Sam, and he placed a kindly hand on his young companion's shoulder.

'Who the blazes are they?' Balatan demanded.

'I don't know,' Faylen replied. 'They haven't answered any of my signals.' She looked at Chayn, hoping for leadership, an idea of what to do next.

But Chayn couldn't help. The shapes were long, slender tubes with a reactor at the rear. Blisters pock-marked the ship at intervals, obviously weapon housings. They were finished in dull black, without markings of any kind. 'Nothing I've ever seen before,' she had to admit. At least, to the best of her knowledge, they weren't Dalek ships. They'd have been blazing away by now if they were.

'Nor I,' the Doctor admitted. 'Though there's a familiar feel to them that I can't quite put my finger on.'

'I told you we should have left earlier,' Sam muttered.

'Yes, you did,' the Doctor agreed, not looking at all contrite. 'And you were quite right. Perhaps there's time to pop back to the TARDIS before trouble begins. It's none of our business, after all.'

Sam sighed. 'Yeah, right,' she replied. 'I know. Not really our style, is it?' She looked hard into his eyes.

'That's the spirit,' he said approvingly. 'And it may not be all that bad. I think whoever they are just want to do a spot of shopping.'

Balatan scowled at him. 'What are you babbling on about?'

'Harmon's down in bay eight,' Chayn informed him. 'He's guarding the pod, and says he's got a customer coming to collect it.'

'What?' Balatan looked furious, and then interested. 'A customer? That's different, then.' He rubbed his hands together. 'I smell profit, after all.' He turned to Faylen. 'Can't you get an answer from them?'

Chayn glanced at the screen, and then at the navigation panel. One of the ships was standing off, the other coming alongside. 'They'll be docking in a minute,' she reported.

There was a buzz of static as the communications channel

sprang to life. A harsh voice ordered, 'You are being boarded. Resist and you will die.'

'Whoever said the customer is always right obviously didn't deal with these people,' the Doctor observed.

The *Quetzel* shuddered as the ship clamped hold of them. The battle cruiser was three times its size, filling the screen now. Faylen turned off the picture, which did little to make them feel better. 'Perhaps we'd better go and meet them,' Chayn suggested.

'Good idea,' the Doctor approved.

Balatan stepped forward. 'This is my ship,' he growled. 'And *I* say who goes to meet them. Chayn, you're with me.' He glared at the Doctor. 'You can come along, if you like, but the girl stays here.' He looked at his son. 'You're in charge here, even if there isn't much you can do.'

Sam looked as if she was going to protest, but the Doctor gave her a short shake of the head and an encouraging smile before following Balatan and Chayn from the bridge. It was a short walk down to airlock three, where the ship had docked. As they hurried, Chayn could feel the vibrations in the floor that meant the locks had been opened. They reached airlock three just as the inner door swung open.

She couldn't help feeling nervous and scared as the first of the suited figures marched into the corridor, their guns held casually, but ready for use. Each looked almost identical to the next, just over six feet tall. The armour encased them completely, only a small face plate showing portions of their faces. The visors were tinted, though, and she could make out little. The figures all had packs on their backs and at their hips, but wore no insignia or markings of any kind. They stood, impassively.

'What is the meaning of this outrage?' Balatan yelled at the first three figures, apparently choosing to ignore the fact that they had guns and he didn't. 'You have no right to be on my ship!'

The lead figure moved forward a couple of paces. Then it touched a connection on the helmet. The headpiece swung back, and Chayn saw the features of the intruder.

He was one of the physically most perfect specimens she had ever seen. Solid, regular features, eyes so blue that they seemed to burn, and short-cropped white hair. He looked to be in his mid-thirties.

'I am Delani,' he announced, staring imperiously about the corridor. 'Your ship is now under my command until I choose to leave.'

'You have no right,' Balatan exclaimed again. 'I demand that you leave my ship immediately!'

Delani raised his weapon. 'This gives me all the rights I need,' he said firmly. 'And if you persist in making a nuisance of yourself, I shall not hesitate to use it. Ayaka, bring in the rest of the troops, and prepare to take over the ship.'

The second figure nodded, and gestured back into the airlock. It then removed its own helmet, and Chayn felt another shock. Ayaka was a woman, and as perfect in her own way as Delani was in his. She had the most beautiful face, better than any entertainment star Chayn had ever seen. Clear-blue eyes, and neck-length hair so pale it seemed to shine.

'The ship will be ours in minutes,' she reported. 'Shall I contact Harmon?'

'Not yet,' Delani decided. 'Secure the bridge first. I want to ensure that there's no trouble. Then we claim the artefact.'

Ayaka nodded, and moved forward. 'Take us to the bridge,' she ordered Balatan.

'No,' he replied, crossing his arms. 'This is piracy, pure and simple, and I will not stand for it!'

'Then don't,' Delani said, firing once.

The projectile slammed Balatan back against the greasy bulkhead, a startled expression frozen on his face. Leaving a smear down the wall, he slid down to the floor, crumpled and broken.

Chayn stared from Balatan's body to Delani in horror. 'You killed him!' she gasped, shaking with shock and anger.

'He was warned,' Delani said impassively. 'Now you understand that I am in charge. You will take my troops to secure the Bridge, or I shall kill you next.' He swung the weapon about to point directly at her heart.

'There's no need for further violence,' the Doctor said smoothly, although his eyes were flashing with anger. He put himself between Chayn and the gun. 'We'll do as you request.'

'Good.' Delani seemed to lose interest, and turned away.

Chayn's heart was beating like an overheating drive unit. She could taste vomit in the back of her throat. These weren't customers – they were butchers, no matter how beautiful they might look on the outside.

Ayaka moved to join them, and six troopers fell in behind her. 'The bridge,' she prompted gently.

'This way,' the Doctor answered. He took Chayn's hand, and tugged her along. Her feet were unwilling to move, but she stumbled after him, trying not to look at Balatan's bleeding corpse as they passed it. 'That was unnecessary,' the Doctor said softly, but Ayaka could still hear him.

'It wasn't my decision,' she replied. Chayn glanced at her and saw something like disgust flit across her features.

'I know you,' the Doctor said abruptly. 'I knew the lines of your ship were vaguely familiar. You're Thals.'

Ayaka studied him with interest. 'You know of my people?'

'Intimately,' he replied. Then he stared pointedly at the gun she held. 'Though I thought they were pacifists.'

'That was a long time ago,' Ayaka answered. 'It's a luxury we can no longer afford. But I didn't know that anyone in this sector of space had ever heard of us, let alone met us.'

'They probably haven't,' the Doctor agreed. 'But I'm not from around these parts. I'm the Doctor.'

Ayaka stopped and stared at him. 'The Doctor?' she breathed.

A low murmur started up among the Thal troops, and some suspicious glances were thrown the Doctor's way.

Chayn was puzzled. 'These… Thals know you?'

'You might say I'm something of a legend to them,' the Doctor replied modestly.

'If you are the Doctor,' Ayaka said, and there was something akin to respect in her voice, 'then you've changed again.'

'A few times,' he answered. 'And I can prove that I'm the Doctor. You'll find the TARDIS is storage bay twelve.'

Ayaka was silent for a moment. 'Interesting,' she finally decided. 'But ultimately irrelevant to our mission here.'

The Doctor gave her a smile. 'You know I'm a friend of the Thals,' he said persuasively. 'What is your mission here?'

The trooper thought, and then shook her head. 'For the moment, my mission is to secure the bridge,' she replied. 'Nothing more.'

'These people are not soldiers,' the Doctor said. 'They're not even armed. There's no need for violence.'

'There won't be any, Doctor,' Ayaka promised. 'As long as everyone does as they are told and stays out of our way, we'll be gone very quickly. We mean them no harm.'

'Tell that to the captain,' the Doctor growled.

Ayaka flushed. 'That was… unfortunate.'

'That was murder,' the Doctor informed her, his voice clipped. 'Are you all like that?'

'No,' Ayaka answered. 'But we are what we must be. And what we are, you created.'

'I?' The Doctor frowned.

'You were the one who taught us to fight, Doctor,' Ayaka informed him. 'What we have become is what you helped to make. If you dislike what you see, you have only yourself to blame.'

Chayn saw a thunderstruck expression cross the Doctor's face. And then he fell absolutely silent, lost within himself.

Sam stared at the screen in horror. Faylen had switched it on to cover the meeting at airlock three, which had comforted Sam somewhat. She hated the Doctor being off on his own without her to look after him. But what she had seen had shocked her.

'Father!' howled Loran, as Balatan was gunned down by the intruders in cold blood. His face blanched, and he looked as though he was going to faint. Then he gripped the back of his chair, struggling to cope with the flood of his emotions.

Sam hadn't particularly liked the captain, but to see anyone shot down for no reason like that… She placed a hand comfortingly over Loran's, and could feel the tension in his body as she did so. What must he be going through now?

'I'll kill them,' he growled. 'I'll kill them all!' He started to turn.

'You're not a one-man army!' Sam exclaimed. 'They'll just

kill you, too, and what will that prove? Don't provoke them.'

'Provoke them?' He gave her a wild look. 'I'll provoke them all right!' He shoved her aside, and stumbled to the door. It wouldn't open.

'I've locked it,' Faylen said calmly. 'Loran, the girl's right. We don't have any weapons. These people will kill you in a second.'

'You're wrong,' Loran snarled. He stormed over to her panel and hit the override codes. 'Sit here and wait to die if you like. I'm fighting back.' Then he was through the door and gone.

Sam stared after him, shocked and concerned. 'Poor little prat... I should have stopped him,' she mumbled.

'You couldn't have done it,' Faylen told her gently. 'He's not thinking straight. He'll end up following his father to the grave.'

'Who are these people?' Sam exclaimed. 'And what do they want?'

'They're called Thals,' said the Doctor quietly from the doorway. 'And they want this ship. Or, specifically, the artefact in cargo bay eight.'

'Doctor!' Sam checked the urge to run over and hug him. 'I was afraid they were going to kill you, too.'

'There will be no more killing,' said one of the soldiers, 'as long as you all do as you are told.'

Sam stared at her, unable to believe what she was seeing. This killer was a drop-dead gorgeous blonde, the kind who'd send any fashion editor's eyes bulging and a photographer into ecstasy. This whole place was just getting more and more horribly ridiculous...

Three troopers, all male, entered the room. Like Ayaka, they seemed to be physically perfect. They were all blond and blue-eyed, like Hitler's dream of an Aryan super-race. But these were real, not an ideal. And they all had weapons held ready.

'You will all continue your duties as usual,' Ayaka informed the crew members. 'Please inform me where the remainder of the crew is. They will be collected and watched, but not harmed. We are not here to make war on a civilian target.'

'Soldiers,' Chayn said suddenly. 'You're not pirates, you're soldiers. What's going on here?'

'War,' said Ayaka simply. 'You've stumbled into the middle of it. I'm sorry for you. But you will be allowed to leave in peace once we have what we need.'

'Whatever's in storage bay eight?' Chayn asked.

'Yes.'

The Doctor rubbed his chin thoughtfully. 'Ayaka, let me come with you when you go to claim it,' he urged.

'It is a military target,' she answered.

'You know me,' he said gently. 'You know I am a friend of the Thals. And I must see this artefact. I have a very bad feeling about all of this.'

Ayaka considered, and then nodded. 'Very well,' she agreed. 'After all that you have done for my people, I cannot refuse you. But you must not interfere. Delani will not allow it.'

'I understand,' said the Doctor as Ayaka turned to walk away from them. He promptly sat down in one of the empty chairs.

Sam flopped onto the floor, and looked up at him. 'Doctor, who are these people? What's going on?' Chayn stayed with them, obviously curious herself.

'As I said, they're Thals,' the Doctor answered. 'Originally, they shared the planet Skaro with the Daleks – or Kaleds as

72

they were back then. Two humanoid species on one
world... and the inevitable happened. War. Long, bloody,
senseless war. In the end, the Thals won the battle and lost
the war. The Kaleds were wiped out, but the Daleks were
created from their ashes. The Thals, appalled by what they
had done, and not knowing that the Daleks still lived, swore
that they would never fight again.'

Sam eyed the troopers. 'They don't keep their word, then,'
she growled.

'And that's my fault,' the Doctor informed her. His eyes
were haunted. 'I fell in with a band of their ancestors
millennia ago.'

'What?' Chayn stared at him, uncomprehending. 'How old
are you?'

'A thousand, give or take a few weeks,' he replied.

'He's a time traveller,' Sam explained. 'That ship in your
hold can go almost anywhere in time and space.'

'A time machine?' Chayn breathed, fascinated. Sam could
see the hunger in her eyes. She was picturing a new toy to
play with, and she could probably do a better job of fixing it
than the Doctor could.

'So what did you do to them?' Sam asked the Doctor. She
could tell that he was very disturbed.

'The Daleks were coming back to life,' he explained. 'The
Thals were simple farmers, looking for fresh sources of food.
They had low levels of technology. The Daleks wanted to
murder them, and they had stolen a vital piece of the
TARDIS from me. I needed to get it back, but I couldn't
manage it alone. So I had to persuade the Thals to help me.
I forced them to fight. I made them stop being pacifists.' He
thumped his chest bitterly. 'I'm responsible for what they've
now become. I'm responsible for Balatan's death.'

Sam scowled at him. 'No you're not,' she snapped. 'You did what you had to.'

'That's no excuse,' the Doctor replied.

'We can't fight every evil in the universe by ourselves, can we?' said Sam. 'You helped them fight back in one situation. You didn't tell them what to do next.'

The Doctor smiled at her, a little distantly. 'Thanks.'

'So then what happened?' she asked him. 'I mean, if these Daleks are all over space, shooting up planets, how come the Thals are still around? Do they still share this.... what's it called? Skaro?'

'No.' The Doctor shook his head. 'The Daleks I helped them to stop were just the first. The Thals took over the Daleks' city and technology. When the remainder of the Daleks burst out of confinement, war began again. The Thals knew they were outnumbered, so they retreated from Skaro and fled. They founded a new home for themselves, and prospered. But they've always felt guilty about the Daleks. You see, in one sense the Thals created the Daleks. Without that war millennia ago, there wouldn't be Daleks today.'

'And that's why you fight?' Sam was addressing Ayaka now. 'Yes,' she said, walking over. She had obviously been listening in to some of the conversation. 'We fight. The Daleks have spread their plague to far too many worlds, and we will not stand by and allow this. So we fight. And, one day, we shall destroy them all.'

'It's such a shame,' the Doctor said gently. 'You're still very young, Ayaka. So are these men and women of yours. You shouldn't be concerned only with fighting and dying. You should be living your lives – not continually fighting.'

'I have a child, Doctor,' Ayaka replied. 'Her name is Rebec; I named her for my ancestor.'

'A good name,' the Doctor said approvingly. 'But why aren't you with her?'

'Because I am a soldier,' Ayaka replied proudly. 'All Thals who are to serve in the military must have a child first, to carry on their lineage. We are not allowed to fight before that.'

Chayn grunted in disgust. 'So you abandon your children?'

'No,' Ayaka answered. 'We fight for them. Rebec will be as proud of me as I am of my father. He was a soldier too.'

'Did you ever know him?' asked the Doctor.

'I do not need to have known him,' Ayaka said. 'He was a soldier. He fought the Daleks.'

'War,' the Doctor snapped. 'Endless, bloody war. Year after year, century after century. Death and destruction.'

'There is no other way!' Ayaka answered angrily. 'We must fight, or we must die.'

'There's always another way,' the Doctor answered. Then he calmed down. 'We just haven't found it yet.'

The whole system sounded appalling to Sam. A race of people who never knew most of their parents because they had all gone off to fight and die in an eternal war against the Daleks... No wonder the Thals were so murderous – it was all the life they knew. She found herself looking at Ayaka in a fresh way.

Ayaka saw this and glared at her. 'I do not need your sympathy or pity,' she said.

'Yes, you do,' Sam answered. 'Yes, you do.'

'Anyway,' the Doctor said, heaving a sigh. 'To get back to your question, Sam. The Thals no longer live on Skaro, and neither do the Daleks now. I helped to destroy it.'

'Destroy it?' Ayaka asked. She looked confused. 'Doctor –' She broke off when a chime sounded from her helmet.

Reaching back, she tapped a button. 'Ayaka.'

'Are the crew confined?' came Delani's voice.

'All but one,' she reported. 'The bridge is secure, and the other crew are being guarded in the dining area. I have two men out looking for the final person.'

'Acceptable,' Delani decided. 'We will now head down to the storage bay and claim our prize. Have one of the crew escort you down there.'

Ayaka turned to Chayn. 'You will show me the way,' she ordered. Sam noticed that her weapon hung straight down. She'd obviously decided that the crew was not a threat. 'Doctor, you may accompany me if you wish.'

'And I'm coming,' Sam said firmly. 'I'm not being left out this time.'

A faint furrow appeared in Ayaka's brow. 'This is not a family outing,' she said. 'This is war.'

'I'm with the Doctor,' Sam insisted. 'And I'm coming. The only way you'll stop me is to tie me up or shoot me.'

'Shall we go?' beamed the Doctor.

Ayaka sighed. 'Very well. But stay quiet. Delani will not be pleased.' She gestured, and Chayn led the way from the overcrowded bridge.

Sam felt both excitement and trepidation. She was going to get to see what this was all about at last. 'Will this be safe?' she asked the Doctor.

'I shouldn't think so for a minute,' he answered cheerfully. 'Rethinking your desire to accompany us?'

'No,' Sam said with determination. 'Just confirming that I made the right choice. You'll need me around if there's trouble.'

'That's my Sam,' he said approvingly.

This sent a shiver through her. It meant so much to her

that he was fond of her in his own, alien way.

They walked in silence the rest of the way through the underlit, musty, oily corridors. Sam could see that the *Quetzel* really was a patched-together junk ship. Most of the systems seemed to have been repaired a dozen times, using non-matching parts each time. But she was starting to get used to it. Sort of like a house that's been lived in for a couple of centuries, she decided. It has character, and something undefinable about it that makes you feel at home. It may be a mess, but with all this recycling going on it had to be the greenest ship in the galaxy.

There were two Thal guards outside the storage-bay door, both stiff at attention, their weapons at the ready. They were both beautiful blonde women. Weren't there any ugly Thals? Sam wondered. Or even non-blond ones? Ayaka nodded to them and then entered the doorway. The rest of them followed her. There was a small area inside to stand, and then a ladder leading down. Ayaka slung her rifle over one shoulder and started down. They followed her.

This bay was pretty much like the one the TARDIS had landed in. It was large, cavernous, and filled with junk. There were a bunch of Thals over by a couple of broken bulkheads, and one of the crew. Harmon, Sam realised. The one who had called in the Thals.

Delani looked up and scowled as they approached. 'Why have you brought all of these civilians?' he demanded. Close-up, Sam could see that he was slightly older than the other Thals. He didn't look like a cold-blooded killer – more like a refugee from *Baywatch*.

'This is the Doctor,' Ayaka said proudly.

'The Doctor?' Delani looked surprised, and then pleased. 'Is it really you?' he asked.

'Yes, I'm afraid it is,' the Doctor answered sheepishly. Delani was clearly sceptical. 'Alydon! Temmosus! Ganatus! I brought with me Ian Chesterton and Barbara Wright, and Susan!'

The names meant nothing to Sam, but Delani was clearly becoming more impressed.

'Come to join us in your TARDIS for the moment of our triumph!' Delani exclaimed. 'You've always managed to turn up when we've most needed you, haven't you?' He laughed, apparently very happy.

'You seem to be very popular around here,' Sam said.

'I'm a bit of a legend to these people,' the Doctor informed her quietly. 'It's a little embarrassing, really. But useful. I may be able to prevent further bloodshed.' He smiled at Delani. 'And what is it you're after?' he asked politely.

'This, Doctor,' the soldier replied, gesturing to something out of sight behind the closest shattered wall.

Sam, the Doctor, and Chayn all moved to see what it was. Ayaka followed. Sam frowned. It was just a large, egg-shaped metal object, pitted and scarred, with burn marks on the outside. 'So what is it?' she asked the Doctor.

'Dalek design,' he replied briefly. 'Some sort of a life pod, which is odd.'

'Daleks don't need life pods,' Chayn pointed out.

'Precisely.' The Doctor ran a hand over it. 'Still powered, too. It must have been floating around out there for a good number of years.'

'About thirty, we believe,' Delani said.

'What's inside it?' Sam asked. 'You know, don't you?'

'Yes,' Delani answered. He turned to one of his men. 'Cathbad, open it up.'

The younger Thal nodded and moved forward. He had a

small instrument in his hand some six inches around and four thick. He clamped it to the side of the egg, where it stuck, obviously magnetically. There were several controls on the upper surface of the device, and coded lights. He tapped away for a moment or two, and paused.

'The computer's overriding the locking mechanism,' he reported. 'It should be open soon.'

The Doctor moved back a couple of paces, frowning. 'I have a very bad feeling about this,' he said softly.

That bothered Sam. If he was worried, she knew that she should definitely be worried too. She stared at the pod, trying to figure out what it could be. There were butterflies in her stomach flying 747 jets.

The pod gave a sigh, and then began to come apart. Fissure lines opened in several places, and then began to fold back with electronic sighs. Air hissed slightly.

'Life supports are engaged,' Cathbad reported. 'The subject has survived and is waking.'

The panels opened downward, acting like legs, balancing the half-egg firmly on the ground now. The metal was several inches thick, obviously serious protection for whatever was inside. A bank of machines was now exposed, all of them lit and functioning. There was still no sign of the occupant. The machines began to fold back out of the way. Some obviously contained nutrients, others mechanisms Sam couldn't even begin to identify. Cryogenics, she supposed, to keep someone or something alive until it could be rescued.

The occupant was revealed as the apparatus peeled away. Sam gasped as she saw the ugly creature exposed. It was barely more than a wizened head and shoulders, embedded in electronic equipment. The skin was yellow-green and wrinkled, eye sockets sunken and blank. The nose was a beak, the mouth a short, dark gash. There was wiring over the skull, a small microphone attached next to the mouth, and what appeared to be some sort of a sensor embedded in its forehead.

The Doctor shook his head. 'Davros!' he breathed.

INTERLUDE
HUMAN SPACE

Space Special Security Agent Dryn Faber stood in the airlock, breathing gently as he began to equalise the pressure. Water cascaded in, flooding the chamber, and then he released the outer door. Light flooded in, diffused through the ocean, as he pushed his way out of his scout ship. As far as *it* was concerned, it made very little difference whether it was in space or underwater. He had programmed it to maintain its position a hundred and fifty feet below the surface of Antalin's ocean world.

An entire planet wreathed in water seemed incredible to him, but it was the case here. No islands or continents broke the unending waters. All life here dwelt in the ocean; there was nowhere else for it to go.

His files on this planet weren't exactly extensive. Antalin had been discovered fifty years earlier and hastily surveyed. With no land masses, it had been considered a poor place for colonization. There didn't seem to be any native civilisations – no way for them to invent fire, for one thing, to get them started on the road to technology – but anything was possible in the depths, Faber imagined. And that had been it, until SSS had detected the shadow of a Dalek contact in the area. It was standard practice to send in teams to investigate, and Faber had been assigned to check out Antalin, even though it had seemed highly unlikely.

And on the way down, his stealth ship had definitely picked up signs of activity below. He'd released a coded satellite that would fly to the edges of the system before it began transmitting. He didn't want to alert the Daleks to his presence. Now he had to take a look at what they were up to, and then disrupt it if possible.

His space suit worked just as well under water as above. The drive unit propelled him at low speed through the ocean. If the Daleks were monitoring – and they most likely were – he wanted them to view him as just another big fish. And there were plenty of those about. A school of silvery shapes flickered past him, each fish the size of his forearm, and bulky.

A larger, darker shape slipped past the school. Some sort of predator? Hard to tell. The fish didn't seem disturbed, however, so it was probably safe. And there wasn't much chance he'd be attacked here. He was extremely unfamiliar life, after all.

Faber broke the surface gently, no more than his eyes exposed. His visor clicked in automatically, binocular vision targeting the Dalek structure ahead. It looked like some kind of drilling rig – splayed floats, a nacelle and several upper decks, topped with a large laser-like drill. That made sense. The Daleks continually needed new supplies of metals and chemicals for their never-ceasing war efforts. And Antalin was completely unmined. The chances of good supplies here had to be high. This single base seemed to be their entire contingency here, though. Well, they were actually in human space here, albeit close to their own border. This had been a test project, most likely, to see whether it was worth exploiting Antalin in full. If these Daleks reported back favourably, then a full-scale invasion might well follow.

It was up to Faber to be certain that this didn't happen.

He'd sent for backup automatically, of course. But in this

82

business, you didn't wait for the cavalry to arrive. He was trained, as all SSS agents were, to act as an army of one. It never occurred to him to scout out the situation and wait for other agents.

He ducked below the surface again, sinking to about fifty feet, and then headed across towards the mining platform. He began to inventory his supplies. He was carrying a couple of magnetic mines, and he had more stored in his ship. His pulse rifle was strapped to his back, and he had grenades in a leg pouch. After a few seconds deliberation, he decided to head back to his ship and get further supplies. He'd get the chance for only one attack on the platform, so he'd have to destroy it the first time out.

Towing a small underwater raft behind him with several more mines and a small deuterium device, he started back towards the platform. He had the advantage of surprise here, but he knew better than to underestimate the Daleks. They were paranoid and obsessively cautious. They'd have some way to monitor beneath the platform, just in case. For all Faber knew, there could be whale equivalents here that might attack a floating station, and the Daleks could be watching for them.

Which meant he'd have to be very careful in his approach. He was helped in one way, in that light didn't penetrate too far underwater. He'd be no more than a vague shape until he was quite close to the platform. But sonar was another matter, and he set his suit's sensors scanning for any such signal – and detected it almost immediately.

That could be a problem. His suit wouldn't register as technology, thanks to its construction, but the raft behind him would. He'd have to disable the sonar somehow before he could set to work planting his mines. And the Daleks were bound to get suspicious as soon as the sonar went out. Unless, of course, he could supply them with a plausible, natural explanation as to what had happened to it.

Another one of the large, dark creatures started to glide past. It was almost twice the length of Faber, and was perfect for what he needed. He released the raft, and, as programmed, it maintained position, waiting to be recovered. Drawing his survival knife from his suit, Faber jetted towards the underwater creature.

It looked like a very large eel of some kind, its body long and sinuous. It had a crest along its back, and swam using several sets of paired fins that ran down the length of its belly. As he drew closer, the eel thing turned to stare at him. It had two eyes, and a large, tooth-filled jaw. It squirmed about in the water, heading towards him.

It was a predator, then, and would attack almost anything. Perfect. Faber waited, unworried, as it closed in on him. The massive jaws opened wide enough to swallow his legs, and several rows of sharp teeth were exposed. There wasn't much chance those teeth could puncture his armour, but there was no point in taking chances. Faber increased the power to his jets, and angled downward slightly, passing below the mouth of the surprised eel. As he did so, he swung over onto his back, and struck out with the knife. It penetrated the creature's skin easily, and he ripped it open several feet.

Dark liquid sprayed out, inking and clouding in the water. Portions of the eel's innards fell free, and he ripped around some more with the knife just to be certain he'd killed the creature.

It shuddered, and then relaxed in death, its fins ceasing to beat. Faber slipped his blade away and grabbed the carcass before it could fall into the depths. He tore at the incision he'd made, widening the gap, and then started cutting out the internal organs, creating a space in there large enough to disguise his own bulk. It was messy work, and the seas started to fill with scavenger creatures, all nipping at whatever he cut free. Well, at least that tidied things up a little. Thankfully, they didn't start tearing at the main bulk of the eel yet. They were probably not quite that brave.

In a few moments, he had what he needed, and slipped into the gap he'd carved. Then he started his jets going again at low power, back towards the drilling platform. He discovered that kicking out with his legs made the tail of the eel wiggle almost realistically.

With luck, the Daleks would see nothing suspicious in an eel approaching the station, and be caught off their guard. Faber grinned happily to himself. The platform grew larger, and it moved from being a dark shape into crystal clarity.

There were three main pontoons holding it up, which were joined by a framework. The work areas were built on this frame, and the laser drill was held suspended below. It wasn't working at the moment, which was one worry fewer for Faber. Dodging a laser beam wasn't high on his list of leisure activities.

Then he spotted the sonar detector, suspended a foot or so below one of the pontoons. A simple device, joined by wires and an armature. Nothing much to it. He cruised up to it, making it seem as if the eel were after food, and then used his knife to sever the cable connectors. His helmet informed him that the signals had ceased. There was a video monitor unit on the next pontoon, and he fixed this in a similar fashion.

The Daleks were now blind below the waterline, so he

threw off his disguise, watching it sink towards the sea bed. The scavenger fish pounced as it fell, and set to work on it. Faber doubted it would ever reach the bottom. Time to recover his raft and plant the bombs.

There was another shadow in the water, and he glanced at it. Another eel?

He realised he was wrong. This was no creature native to Antalin. It was wide, about six feet across, and two thick at the centre. It swam by undulating its entire body, like a ray. Twin stalked eyes stared at him, malicious intelligence evident.

A Slyther...

This was a creature from the Daleks' home world. They must have released one to patrol the sea about the platform. It would envelope its prey like a jellyfish, grabbing hold and then absorbing it through its membranes. It could pump stomach acids from the underside of its body to weaken its prey and partially digest it. Those acids would be able to penetrate his suit if it enveloped him.

The creature swam closer, and he unsheathed his rifle. There was the possibility that the Daleks might detect an energy discharge underwater, but he had to weigh this against the certainty that the Slyther would kill him otherwise. As it drew closer, Faber could see it preparing to extrude its stomach and envelope him. At the last second, he opened fire, raking that disgusting organ with a white-hot beam.

The Slyther thrashed in agony as he opened it up. He moved to one side as it dirtied the water with its outpouring blood, squirming in agony as it perished. Then it stopped moving, dead in the water. The little scavenger fish closed in again, tearing away at the creature. If he kept this up, he was going to have his own piscine fan club.

There was now no time to waste. The Daleks might well have detected his rifle's discharge, so the need for subtlety was gone. He sent a signal for the raft to join him, and moved to the closest pontoon, planting the two mines he carried, and adding the grenades for good measure. The raft closed in, and he started using the explosives there on the second pontoon.

A pressure wave slammed into him, and the water thrashed. He hit the pontoon with a bone-jarring force.

The Daleks were dropping depth charges at him. Damn.

He placed the three mines he had as a second detonation slammed through the water. There was no time for any more precision work. He locked the raft on to a collision course with the final pontoon, set his jets to maximum and shot himself out of the immediate area. A third explosion slapped his back, giving him a little extra thrust, but doing no damage.

He had to get out of range before triggering the mines. But if he waited too long, the Daleks might have time to remove or defuse them. And then, in the water ahead, he saw another shape. This was no Slyther. It was larger, bulkier and rounder.

Marine Dalek...

It was torpedo shaped, with the eye stalk at the point, scanning forward. Halfway down the streamlined body, parallel to itself, were the gun stick and a grappling arm. The inevitable sensor globes flowed towards the reactor at the rear that propelled the Marine Dalek through the water.

Hell... There was no time to waste. Faber triggered all of his explosives at once.

The pressure wave slammed into him, driving him

towards the Marine Dalek. His sensors were overloaded in the blast, and he couldn't get a clear lock on it. Thankfully, its own equipment seemed to be scrambled, too. It opened fire on him as he drew closer, but the laser fire couldn't target him properly. The water was churning and bubbling ferociously, no doubt helping to hide his shape and exact position. It also made it difficult for him to make out the Dalek clearly. He managed to free his rifle, though, as his readings started to come back on line.

If his were, then so were the Dalek's. He didn't dare wait for a clear target. Instead, he laid down a pattern of fire in the general direction of the Dalek, hoping for a lucky shot.

He didn't get one. Pain lanced through his arm as the Dalek returned fire, only with greater accuracy. His right arm lost all feeling, but he was left-handed, so he still had a hold of his rifle. And now, he'd seen the flash of the blast, he knew where the Dalek was.

His return fire tore across the belly of the Marine Dalek. Metal howled ferociously in the water, ripped apart and falling. Oil or some other liquid gushed out, like the ink from an octopus, blurring the waters. He kept firing anyway, and was rewarded with a ball of flame. He jetted on, and saw the bulk of the Dalek falling slowly out of its own cloud, towards the waiting sea bed. Its belly had been torn open, exposing the green, writhing creature within.

The omnipresent scavengers closed in, tearing at the Dalek creature as it slowly drifted down to the seabed.

His arm was starting to hurt badly now, and he headed towards his waiting scout ship. As he did so, he glanced back through the waters. They were filthy with clouds of darkness, but he could see something bulky tearing itself apart, and sinking slowly into the ocean behind him.

He'd succeeded in destroying the platform – hopefully, before the Daleks could send out word of his attack. With any luck, Dalek Central would simply assume something had gone wrong with its platform, and that Antalin wasn't a suitable place for mining operations.

Faber made it back to his ship, and was inside again in moments. He stripped off his suit, taking great care with his injured arm. He'd been hit across the biceps, which explained the horrible pain. He gave himself a shot of painkiller, and then put a regenerative pad over the wound, fixing it in place with a bandage. As he worked, the throbbing fire seemed to die down in it, and he focused now on preparing to lift off.

But were all of the Daleks destroyed? His quick glimpse of the platform on the way down hadn't revealed any starships moored there, but he hadn't had the chance to do a proper scan. Leaving the ocean might expose him to withering fire. On the other hand, if there were any Dalek survivors, staying here was suicide.

He powered up his scout, and armed all of his weapons. Then, grinning savagely to himself, he gunned the engine and shot towards the skies.

As he broke water, fire erupted all about him. He shot back, though he could see no targets a first. As he rose, his ship shuddered, but the shields held. His sensors had started to make sense of what was happening – two Dalek hoverbouts, their single Dalek occupants blasting at his ship. They had to be all that was left of the Dalek base, and they were trying to take him out. Faber spun his ship over, and launched one of his heat-seekers.

The first hoverbout exploded, showering metal and burning fragments towards the boiling sea below. The second Dalek fired again, and then Faber targeted it, too. Pathetic, really. They didn't have the fire power to take out his ship, but it had never occurred to them not to bother attacking. It would have been totally against their nature.

Alone in the skies, he banked about, and examined his handiwork.

The seas frothed and boiled below him. Chunks of metallic debris floated on the surface, and a slick of oil was spreading. The drill platform had vanished beneath the waves, still roiling where it had been.

Faber felt an intense satisfaction at another payback on the Daleks. 'That one was for you, Marc,' he murmured to himself, honouring the memory of his fellow agent and best friend who had fallen to the Daleks not long ago. 'And there's more where that came from. Much more.'

Turning his scout's nose towards the stars, Faber began the voyage home.

PART 2
PRISONERS OF WAR

'The art of war is simple enough. Find out where your enemy is. Get at him as soon as you can. Strike at him as hard as you can and as often as you can, and keep moving on.'
Ulysses S. Grant, *On The Art Of War*

CHAPTER 4
MADMEN ALL

'Doc-tor…'

The voice was more mechanical than human, and Sam hated it instantly. The creature, Davros, was utterly disgusting. There was little human left of him, it seemed, except for some of his emotions. The word had been purred almost affectionately, but Sam could tell that there was no love between the Doctor and this creature.

'It had to be you,' Davros said, reviving more each passing second.

'Yes,' the Doctor agreed. 'I suppose it was inevitable, really.'

'Doctor,' Sam asked in a stage whisper. 'Who is this?'

'Excuse me, I've been very remiss.' The Doctor smiled, and gestured towards the figure. 'Genocidal, xenophobic maniacs, number one in a seemingly endless series. Sam, this is Davros; Davros, this is Sam.' He lowered his voice very slightly. 'He doesn't shake hands,' he confided. 'You should just curtsey.'

'I know his name,' Sam said, trying to muster her patience. 'You mentioned him on Tractis. You don't exactly sound like old friends.'

'Quite the opposite,' he replied. 'Davros is the person who created the Daleks. And, like all would-be gods, he created them in his own image. That's why they're twisted creatures, without conscience or mercy.'

'Without weaknesses, Doctor,' Davros stated. The light in his forehead was pulsing softly.

'Without strengths,' the Doctor countered. 'Without a future.' He sneered. 'Without a hope.'

Davros gave an electronic rattle that Sam realised was a laugh. It chilled her, because it sounded both mechanical and insane. It was quite clear that Davros was completely barking.

'Much as I enjoy sparring verbally with you, Doctor, I can see that you are not alone.' Then his voice took on a note of alarm. 'Thals?'

'Thals,' agreed Delani, stepping forward. There was a smile on his face, and Sam could understand it. The Thals must really have it in for Davros for creating their greatest foes. 'And you are in our hands now. Your Daleks will not be able to rescue you.'

'His Daleks are dead,' the Doctor said flatly. 'He destroyed them.'

'Yes, Doctor,' Davros agreed. 'You tricked me into using the Hand of Omega to destroy them.'

'No, Davros,' the Doctor countered. 'You tricked yourself. I told you nothing but the truth. You unleashed its power and destroyed your world and your army. You're powerless now.'

Sam sighed. 'I feel like I've come in at the middle of a film,' she complained. 'None of this is making much sense to me.'

'Nor to me,' Chayn admitted.

'I'll explain it all later,' the Doctor promised. He turned to Delani. 'Are you telling me that your whole mission here was to capture Davros and take him for trial?'

'No, Doctor,' Delani answered, a smug smile still on his face. 'I'm not here to try Davros. I'm here to make him an offer.'

'What?' Sam had rarely seen the Doctor speechless – quite the opposite, if anything. But now he stood there, his mind clearly in a turmoil, his mouth slightly open but without a word coming forth.

'An offer?' Davros sounded intrigued. 'I have expected nothing but violence from your kind, Delani. I know you of old.'

'I'm sure you do,' Delani agreed. 'But circumstances change.'

'And politics make strange bedfellows,' the Doctor finally said. His body was tense, and he seemed almost ready to jump up and down on something – or someone. 'Delani, we have to talk.'

The Thal commander eyed the Doctor. Sam felt he should have had the sense to look more worried. Instead he simply nodded slightly. 'Very well.' He turned to Cathbad. 'Monitor Davros, and let me know when he has powered up sufficiently to be transported to our ship.' To Ayaka, he added, 'Watch those two aliens. Don't let them interfere in any way.' Turning back to the Doctor, he said politely, 'Let's get some privacy, shall we? I never imagined that I would ever meet a legend.' The Doctor shot him a dark stare, but followed him out of earshot across the storage bay.

Sam didn't know what to do. There was still so much that she didn't know. Davros was obviously somebody very dangerous, and the Doctor was extremely concerned about him. Still, there was nothing she could do about it at the moment. And these Thals really bothered her. Delani had killed the poor old captain without hesitation. What would it take to trigger a wholesale massacre of the *Quetzel*'s crew by the rest of the Thals? She eyed Ayaka nervously. The young woman seemed to be a little different from Delani, lacking some of his fanaticism. And she had promised there would be no more bloodshed. But could Sam believe that?

'What's it like to kill people for a living?' she asked the Thal. They had moved away from where Cathbad was running some kind of diagnostic on Davros.

Ayaka's eyes hardened. 'I do not kill people,' she replied coldly. 'I kill Daleks.'

'And they're not people?' Sam asked.

'No.' Ayaka stared at her. 'You do not know the Daleks?'

Sam shrugged. 'The Doctor's talked about them, and I've read a bit about them, but I've never met a living one. Can't say I'm dying for the pleasure, either.'

Ayaka nodded. 'A sensible wish. Daleks *are* death. There is only one way to avoid being killed by a Dalek, and that's to kill it first. One day, I shall die fighting them. But I will have taken many of them with me.'

'And that's a fair exchange?' asked Sam. 'Kill until they kill you? That's it? That's the sum total of your life?'

'It is a noble cause,' Ayaka answered. 'We fight to save our people – and other peoples – from the Daleks. If we did not fight, the Daleks would overrun the galaxy and slaughter every race they encountered in a matter of years. We have to destroy them.'

'And innocents, like Balatan?' Sam jibed.

Ayaka flushed. 'That was… unfortunate,' she agreed. 'He was stubborn. And Delani had no choice.'

Chayn had obviously picked up on what Sam was doing here. 'Would you have killed him?' she asked the Thal.

For a moment, Ayaka didn't reply. Sam could see from her eyes that she was troubled. Struggling with her conscience, perhaps? Finally, in a whisper, she admitted, 'No.'

Sam sized her up afresh. 'Look, I know I don't have any right to say this. I'm not in the position you're in, fighting a war for my life, and the life of my whole world. But surely, if you let it, this war will take away everything that makes you what you are –'

Chayn cut across her, her voice bleak. 'My father was a soldier,' she said. 'He fought the Daleks, along with other races. He hired himself out to kill for money. I only saw him three times in my life. The last time, he was in a medlab, strapped to a bed, dying. His body had been shattered, but he wanted to tell me that he loved me before he died.' Her voice became very quiet. 'He did. And I couldn't believe him. If he'd loved me, he'd have been with me, raising me.' She glared at Ayaka. 'I hate war, not because of what it does to my enemies, but because of what it does to those I love. It took my father away from me and killed him. But before it did that, it made him forget about everything that was important – really important – in life. He told me that he loved me, but by then he'd forgotten what love is.' She swallowed. 'I've heard it said that the first casualty of war is the truth. That's not so. The first casualty in war is love.' She looked into Ayaka's eyes. 'Perhaps your child will be able to forgive you for not being there for her. Perhaps she'll even grow up thinking you're some kind of a hero. She may even be right. But that doesn't matter. Because war has already killed everything important inside of you. You've lost your love.' She paused, waiting for that to sink in. Ayaka said nothing. 'Your little girl isn't a real person, with needs and hopes and fears. She's simply a symbol of what you're fighting for now, a sacrifice you've made. A part of you you've chopped off. Like your conscience. You know what Delani did was wrong, and yet you said nothing.'

'He's my superior,' Ayaka said quietly.

'He's nobody's superior,' Chayn snarled. 'He's just some soulless bastard who kills innocent people who get in his

97

way. If he weren't in a uniform, he'd be on trial for murder right now. But because he's a soldier, instead he's a hero, and you all obey everything he tells you to do.'

'She's right,' Sam said, beginning to feel a little detached from the conversation. She reminded herself that six months ago her oratory skills had been confined to a poorly attended sixth-form debating club. 'If you let it, this fighting will kill everything that's good in you.'

'It hasn't,' Ayaka insisted. 'And it won't.'

'It has,' Chayn said bitterly. 'When was the last time you fell in love? Allowed yourself to be vulnerable, to –'

Ayaka shifted uncomfortably, and interrupted her. 'I am a soldier, and could die any moment. Emotional entanglements are an unnecessary complication.'

'Emotional entanglements are what makes life worth living,' Chayn answered, then she paused. 'It's the answer I expected from you.' She turned away in disgust.

Sam could see that Ayaka was troubled, but was it enough to win the woman over? 'Don't you have any friends?' she asked gently. 'People you are close to, at least?'

The Thal thought about this for a moment. She'd clearly been about to pontificate along the lines that friends are also emotional entanglements a soldier doesn't need, but she thought the better of it. Finally she nodded slightly. 'I have two,' she admitted. 'Dyoni, who commands one of our ships waiting for us. And Cathbad.' She gestured towards the solider with Davros. 'But they are luxuries I cannot afford. They could die any time, and if I stopped to grieve, then I would probably die, too. It is better not to care.'

'Bugger off,' retorted Sam. 'It's simpler not to care. But better? No way.'

'You are trying to disturb me,' Ayaka answered. 'I don't

know why. But it is wrong. A soldier should not be asking these sorts of questions.'

'A soldier shouldn't,' Chayn agreed, turning back. 'But a human being – or even a Thal – should. You have to decide whether you're a Thal first, or a soldier first. And then learn to live with the decision you make.' She looked over to where Delani and the Doctor were deep in heated discussion. 'Delani is a soldier first. That's obvious. He can even sublimate his hatred if he thinks it necessary.' She glanced at Davros. 'I don't know the history of your people very well, but I would assume that Davros is not well liked.'

Ayaka clearly felt on safer ground here. 'He is despised, feared, and spat upon. He alone is responsible for the evil of the Daleks.'

Chayn shrugged. 'Then why hasn't Delani ordered him executed?' she asked. 'Delani killed Balatan, who did nothing to your people. Yet he's willing to offer this monster a deal?'

'Right,' Sam agreed. 'Do you agree with this plan?'

'I do not have to agree,' Ayaka snapped. 'I am a soldier. I have to obey.'

Sam rolled her eyes. 'We're back to that again, are we? You have to obey? What if Delani tells you to do something that you know is wrong? Then what do you do?'

Somehow, Sam realised, she'd asked a question deeper than she had known. A tear formed at the edge of Ayaka's eye. She made no move to brush it away. Her beautiful face was frozen in the grip of some deep emotion. Finally, she stood taller. 'I am a soldier,' she replied. 'I do what I must. And I will speak no more about this.'

'What will you do if *we* speak more about it?' Sam pressed. 'Kill us?'

Ayaka turned her back on them and walked to join

Cathbad. Sam sighed, and looked at Chayn. She was starting to understand and like the engineer. 'I really pushed her buttons somehow,' she said. 'I wish I knew why. It might help us.'

'It's a start,' Chayn said. She glanced over at the Doctor. 'And we seem to have done better than the Doctor has managed.'

Sam followed her gaze, and saw that Delani was yelling at the Doctor, who appeared resolute. Now what had happened?

Delani was feeling very pleased with himself when he led the Doctor aside to talk with him. He had already succeeded in his objective: to locate and recover Davros. That would look very good on his record, especially after the victory on Terakis. He was bound to get his long-deserved promotion for this. And to run into the legendary Doctor, too! Here of all places in the universe. The mysterious traveller who appeared at times of crisis and great significance, here to help him with his plans. It would add the last extra little polish to his record.

'I am so glad to see you, Doctor,' Delani said warmly.

'You may not be so glad soon,' the Doctor answered bluntly. 'What are you doing?'

Delani was puzzled. 'I am taking Davros back to our home world, where he will aid us in our struggle against the Daleks.'

The Doctor stared at him, his eyes troubled. 'Are you a madman or simply a fool?' he asked. 'Davros is far too dangerous to be trusted.'

'I have no intentions of trusting him, Doctor,' Delani answered. 'Rest assured of that. But he will be compelled to

100

work for us. He already has a motive: his loyal Dalek forces have been annihilated, and he is sought by the rest as a criminal.'

'I know that,' the Doctor said. 'I helped engineer his losses. But you can't count on his hatred of the Imperial Daleks to make him work for you. He's too devious for that. If you give him the opportunity, he will most certainly betray you. It's his nature, he can't help it.'

Delani could see that the Doctor was concerned, and sought to put his mind at ease. 'He will not be given that chance, I promise you. We are going to fit an explosive collar to his life-support chair. At the first hint of a problem, it will be detonated, killing him. He will have to cooperate to stay alive.'

'A bomb?' The Doctor snorted. 'You think *that* will keep Davros in line? He's also been exterminated, blown up, frozen and heaven knows how many more fates. And he's escaped each one of them. A bomb isn't going to worry him greatly. He'll find a way around it.'

'Are you always such a pessimist, Doctor?' Delani inquired, refusing to be baited. He was in too good a mood for that.

'On this occasion I'm being a realist,' the Time Lord replied. He blinked slowly. 'And what is it that you want Davros to do, exactly?'

'That's a military secret, I'm afraid,' Delani said. He spread his hands and smiled. 'If I could tell you, I would, but...'

'But it's obvious anyway.' The Doctor studied Davros from across the room. 'He's an all-round genius and maniac, but his speciality is genetic warfare. You and your superiors want Davros to help breed a biological deterrent, don't you?' He studied Delani's face, and then shook his head. 'No, nothing that sensible. You want Davros to alter your species, don't you?'

So the Doctor had already guessed. Well, it would do no harm to confirm the man's suspicions now. 'Yes.' He gestured at himself. 'We are flesh and blood, Doctor. Perfect specimens, perhaps, and enhanced by careful breeding. We are faster, stronger, more endurable than most humanoid species. But we are still no match for the Daleks. What we need is a biological edge, and we lack the knowledge. Davros can give it to us.'

'You are insane,' the Doctor decided finally, a look of horror on his face. 'You know what Davros has done to the Daleks, and yet you're willing to allow him to do the same to you!' Agitated now, he exclaimed, 'You can't defeat the Daleks by becoming the Daleks!'

Delani, too, was starting to get irritated. The Doctor, for some reason, didn't seem to be understanding and appreciating the plan. 'We don't intend to become the Daleks,' he growled. 'We will not allow Davros to remove the nobler emotions or drives of our people. But we must become stronger and better.'

'You will not *allow*?' Now the Doctor was getting very excitable. 'Delani, Davros will find a way to pervert whatever mad plan you're thinking up into something even worse!' He pointed to Ayaka. 'Would you turn *her* into *that*?' He gestured at Davros.

'If it will help us to finally annihilate the Daleks, yes!' Delani said with passion. 'Anything is worth that aim.'

The Doctor was suddenly very still, which bothered Delani more than his passion. 'No,' he said softly. 'No, it isn't. Some things are not worth the price.'

'Victory is worth any price,' insisted Delani. 'Would you sooner see us perish?'

'Than become *that*?' The Doctor turned worried eyes on

to Davros again. 'Yes. I'd sooner see the entire Thal race exterminated than have them become like that. It would be better for them in the end.'

'Then you're a fool, Doctor,' Delani decided.

'No,' the Doctor disagreed. 'An idealist, perhaps. But not a fool. I'll leave that job to you. Is there nothing you wouldn't do to gain your victory?'

'Nothing,' Delani agreed with complete conviction.

'Then you've surrendered the moral high ground, and I have nothing more to say to you.'

Delani had heard such talk before, from Thal civilians, and he had nothing but contempt for it. He sneered. 'Doctor, in war, there is no moral high ground. There is only survival or death. Either the Daleks perish, or the Thals do. And I intend to make certain it's the Daleks.' He tried once more to reason with the saviour of his people. 'You know the Daleks, Doctor, perhaps better than anyone outside the Thal race. You know they cannot be reasoned with, or intimidated, or bribed. The only way to stop them is to annihilate them utterly.'

'Perhaps,' the Doctor conceded. 'But I was wrong. You aren't turning into a Dalek – you've already become one.'

Delani was stung, and almost furious enough to backhand the Doctor. It took all of his self-control to restrain his fist from striking. 'I am sorry you feel that way, Doctor,' he grated. 'But you are wrong. We can do what we plan. Davros will work for us. The Daleks will be defeated. As soon as he is able to be transferred to my craft, I am taking Davros and returning home.'

The Doctor shook his head once. 'I cannot allow that.'

Delani stared at him in anger. 'You cannot allow it? You have no say in the matter! And if you try to interfere in any way –'

'What?' the Doctor demanded. 'You'll have me killed? And the rest of the crew? And anyone who stands in your way? Delani, tell me – what are you fighting for?'

The question caught him off guard. 'To destroy the Daleks, of course,' he replied honestly.

'That's what I suspected.' The Doctor gazed thoughtfully at Ayaka. 'She, at least, is fighting to save the Thals.'

'It's exactly the same thing,' Delani snapped, irritated again.

'No. No, it isn't. She's fighting for a positive goal; you for a negative one.' He smiled sadly. 'I know you can't see the difference, but it's real.'

Delani was confused and angry. He had been expecting the Doctor to back him up, and encourage him. Instead, he was ranting on with nonsensical pacifist muck and threatening him. 'It's time we returned to the others,' he decided coldly. 'I'm sorry, Doctor, but you leave me no choice.'

'And you leave me none, either.' The Doctor's eyes were sad. 'And you have no idea how much that pains me.'

Ignoring him, Delani marched the Doctor back to his companions and Ayaka. She came crisply to attention. She was a good soldier, and loyal to the core. 'Ayaka,' he barked. 'The Doctor and his companions are to be locked somewhere secure until we return to our ship. Stay with them, and guard them.'

Ayaka looked puzzled. 'I… don't understand,' she confessed. 'Is the Doctor not on our side?'

'No,' the Doctor replied, saving Delani the trouble. 'The Doctor most assuredly is not. You'd better do as he says.'

Delani smiled in satisfaction. 'Do it,' he ordered. Ayaka nodded her understanding. With her rifle, she gestured for the Doctor, Sam, and Chayn to precede her. Wordlessly, they did. Delani ignored them now. The Doctor had been neutralised, at least. He turned his mind to more important matters, addressing Cathbad. 'How is Davros doing?'

'His systems are up to forty per cent power,' Cathbad reported. 'It will be only a short while before he is able to be transferred.'

'Excellent.' Delani studied Davros's impassive face. 'Attach the collar now.' Cathbad pulled the device from a pouch in his suit, and clicked it into place about Davros's throat.

Davros came to life again. 'An explosive device to secure my cooperation?'

'Precisely.'

'A wise precaution,' Davros approved. 'You have clearly thought this through.'

'Thank you,' Delani said, pleased with himself. The Doctor was worrying unnecessarily. Davros was impotent, and could do nothing. All of the cards were in Delani's hand, and the game was now his. Nothing could possibly go wrong.

'I'll kill them all,' Loran muttered to himself. 'I'll kill them all.' It was an incantation he needed to focus his mind. Part of him wanted to grieve the death of his father, but there was no time for that now. These Thals had invaded his ship, killed his father, and were holding his crew hostage. They had to be stopped. They thought they had the upper hand because they possessed the only weapons aboard, but they were wrong.

In storage bay twelve was another weapon, and Loran had made his way there to secure it. He wasn't an engineer, and could have done with Chayn's help in this, but dismantling the wrecked Dalek wasn't too difficult a task. The blaster was a single unit, and could be removed for replacement or recharging quite simply. It didn't take long for him to free it from the casing, and he checked its charge. There was still power in it, perhaps not very much. But certainly sufficient for the time being. He hefted the gun, a long, balanced barrel on a universal mount, attached to the power pack and trigger – a small button to depress. He checked that it would work, and energy lanced from it, exploding a small section of one of the wrecked bulkheads.

Now he was armed, and he could begin taking back his ship.

He hurried to the exit, forced to climb the ladder one-handed while carrying the gun, and then into the corridor beyond. The Thals were bound to be searching for him, he realised, but they were convinced he was helpless. They'd soon discover the truth.

He heard the sound of footsteps ahead, and knew it must be his foes. Grinning, he paused, the Dalek gun at the ready. Two Thals came around the corridor junction, their weapons held casually until they saw him. Both men then looked shocked, and started to raise their rifles.

Loran depressed the firing trigger, and exterminated them both. The Thals danced in electronic flame, and then collapsed to the deck. He almost giggled at the macabre sight, and found himself wiping tears from his eyes. Hurrying to their steaming corpses, Loran stripped them of their rifles. Both had pouches attached to their armour containing small percussion grenades, which he also took.

Now he was better armed, his next task was to try to free some of the crew. The more of them there were to continue the fight, the better. These Thals were about to learn that they had taken on the wrong foe this time. They would pay for what they had done, all of them. 'Rest in peace, father,' he muttered. 'Soon you'll have plenty of company.'

CHAPTER 5
COUNTERSTRIKE

'He's quite insane, you know,' the Doctor said brightly.

Sam gave him a sour glance. 'Davros?'

'Delani. He thinks that he can compel Davros to build him a better Thal.' The Doctor turned and looked at Ayaka. 'How would you like to end up looking like Davros? Or a Dalek?'

'I do what I have to do,' Ayaka said simply. 'I do not make the policy; I only obey orders.'

'Then you're a fool, Ayaka,' the Doctor said without rancour. 'Obeying evil orders is wrong. And avoiding thinking about the moral implications of what you're doing is worse. And following the orders of a madman makes you no better than a hired killer.'

'That is not true!' she snapped.

'Which bit of it?' the Doctor asked her with a smile.

'All of it,' Ayaka insisted. But even Sam could see that the woman was worried.

'Delani wants to turn her into a Dalek?' Sam asked. 'Talk about a waste. I'd kill to look like that. Why does he want to do it?'

'He's convinced that the Thals as they are can't defeat the Daleks,' the Doctor explained. 'So he intends to force Davros into modifying their biology to make them better killers.'

'Is he right, Doctor?' Chayn asked.

'That the Thals can't defeat the Daleks as they are?' He shrugged. 'Possibly. That he can force Davros to do what he wants? Absolutely not. He doesn't know Davros like I do. He always scrapes through, and he always leaves the corpses of others in his wake. Delani will discover his mistake eventually, but I can't allow him to make it. Davros has caused enough deaths. We've *got* to stop him. His insanity *cannot* be allowed to spread.' He turned to Ayaka, giving her his best smile. 'Be sensible, Ayaka. Please. Help us.'

Ayaka gestured with her rifle. 'That door ahead,' she said to Chayn, ignoring the Doctor. 'What's behind it?'

'It's one of the crew's quarters,' Chayn replied. 'Faylen's, I think.'

'That will do. Open it.'

Chayn did so, and Ayaka gestured again with her weapon. 'Inside, all of you.' As they obeyed, she said to the Doctor, 'I cannot do as you ask. I am a solider, and must obey orders.'

'No,' he replied gently. 'Think.'

She closed the door in his face.

'Pity,' the Doctor said. 'Just as I thought I was getting through to her, too.'

'She's a soldier first and foremost,' Chayn commented. 'You'll never turn her against Delani.'

'Perhaps not.' He surveyed their surroundings. 'Let's look for another way out of here, shall we? It's vital I stop them from removing Davros.'

Sam had a quick look around, but there wasn't much to see. An unmade bed in the corner, a small table with a couple of chairs, and an entertainment unit of some kind. A small computer was built into one wall. 'Not exactly the Ritz, is it?' she asked. There were two doors, which she opened. One was a tiny wardrobe, the other led to the bathroom. It held a toilet and a shower.

Chayn shrugged. 'The *Quetzel* never made much money,' she confessed. 'We don't have access to much. It's a life. Not much of one, but a life.'

'You must get bored out of your skull here,' Sam said sympathetically.

'A lot of the time,' Chayn admitted ruefully.

'Excuse me,' said the Doctor politely interrupting them. 'But we really do have to escape.' He looked up at the ceiling, which was metal, like the rest of the room. 'Are there conduits up there? Access tunnels? Another room above? Anything we could break into?'

'Outer hull,' Chayn informed him. Then she grinned and pointed to the floor. 'Down here's another matter, though. She pulled out her palm comp and accessed the ship's layouts. 'There's an access shaft for the power couplings right below us.'

'Sounds perfect,' the Doctor said. 'Now, let's see about getting into it, shall we?' He smiled, and fished something out of his pocket. 'At least Ayaka didn't think to search us. I suspect she's too bothered by her conscience. Swiss Army knife!'

Chayn matched his grin, extracting a tool from her own pocket. 'And what engineer would be without a screwdriver?' She indicated a section of the floor. 'This one.'

The two of them set to work removing the screws holding the six-by-six section of metal in place. Sam felt a stab of jealousy, seeing how well the Doctor and Chayn were getting along. The Doctor admired Chayn's skills, she could tell, and it was beginning to make her feel inadequate. Chayn looked similar in age to the Doctor's physical appearance, and she seemed to know exactly what she was doing. To distract herself, Sam asked the Doctor, 'What was all that you were saying about Davros not wanting to be rescued by the Daleks? If he created them, that doesn't make much sense.'

The Doctor pursed his lips. 'I'd better fill you in on the basics of Dalek history,' he decided. 'As I mentioned, Davros created the Daleks in his own image. He used his genetic techniques to make them without mercy or consciences, and to believe that all other forms of life were inferior and fit only for enslavement or extermination. He forgot that, to the Daleks, he's an inferior form of life. They tried to kill him, not realizing that he'd built a backup life-support system in his mobile unit. That put him into stasis for quite a while.

'The Daleks managed to embroil themselves in a war with a robotic race known as the Movellans, and reached an impasse. To break it, the Daleks realised that they needed Davros's mind. They rescued him from the ruins of Skaro, and aimed to use him to defeat the Movellans. But I managed to engineer his capture, and he was taken to Earth for trial and imprisonment.

'But he was rescued again. I met him again in a holding house for the recently deceased and terminally ill stored cryogenically until they could be cured by any advances in medical sciences. Davros was converting the stored bodies into Daleks, this time absolutely loyal to him. He intended to use them to regain the Dalek empire. The Imperial Daleks – those not loyal to him – captured him, but he somehow escaped and finished the creation of his army on Skaro.'

The Doctor glanced up at his rapt audience. 'That's when I laid a trap for him. I had left on earth a Time Lord device called the Hand of Omega. Very powerful. It's used for customising suns. Through information I let slip, Davros believed he could use it to turn Skaro's sun into a source of power that would enable him to take on even the Time Lords in a spree . of destruction. In fact, I had already

112

programmed the Hand to destroy Skaro's sun if it was deployed. Davros, secure in his arrogance, used the Hand. It wiped out Skaro's solar system and shattered his army totally.

'That was a pretty sneaky thing to do, wasn't it, Doctor?' said Sam.

'But necessary, Sam. So you see,' he summed up, 'the Daleks that are left alive are the Imperial Daleks, the faction that hates Davros. There can't be many of them left. And if they ever discover him alive...'

Sam grimaced. 'I can see why you don't want him in the hands of the Thals,' she said. 'He isn't going to do what they want, is he?'

'Not Davros,' the Doctor agreed. 'He'll find a way to try to seize power once again. He's done this once to the Daleks, and I'm not going to allow him to do it again to the Thals. They happen to be friends of mine.'

'With friends like those,' Sam observed, 'you don't need enemies.'

'Think of it, Sam,' the Doctor insisted, a little harshly. 'This war of theirs with the Daleks has dragged on for centuries, maybe even millennia. Imagine the lives they've led. Ah, there we are.'

Sam dropped her head and looked at the floor, a little embarrassed. She saw that the floor panel had finally come free, and the Doctor and Chayn swung it up. Below, as Chayn had said, there was an access tunnel, large enough for them to move about in if they walked at a half-crouch. They all slipped down, and then the Doctor lowered the floor section back into place.

'Where to?' asked Chayn, studying the layout on her comp.

'Storage bay eight,' the Doctor said. 'I've got to get to

Davros before the Thals can move him.'

'This way, then.' Chayn set off in the lead. She called back. 'There's just one thing I don't understand, Doctor. You say that Davros's Daleks are all wiped out, and that the Imperial Daleks are a shadow of their old selves. So why haven't the Thals been able to simply eradicate them?'

'That's a very good question,' the Doctor answered. 'And here's another – how do these remnant Daleks possess so many ships? You've got parts from at least four different killcruisers in your holds. One of them is Davros's own that the Hand destroyed. Three more, in such a small section of space, is a trifle odd.'

Sam sighed. 'There's obviously something going on that you don't know about,' she concluded.

'Precisely,' agreed the Doctor. 'And if there's something the Daleks are up to that I don't know about, it worries me.'

That didn't exactly reassure Sam.

Davros waited until Cathbad was occupied with his equipment before sending out a simple pulse to the collar he wore. Delani was a fool, just like all the Thals. Imagine thinking a simple device like this could hold Davros ransom! He used the circuits in his chair to analyse the collar, and almost laughed. It was pathetically simple to defuse, and would take only minutes. His support systems were up to only sixty per cent strength, but that was quite enough to generate controlled electric charges that he could use to reprogram the collar. Once that was done, he would deal with his Thal guard. Then he would take over the ship.

All of this was ludicrously simple for him. The only real problem here was the Doctor. Always in the past the Doctor had managed to interfere with Davros's plans. He'd even managed to dupe Davros into destroying Skaro and his Dalek army. That was a setback, true, but nothing more. Once he was free, he would create a new army.

But first, he would deal with the Doctor…

Barydon was worried. The patrol hunting for the last crewman had been gone too long. Rounding up a single unarmed man should have been very simple work. Irritated, he checked their signals, and discovered that they had stopped in a corridor. He attempted to contact them, but there was no reply.

Now worried, he went to investigate cautiously. He found their dead and stiffening forms where they had fallen, and growled in annoyance as he realised what had happened. He called Delani immediately. 'The crewman killed two men,' he reported. 'Unless we have Daleks on board, he must have salvaged a Dalek blaster. With their helmets off, they didn't stand a chance.'

'Begin a new sweep,' Delani ordered. 'Full armour, helmets closed. Take four men, and find him. Then take him to where the crew is being held and execute him so that they get the message.'

'He has their weapons,' Barydon added.

'He's a scavenger!' Delani snapped. 'You're trained soldiers. You should be able to find him without trouble. Do it.'

Barydon acknowledged and signed off. Delani was right. The fugitive had simply been lucky. He would not be so lucky again.

Sam was feeling worse and worse about this whole situation. The Doctor seemed to have sunk into introspection, and Chayn was silent as she led the way through the underworld of the ship. About the only good thing Sam could see here was that there were no Daleks actually involved. The Doctor might think the Thals were friends of his, but Sam was under no such illusion. They were soldiers, and they would do whatever they were ordered to do. Delani had already proven that he had an itchy trigger finger. And if this Davros character was half the monster the Doctor seemed to think he was, then he was definitely trouble.

He certainly looked evil. Sam knew from her time with the Doctor that appearances were definitely deceptive when dealing with alien creatures. But there was something about the misshapen creature that made her feel sick. She could understand the Doctor's sense of urgency. She'd have preferred to return to the TARDIS and get the hell out of there, but she knew that wasn't an option for the Doctor. He was on another crusade to save a sizable portion of the Universe. And for all his being a Time Lord and a thousand years old, she knew that he still needed her around to look after him and watch his back. Although Chayn, too, seemed to be quite happy to take on that role.

Again, Sam resented the older woman and her skills. She could only hope that the Doctor wasn't foolish enough to reciprocate the interest that Chayn clearly had in him. No matter how compatible they might look, it was obvious that they weren't really suited to each other.

Chayn stopped by an access panel. 'Storage bay eight,' she whispered. Sam thought this was a bit silly. It was rather unlikely there would be anyone standing on the other side of the panel, listening for them. Unless, of course, Ayaka had discovered that they had escaped. Chayn looked worried.

'There may be several Thals guarding Davros.'

'I doubt it,' the Doctor replied. 'Delani is arrogant, and thinks he's got Davros firmly in hand. But we have to take that chance.'

Nodding, Chayn eased open the panel, and then the three of them slipped out into the storage bay. There was nobody in sight, and she closed the hatch behind them. They had emerged behind the debris, hiding them from Davros and Cathbad. The Doctor now took the lead, hurrying silently through the maze of wreckage to where Davros had been sitting. As they rounded the final wrecked bulkhead, Sam saw that Cathbad was working on some instruments, his back to Davros.

And Davros was moving. He seemed to have regained his mobility by now. A mechanical hand-like device was protruding from a portion of his shell, and it was definitely aimed towards the unsuspecting Thal.

'Cathbad!' the Doctor yelled. 'Look out!'

Cathbad dived and rolled, his instinctive reaction as a soldier. A lance of electricity shot from the mechanical hand, aimed at the spot where the Thal had been standing. The machine he'd been tending exploded in incandescent flames. The blast rocked the floor slightly, making Sam stumble. The Doctor kept his feet, though, and made it to Davros.

'That's quite enough from you,' he said, his fingers tapping controls in Davros's shell. 'I think it's time to subvert your control systems.'

Chayn hurried to Cathbad's side, grabbing the Thal's rifle, and then helping him to sit up. 'Are you all right?' she asked him.

'Yes,' Cathbad gasped. 'Fine.'

'Good.' Chayn pointed the rifle at him. 'Now, sit still, there's a good fellow.'

Sam reached the Doctor's side. She glanced at Davros, and saw that some of the mechanical lights on his casing had died out. 'What have you done?' she asked the Doctor.

'I've shut down all of his power functions, leaving only life-support,' the Doctor explained. 'It means, among other things, that we won't have to listen to him ranting.'

'No,' said a fresh voice. Sam whirled around, to see it was one of the crew members. He was a tired-looking man, but he held a rifle on them all.

'Harmon!' Chayn exclaimed. 'You traitor! You sold us out to the Thals!'

'I didn't know they were going to do this,' Harmon said bitterly. 'I thought they just wanted that Dalek artefact that we found. They never told me that it contained Davros.' He spat on the metal floor. 'The Daleks wiped out my entire family. Now it's time to switch him off for good.' He gestured with the rifle, and Sam and the Doctor moved slowly out of his way. 'How do I do it, Doctor?'

The Time Lord said nothing. 'Tell me or shc dies.' Harmon indicated Sam.

Almost immediately the Doctor rejoined, 'Those two switches on the right.' Sam looked at him quickly. Was his haste from the threat on her life or from finding someone prepared to bump off Davros without compunction?

Harmon moved in, and shot home two final switches on Davros's control panel. Instantly, Davros shuddered, and the rest of the lights died out – and Sam got her answer.

'No!' the Doctor snapped, starting forward. Harmon held up the rifle threateningly. The Doctor halted, his face torn by emotions. 'Harmon, killing Davros won't solve anything.'

'Wrong, Doctor.' The man sighed. 'It'll stop some of my worst nightmares. And he'll never cause the death of another living being.'

Sam glanced at Davros, who seemed frozen in place. Was he already dead? She knew that she was witnessing murder, and that she should do something. But what? And did she really want to risk her life to try and save a mass murderer? She was torn between her principles and her knowledge that Davros was utterly evil. The Doctor, too, seemed to be undergoing the same agonizing choice, his eyes flickering back and forth from Davros to Harmon.

'That's enough,' Delani called. Sam whirled around, and saw that he was standing in the open hatchway to the bay, two other Thals flanking him. All three had rifles trained on them. 'Harmon, turn him back on immediately.'

'Drop your weapons, or I kill him,' Chayn called, tapping Cathbad under the chin with his own weapon.

'Kill him, then,' Delani said, emotionlessly. 'He's a soldier, and expects to die.'

Chayn stared at Cathbad, her knuckles white. Then she laid down the gun. 'I'm sorry, Doctor,' she said.

'I'm not,' he told her.

Harmon had made no move to obey Delani. Instead, he started to turn and raise his rifle, clearly intending to fire at them.

Three bolts cut him down where he stood. He looked startled, and then fell, smoking, to the deck.

The two Thals were hurrying down the ladder, Delani keeping the small party covered from his vantage point. 'Turn Davros's life support back on, Doctor,' Delani ordered. 'Or I kill your friends.'

The Doctor looked from the gun to Davros to Sam and

back to Delani. 'So you can continue with your insane plan?' he asked. 'I will only do as you ask if you give me your word that Davros will be held for trial.'

'No deal, Doctor,' Delani snapped. His finger tightened on the trigger.

Cathbad pushed past Chayn, and started to tap in commands on Davros's carriage. The lights began to return to their normal colors, and Davros took a long, deep breath. 'It's all right, sir,' Cathbad called. 'I've repowered him.'

'Good.' Delani started down the ladder now, as Cathbad and the other two Thals had the Doctor, Sam and Chayn covered.

Cathbad gave Chayn a slight smile. 'It was sensible of you not to kill me,' he complimented her. 'Delani would have killed you immediately in retaliation.'

'That wasn't what stopped me,' Chayn snapped. 'He's probably going to kill me anyway.'

Puzzled, Cathbad asked, 'Then what did stop you?'

'Killing you in cold blood would have made me as bad as you,' she replied defiantly. 'And I won't sink that low.' She seemed to enjoy the confusion on his face.

Delani hurried over to join them, his expression a mixture of satisfaction and anger. 'So, Doctor,' he said, mildly enough, 'you had to interfere. And you managed to get away from Ayaka. She's not normally this careless.'

'I think she was a little preoccupied,' the Doctor answered. He looked at Harmon's body. 'Another death you've caused. I hope you're feeling proud of yourself.'

Delani grunted, and then turned to Cathbad. 'What happened?'

'Davros tried to kill me,' the young Thal replied. 'The Doctor called a warning which saved my life. While I was stunned, they captured me, and Harmon then tried to terminate Davros.'

Delani gave the Doctor a slight smile. 'Contradictory messages,' he murmured. 'Saving my man's life and attacking my prize.'

'I'm a complicated person,' the Doctor answered.

'So I see.' Delani examined the explosive collar still around Davros's neck. 'It seems that the Doctor was right. You have been busy.'

Davros said nothing. He clearly regretted only that his attempt had failed.

Delani turned back to Cathbad. 'Watch him from now on,' he ordered. 'Put a power lock on his chair, with a dead man's switch. If anything happens to you, I want his power packs to be drained instantly, killing him.' He turned back to Davros. 'You understand that I will give you no more chances?'

'Perfectly,' Davros grated. 'However, I am willing to work with you as you desire, on one condition.' His head turned. 'Kill the Doctor.'

Delani raised an eyebrow. 'You will work for me without any conditions,' he stated. 'And what happens to the Doctor will not be because of your desires.' He turned to one of the guards. 'Stay here and help watch. We move out as soon as this ship is secure.'

'Secure?' The Doctor's ears perked up. 'Having a little trouble, are we?'

'Very little,' Delani snapped. 'One crew person has managed to kill two of my men. He is being isolated and punished. Now, Doctor, you and your friends will precede me. We are going to the dining area where the crew is being held. Ayaka will join us there. Move.'

The Doctor shrugged, and gestured politely for Sam and

Chayn to go before him. Sam knew that Delani had something planned, and she suspected that, whatever it was, none of them were going to like it very much. But she was glad to get away from Harmon's dead body and the cold, calculating evil of Davros.

Loran waited for the inevitable search, prepared. He'd holed up in the doorway to the reactor chamber, knowing that the next Thals he saw would be more prepared for him. Or so they thought.

The Dalek weapon would be useless now, he knew. The power pack was running low, and it stood to reason that the Thals had some form of defence against it. But their own weapons were another matter.

It was just a matter of time now. He had hoped to be able to free some more of his crew, but had been forced to abandon that plan. They were too well guarded, and the Thals were expecting trouble. Loran was under no illusion that he could win this battle, but that wasn't really his intention. He knew he was a dead man; it was merely a matter of taking as many of the enemy with him as he could before they killed him. Two so far, but he had no intention that they would be the last.

Then he heard footsteps in the corridor, and he brought up one of the stolen rifles, aiming carefully. He'd placed several of the magnetic grenades ready for the impending attack. They were attached to the ceiling of the corridor, hidden in the shadows caused by burnt-out bulbs. This was the first time he'd ever been thankful for the lousy maintenance on the *Quetzel*. All he needed were targets...

Suddenly four Thals were advancing on him, their own rifles raised and ready to use. Loran smiled to himself. If he could take these out, then his father's and his own deaths would be avenged. He waited as they came closer. Their armour was closed, he noted, and they were ready for an attack. Well, he'd see just how ready they were...

He fired at the first of the ceiling grenades. The device exploded, a flash charge that slammed downward. Three of the Thals were knocked from their feet, and sent tumbling in the dust and smoke. Loran laughed, and fired again, this time at the grenade pouch on the closest target.

All the soldier's grenades detonated at once. It didn't matter how good his armour was, there was no surviving that explosion. Loran hit a second target, who also erupted into a column of fire and pain. The third soldier managed to roll for cover.

The fourth, still on his feet, fired back. The shot missed Loran, but hit the door frame above him. Molten metal sprayed across his back. The agony of the burns made him scream and roll to fight the pain.

He never saw the next shot, but the pain was gone forever...

Ayaka was waiting for them in the dining room, her face flushed with embarrassment. Delani motioned for the trooper he'd brought with him to wait outside the door, and then ushered the Doctor, Sam, and Chayn in to join the rest of the captives. Then he sealed the door behind him.

'I'm surprised at you, Ayaka,' he said mildly.

Ayaka hung her head in shame. 'I'm sorry, sir,' she replied in a quiet voice. 'I neglected to search them.'

'Yes, you did.' Delani shrugged. 'However, even if you had, I doubt it would have changed much. The Doctor is a dangerously resourceful person.'

'It's nice to be appreciated,' the Doctor murmured.

Sam was definitely getting a very bad feeling about this, and she suspected that this was the worst possible time for the Doctor to be needling Delani. The Thal wasn't too well hinged right now, and any small thing might set him off.

Delani studied the forty or so people in the mess hall. They were sullen, tired and cramped, but still somehow defiant. 'One of your number,' he said slowly, 'has managed to kill four of my troops. I had hoped to have him brought here alive and executed as a lesson. However, my troops were forced to kill him.'

'What a shame,' the Doctor murmured. 'It's so much more fun when you make execution a spectator sport, isn't it?' Sam wished he would just shut up, and stop provoking Delani further.

Delani turned to the Doctor and looked pointedly at him. Then he turned to the crew. 'It appears as though I shall have my example for you after all.' To Ayaka, he added, 'This vessel is under military jurisdiction, and the Doctor is attempting to defy my command. Kill him.'

'What?' Sam jumped forward, furious and scared. 'You can't do that! He's unarmed. You're asking her to commit murder for you!'

'No,' Delani said coldly. 'I am enforcing discipline, without which power cannot stand. Ayaka, your orders have changed. Kill the Doctor – and the girl.'

Sam felt sick, realizing she'd been baited into opposing him, too. She couldn't think of a thing to say, and turned to stare at Ayaka. The beautiful Thal appeared torn and confused. Chayn seized the opportunity to step forward, her face grim.

'You'd better order her to kill me, too,' she said coldly.

'Because if you don't, I can promise you that I'll continue the Doctor's mission.'

The Doctor gave her a wan smile. 'There's no need for these heroics,' he said gently.

'You're wrong, Doctor,' Chayn answered. 'There's every need for me to take a moral stance.' She crossed her arms and glared at Ayaka.

Delani sighed. 'Very well. You leave me no option.' He glared at Ayaka. 'Execute them,' he ordered.

'You can't do it,' Sam said, not really believing it, but forced to say something.

A tear trickled down from Ayaka's eye. 'I'm sorry, Doctor – Sam,' she apologised, raising her rifle.

Sam stared into the barrel, wishing she could simply faint. Her stomach was cramped, her throat dry, her heart pounding. It was clear that Ayaka didn't want to pull the trigger. Somehow, though, it was no comfort to know that she was going to be murdered by someone who really didn't want to do it.

CHAPTER 6
SIGNAL

Sam swallowed, waiting for the final shot. Her body shook as Ayaka's finger tightened on the trigger.

'I'm sorry,' she repeated. Then she moved the barrel and fired.

The top of Delani's head exploded, splattering over half of the wall behind him. There was a sickening scent of blood. His dead body collapsed into a dribbling heap.

'I'm sorry, Doctor, Sam,' Ayaka sighed, lowering her rifle. 'But you were right. He was no longer fit to be our commander.'

Chayn stared at the woman in shock. 'You killed him!' she exclaimed. She didn't dare look at the body again, afraid that this time she would faint.

'Of course I did!' Ayaka snarled. 'What did you expect? You didn't think I could just ask him politely not to have you murdered, did you? If I'd tried, he'd have killed me and then the three of you.'

The Doctor stepped forward, his eyes burning. 'There must have been another way,' he said gently.

'There wasn't, Doctor,' Ayaka said. She was still wet-eyed, but resolute. 'I knew Delani better than anyone. There was no other way.'

After a moment, the Doctor nodded slightly. 'Right, then, we'd better get to work.'

'No.' Ayaka held up the weapon again. 'Doctor, I would not obey his orders to kill the three of you, but my primary loyalty has not changed. Guards!'

The door opened, and the three guards on duty came in. They'd clearly been expecting to see a corpse on the floor, but none of them were prepared to see whose it was. Ayaka held out her rifle.

'I have killed our commander,' she said firmly. 'You must now arrest me and hold me for trial.'

One of the women looked at her in consternation. 'But… with Delani dead, you are now in charge,' she protested.

'No,' Ayaka said, forcing the woman to take her rifle. 'I cannot be. Dyoni must now take command of the mission. I will contact her and inform her of the situation.'

Sam could see that the troopers were having as hard a time understanding what was happening as she was. She'd hoped that Ayaka would understand that what Delani was doing was wrong, but she had never expected this to happen. Was his death in some part her fault? She had baited and prodded Ayaka into rebellion. Sam felt hollow inside, her emotions too tangled to sort out quite what she felt. Except distinct relief that she was still alive.

Ayaka triggered her transmitter, and contacted the main Thal ship. 'Ayaka to Dyoni.'

'Dyoni,' came the reply. 'What's your status?'

'Delani is dead,' Ayaka reported. 'I… killed him. I have ordered myself arrested, to be held for military tribunal. I formally pass command of this mission on to you.'

There was a stunned silence from the other end, and then Dyoni's startled voice, 'You did what?' Ayaka didn't bother replying, and Dyoni demanded, 'Why?'

'Because he wanted me to murder innocent hostages,' Ayaka replied simply. 'I could not obey the order.'

There was another pause, and then Dyoni's voice sounded

harsher. 'Very well. You have made the correct decision. I am coming over to the ship. The mission will be completed.'

'No!' the Doctor exclaimed. 'You can't continue!'

But Ayaka had already cut the connection. She regarded the Doctor coolly. 'Personally, I believe you, Doctor. I feel that taking Davros back to our home world is madness. But it is what we were ordered to do, and we must obey those orders.'

The Doctor looked as if he were about to tear his hair out in frustration. 'I thought you were finally starting to understand!' he exclaimed. 'I had to provoke Delani so that you'd see how crazed he was. Why are you stopping with the job only half done?'

'Because I can bring myself to do no more,' Ayaka answered simply. There was another tear trickling down her cheek. 'I have killed my commander, and betrayed my people once. I cannot do it again. There is no use in asking more of me.' She began to unfasten her armour, and turned to the female trooper. 'I will surrender all of my equipment, and stay here for now with these aliens. When the time comes to return to the ship, I will accompany you.'

'Understood.'

Ayaka stripped off the armour, handing it over to the Thal. Sam couldn't help feeling another burst of envy when she saw Ayaka without the bulky clothing covering her. She was dressed in simple leggings that were held together all the way up the side of her legs by leather thongs. Above this, she wore a Y-shaped tunic, the upright up her spine, the two bars across her shoulders and down her front. These, too, were laced together with thongs. The clothing covered only what it had to, and showed that the rest of Ayaka's figure matched the perfection of her face.

129

Ayaka caught Sam's look and said, 'It is our traditional fighting costume, handed down from the time of our ancestors who first fought the Daleks.'

You wouldn't catch me dead in it, Sam thought to herself. Not that I've got the body to fill it out... She glanced at the Doctor, worried that he'd be staring at Miss Universe Whatever-Year-It-Was, but he didn't seem to be giving Ayaka a second glance. He was brooding deeply, obviously trying to figure out how to get to Davros again.

The three troopers now left and sealed the door again, leaving the captives all alone once more. Sam didn't know what to do, so she collapsed into the nearest chair, trying to sort out her thoughts. She wished that Delani's body had been removed, too. His eyes were staring wide open under the mess of blood and bone the blaster had left behind.

The communications officer, Faylen, crossed from the frightened group of the crew to stand in front of Chayn. 'Both Balatan and Loran are dead,' she said simply, her face pale. 'We don't know who that leaves in charge.'

Chayn made an obvious attempt to bring her mind back from wherever she'd been thinking. 'Oh. Well, I guess it might as well be you as anyone,' she said. 'It really doesn't make much difference, does it, right now? When the Thals leave, if we're still alive, then we can worry about it.'

'Maybe,' Faylen agreed uncomfortably. It looked like she'd been hoping Chayn would volunteer for the job. 'But there's something odd happening.'

Chayn gave a very bitter laugh. 'We're occupied by Thals, the captain and his son are dead, there's a resurrected monster in our hold and you say there's something odd happening?' Faylen flushed, and Chayn was immediately contrite. 'I'm sorry, that was cruel of me. It's just that my nerves are so tight… What is it that's odd?'

'Take a look.' Faylen held out her palm comp.'I tried to get an outside signal, figuring maybe I could call for help.' She snorted. 'Who, don't ask me. But I had to try something. Anyway, when I patched into the communications system, I found that.'

'What?' asked the Doctor, suddenly springing to life. He put a hand gently on Chayn's shoulder and stared down at the palm comp in her hand.

'A signal,' Faylen answered.'Someone's already managed to set up a distress call. It must have been Loran, before they killed him. So maybe there's a chance of a rescue.'

'I don't think so,' Chayn replied. 'How would Loran have sent a signal? He's… was… hopeless with anything mechanical.' She bit back her emotions. 'It ccould't have been him.'

'Can you tell where it's being sent from?' the Doctor asked, flashing Faylen a high-wattage smile.

She almost simpered, and Sam rolled her eyes.'Storage bay eight,' she said.

The Doctor's face clouded. 'And Davros is in storage bay eight,' he said grimly. 'Somehow, I can't see this being coincidental. Do you know when it began?'

Faylen shrugged.'If I were at my station, I'd be able to tell you to the second. Here… Well, within the last couple of hours, I'd say.' She looked worried.'You don't think that's a call for help, then?'

'Oh, yes,' the Doctor replied.'But good help is hard to find.' He turned around. 'Ayaka.' When the Thal didn't move, he went over to her and placed a hand gently under her chin, lifting her face to look up at him. 'Ayaka, this is very important. Where are we?'

131

She blinked, and focused in on his face. 'On this junk ship,' she answered.

'No, no, no,' he said impatiently. 'What area of space? Who controls it?'

'No one, at present,' she replied. 'It's on the border between our space and Dalek space.'

'Dalek space…' he breathed, thinking furiously. Then he let her go. 'Ayaka, you've got to contact Dyoni immediately. We're in very grave danger.'

'What are you talking about?' she asked, confused.

'That signal.' The Doctor gestured to Chayn's palm comp. 'It began when Davros was resuscitated. It can only be heading in one direction.'

Ayaka went pale. 'The Daleks.'

'Right.' The Doctor was very disturbed now. 'And it can't be Davros's doing. He knows his forces were wiped out when I destroyed Skaro. That means it must be the Imperial Daleks. They must have found his pod and planted a signalling device on it. But why didn't they simply take him with them?' He looked confused.

'Doctor,' Ayaka said, troubled. 'About Skaro –'

'There's no time for that now,' he told her. 'Get Dyoni moving. I'm certain that the Daleks are already moving in on us.'

Sam could see how worried he was, and how unsure. Clearly the Daleks were up to something, and, equally clearly, he couldn't figure it out. But Sam knew the source of his urgency. If he was correct in his beliefs, then the Daleks could be here at any moment. And, from all she'd been told about the Daleks, that would sign everyone's death warrants.

Dyoni strode into cargo bay eight keeping her emotions in

tight check. How could Ayaka of all people have behaved so insanely, killing their commander and endangering their mission? It was almost unthinkable. Ayaka had been her best friend and confidante for two years. She thought they had no secrets from each other. And now – this! It made no sense.

'Cathbad,' she snapped, as she walked across to him. 'I don't care if Davros is powered up fully or not. Transfer him over to your ship and prepare to get under way. I want to see the back of this garbage scow as soon as possible.' She glared at the creature who had created the Daleks without disguising the hatred and contempt she felt for him. 'There's no need to be gentle with him.' She added, thoughtfully, 'The Doctor is aboard, and I understand his vessel is in cargo bay twelve. Have that removed to your ship also.'

'Understood,' Cathbad agreed. He hesitated for a moment. 'And the crew of this ship?'

'They're immaterial,' Dyoni answered. 'I'll have them freed when we leave. They can get on with their miserable little lives like before.'

He looked relieved at this. Dyoni briefly wondered why, and then dismissed the thought. It didn't matter.

There was a signal from her ship, which she answered as she began moving again, heading this time for the room where Ayaka was being held prisoner. She'd have to transfer her friend back to a holding cell on her own ship until a tribunal could be convened. If Ayaka had done what she claimed, however, there was little doubt in Dyoni's mind that she would be swiftly executed. She felt a pang at the thought. But what else had Ayaka expected?

The call was from her communications officer. 'We're picking up a signal,' she reported. 'Another ship is approaching.'

'One of ours?' Dyoni demanded.

'We're not getting a recognition code,' the officer replied. He paused. 'It is possible that it's another neutral vessel, like the one you're on…'

'But we'd be fools to assume it,' Dyoni finished for him. 'Very well. Go to full alert, and prime all weapons. Assume it's a Dalek ship unless it manages to identify itself first.'

'Understood.'

Damn. Dyoni paused for a second, and then hit her communicator again. 'Dyoni to all occupying forces. Return to your vessels and prepare for combat.' She didn't wait for acknowledgement, but finished the trip to the makeshift prison on the run.

Dyoni burst into the room, glancing around, taking in the crew, and then the smaller group with Ayaka. They had to be the Doctor, Sam, and the female engineer that Delani had been having trouble with. 'All right, listen to me, everyone.' All attention was hers in a moment. 'The Daleks are heading this way, and I don't need to tell you what that means if they get here and find an unarmed vessel. I'm setting you all free so that you can at least try to make a run for it.' She gestured with her rifle at the Doctor, Ayaka, Sam, and Chayn. 'Not you four. You're coming with me. Any argument, and you die here and now.'

'Dyoni, listen to me,' the Doctor began. Dyoni pointed her rifle at him and held the trigger.

'Is that an argument?' she asked, softly and dangerously.

He saw the determination in her eyes and shook his head. 'No.'

'Good.' She glanced at the crew. 'If you value your lives, move.' They didn't need any further urging. Like frightened

134

animals, they streamed past her. Then she gestured with her rifle. 'Come on.'

They moved quickly through the ship to the airlock where Cathbad's ship was docked. Since none of them were wearing armour, they couldn't get across to her ship. Instead, she greeted the troopers at the airlock.

'Transfer these four to a holding cell,' she ordered. 'Once we've dealt with the Daleks, I'll let you know what to do with them. As soon as they're aboard, cast off and prepare for engagement. I'm returning to my own ship.'

'Understood.' They took command of the prisoners, and closed the airlock door.

Dyoni sealed her armour. As soon as the ship pulled away, she started her flight pack, and returned to her own vessel.

Battle was about to be joined.

The whine of the signal for battle stations was in her ears as she raced for the bridge. She split her armour open as she ran, but there was no time to remove it now. She entered the bridge at a run, and flopped into the command chair. 'Status!' she demanded.

Ioki turned from her station at communications to face her new commander. The bridge was circular, with all stations laid out in a two-thirds of circle about her, so that she could have immediate access to any of them. 'We're at full alert and ready,' she reported. 'We can have drive whenever you command it.'

'Good. Stand by for manoeuvres.' Dyoni lit up her own console, which was tied in to all of the rest. She could call up any information she might need here. She wanted to know where the Dalek ship was coming from. Should she fight? It was tempting, but she had their prize on Cathbad's ship to think about. It was more important to get Davros to the home world than to kill a few more Daleks. Regretfully, she ordered Navigation, 'Prepare a course to take us home, and have our sister ship lock trajectories with us.'

Preparations were begun. Dyoni knew that they had time. The Dalek ship was at extreme range, and couldn't be upon them in less than half a unit. Plenty of time for them to retreat, no matter how bitter the decision tasted. As soon as Navigation reported the course laid in, Dyoni ordered the drive started.

Two seconds later, Ioki called out, 'I'm picking up multiple contacts.'

'Multiple?' Dyoni sat straight in her chair, and called up the screen on her panel. Ioki was correct. There were at least five more ships closing in on them – from the direction of home. Reinforcements? If so, why hadn't they contacted her?

No, there was only one possible answer. It was a Dalek trap, and it was closing in neatly about them. They had known she would order a retreat, and had been waiting for it. They must have been arranging all of this while the Thals were occupied on the *Quetzel*. Five more ships… they were outnumbered three to one. Now what?

She wished Delani were here to take charge. Or even Ayaka. She had more confidence in their abilities to plan than in her own. But she was all they had now. 'All hands to battle positions,' she announced. 'We fight.'

Ioki looked startled, and stared at her. 'I'm getting a signal… from the Dalek vessel behind us.'

'A signal?' This made no sense. The Daleks never talked. They simply killed. 'What do they want? Relay it to me.'

The speaker in her console lit up, and the familiar, hated Dalek tones grated forth. It said only one word, but it was one word she never expected to hear from a Dalek.

'Surrender!'

Dyoni stared at her console, and then at Ioki. This was totally unprecedented. In generations of warfare, the Daleks had never before demanded surrender. They simply annihilated all opposition or died trying.

What was going on?

What was going on? Sam wished she knew. It was bad enough being a prisoner of the Thals without knowing that they were going up against the Daleks. 'This is what you call a lose-lose situation, isn't it?' she asked the Doctor. 'Whether the Thals or the Daleks win, we've still had it.'

They were in a small Thal holding cell. Since joining the Doctor, Sam had become quite familiar with the interior of almost all kinds of jails. As far as they went, this wasn't bad. It was intended for only one person, so it was rather small. Apparently there weren't too many criminals or prisoners on Thal ships. There was a small bed, on which Ayaka and Sam were currently sitting. There was a small unit that was clearly a toilet, and a small washbasin. Nothing else at all, except the locked door out of there.

'I think that sums it up,' the Doctor agreed, and then smiled. 'Of course, that's without taking into account that we're four very resourceful people in here.' He glanced at Ayaka, who seemed sunk in depression. 'Well, three at least. And that we passed the TARDIS, which is now stored just inside this ship. All we have to do is to get out of this cell and we've as good as escaped.'

Trust the Doctor to look on the bright side of things. But at least his optimism gave Sam hope. Maybe they would make it out of this alive, after all. 'So, can we get out of here?' she asked.

He grinned and held up a familiar device. 'Sonic screwdriver,' he announced. 'Now, all I have to do is work on the lock, and...' He bent to do precisely that when the door slid open, catching him by surprise.

It caught the Thal guard by surprise, too. His rifle was up, though, and he stuck it under the Doctor's nose. 'I'll take that,' he said. Meekly, the Doctor handed him the device, which the guard slipped into a tunic pocket. He was dressed in the same style of thonged leggings and Y-shaped tunic as Ayaka, and was holding out a communicator. 'Ayaka,' he said. 'Cathbad wishes to speak to you.'

Ayaka's mind seemed to stumble back to awareness. 'With me?'

'Yes.' He tossed her the communicator, which was shaped like a bracelet. He then closed the door again.

'There goes that escape,' Sam said with a sigh.

The Doctor shook his head and opened his hand. The sonic screwdriver was nestled there. Sam grinned. Good old sleight of hand!

'Ayaka,' the communicator said. 'I'm out of my depth here. I need your advice.'

'This has to be a first,' the Doctor murmured. 'The captain of a ship asking his model prisoner for advice.'

'Cathbad was never interested in command,' Ayaka said simply. 'He's good at following orders, but not too innovative.' She tapped the control. 'Ayaka here. Cathbad, I cannot command a battle from a jail cell. You will have to cope.'

'It's not that,' Cathbad answered. Sam could hear the strain in his voice. He'd seemed like a nice guy, and very young. He had to be feeling totally inadequate for this. 'The Daleks want us to surrender.'

'What?' Ayaka was startled. 'Are you sure?'

'I heard the signal,' he said, troubled. 'Ayaka, they've never requested a surrender before.'

'It must be a trick,' Ayaka decided. 'They wish to avoid a fight. They will kill us all afterwards.'

The Doctor placed a hand over hers. 'I don't think it is a trick as such,' he said softly. 'They know we have Davros aboard. They must want him alive for some reason. Maybe the same one Delani had in mind. Maybe they're having more trouble with the Movellans. I'm not sure. But they obviously don't want to destroy this ship and lose him.'

Ayaka nodded. 'That makes sense, Doctor. But surrender is hardly an option. They will kill us all when we have laid down our weapons. It's better to die fighting.'

'That may not be your best option,' the Doctor warned her.

'It is all we can do,' Ayaka said simply. To Cathbad, she added, 'You must fight while you can.'

'Understood.' He sounded relieved. 'Thank you, Ayaka.' The line went dead.

Chayn snorted. 'Are you sure you don't want to take command back again?'

'I am dishonoured,' Ayaka answered. 'The troops would have no confidence in me.'

'It didn't sound that way just now,' Chayn informed her.

'Cathbad is my friend,' Ayaka said. 'He values my opinion. The rest of the crew would not be so considerate.'

Sam tapped the Doctor on the shoulder. 'Isn't it time for the great escape?' She tried not to sound too scared. 'Right now, I'd really love to be back inside the TARDIS.'

'That may not be our best option, either,' the Doctor answered. He was clearly very troubled. 'I don't understand what's happening here. Is leaving this cell really the best thing to do?'

'Speaking for me, yes,' Sam replied. 'Let's get back to the TARDIS and scarper before they blow us all to smithereens.'

'Good point,' the Doctor agreed. He moved back to the lock, and started to work on it.

Sam turned to Chayn and Ayaka. 'Are you two coming with us? The TARDIS can get us away from here in safety.'

Chayn grinned. 'That's the Doctor's time and space machine? Sam, you'd have to lock the doors to keep me out of there! I'm dying to take a peek at what makes it tick.'

Ayaka shook her head. 'I shall stay here,' she replied. 'These are my people, and I should be with them.'

Sam couldn't believe her. 'Look, if you stay, you've got two options. First, the Daleks blow up the ship and you die. Second, the Thals get you back home, they put you on trial and you die. Either way, you die. Is that really what you want?'

'No, of course not,' Ayaka admitted. She looked wistful. 'I should dearly love to see my daughter again now. But I cannot abandon my people. I have committed a crime and I must be prepared to account for my actions. If I am sentenced to die, then so be it. But I will not be a coward and run away.'

'More fool you, then,' Sam informed her. But, at the same time, she supposed there was something admirable in the Thal's conviction and courage. She turned back to the Doctor. 'How's it going?'

He tossed his sonic screwdriver into the air and then caught it. Slipping it into his pocket, he said, 'The matter has become academic. The guard fused the lock. Perhaps he discovered I'd picked his pocket, and he's taking no chances. We're all of us stuck here for the duration of the battle.'

Sam sighed, and collapsed back on to the bed. Bad news and more bad news. Was the universe against them, or just this one small portion of it? They were stuck here, in this jail cell, while their ship took on forces three times their size...

Her mum and dad had always warned her about going off with strangers.

Dyoni sent a single-word answer to the Daleks – 'No!' She would prefer to die than to spend the rest of her very short, painful life as a slave. She turned her ship to the attack. With Cathbad's support, perhaps they could hammer their way through the waiting ships and escape. It wasn't much of a hope, but it was the best they had.

Tension rose as they closed in. The bridge was a hive of activity, and Dyoni knew it would be matched throughout the ship. Adrenaline was flowing, and she felt gloriously alive. This was what she had be born to do – face the Daleks. Maybe this would be the day she'd die; if so, she'd take plenty of the enemy with her.

The closest Dalek ship opened fire, impacts slamming into their force shields. Dyoni knew that this was only a testing; the Daleks didn't expect to cause serious damage at this distance. 'Hold your fire,' she ordered quietly, as the ship shook under the barrage. A second killcruiser joined in, the combined fire power causing a rolling effect similar to that of being on water. Still too far for her to consider wasting their ammunition. She gripped the edges of her monitor, her knuckles white, as she stared at her displays. Almost within range... The shelling on their shields was increasing in intensity, but that was to be expected.

'Ready,' she called to the weapons officer. And a moment later, 'Fire!'

Her ship's missiles began to streak out, dots of light against the blackness of space. Several exploded in the Dalek fire power, but most made it through to their target, the closest killcruiser. The Daleks' shields flared almost white as they strove to absorb the impact, and then Ioki reported: 'They've lost power to their forward shields. It's down almost fifty per cent.'

'Again!' Dyoni ordered, the scent of death heady. This could be their first victory of the day... As her ship shuddered under the continued impacts, they fired again and again. She was dimly aware that Cathbad's ship had engaged one of the other killcruisers. She focused all of her attention on their own target. The second killcruiser was closing, and the faster they could finish the first, the better.

'They've launched hoverbouts,' Ioki reported.

'Order the secondary gunners to target them,' Dyoni called to the weapons officer. Hoverbouts couldn't do a great deal of damage, but two or three together might be able to penetrate a shield somewhere, and make them vulnerable to the main batteries.

Space about their ships became a seething cauldron of fire. Lasers, masers, missiles, and anything else either side could throw against the other lit the inkiness almost constantly. The ship shuddered and groaned under the assault.

'Dalek forward shields are down,' Ioki reported jubilantly.

Dyoni leaned forward, staring at her monitor. The enemy was vulnerable now... Her gunners targeted the bow of the enemy ship, pouring everything they could into an intense hammer. There was a momentary pause, and then space lit up as the killcruiser came apart at the seams, billowing outward in a mass of flames and debris. The shields shook harder as the debris battered against them.

'We're down to two-thirds strength,' Ioki reported.

'Continue,' Dyoni ordered, her eyes fastened to her own displays. Cathbad was taking on two ships and struggling. The fifth now moved to press home the attack on Dyoni, and the one that had been chasing them into the trap was also closing in. Still, there was nothing to do but to fight on.

Brief flares showed where hoverbouts were being destroyed, but still the individual killers came on. Their puny fire power still rocked the ship, adding to the main blasts from the two killcruisers.

'Shield-power draining,' Ioki reported, her voice strained. 'We can't hold them all off.'

'No,' agreed Dyoni, resigned to death. 'But we can make them know they've been in a fight. Close in on the nearest target.'

The engines fired, moving them closer to one of the killcruisers. The intensity of the attack increased. Her panel was showing massive damage to several decks, but she ignored it. It hardly mattered at this stage of the game. As long as her guns and her engines worked, the rest of the ship could fry.

'Shields failing,' Ioki reported. She coughed as her panel started to smoke and sputter fire. 'We won't hold together much longer.'

'I know,' Dyoni nodded. To the engineer, she ordered, 'Full thrust.'

She was dying, but she would not die alone…

Cathbad was going frantic, attempting to keep up with the flow of data to his station. He didn't want to be in command, but there was no one else to take his place. He desperately wished that Ayaka were here, but that was impossible.

What should he do? He was no tactician. He could follow orders without a problem, but originating some brilliant plan to save their lives was beyond him. Still, it didn't take any great brains to realise that the Daleks were not trying to destroy his ship. Oh, they were fighting, and parrying his attempts to destroy them, but he could tell that they were simply trying to shake him up, or cause minimal damage. Dyoni was not as lucky.

He saw the first killcruiser explode, and for a second wondered whether victory might be posible after all. Then Dyoni's ship powered up and began to move. The intensity of the blasts about it increased, and it became obvious that it could not withstand such concentrated fire for very long.

Cathbad suddenly realised what Dyoni was up to, she was about to ram the closest killcruiser. The Daleks must have deduced that also, because the bombardment of her ship increased. A gout of flame erupted close to her engine room, but it didn't slow her ship down. Cathbad watched, spellbound, as the Thal ship closed with the killcruiser.

They were almost touching when Dyoni's ship exploded. That close in, the Dalek shields couldn't take it. A line of fire burst out down the length of the craft, and then it, too, exploded. Twin fireballs merged incandescently, blooming like some beautiful, deadly flower, before collapsing in on themselves and snuffing out.

Dyoni was gone...

'Incoming message from the Daleks,' his navigation officer reported.

It was that one word again, 'Surrender.'

Cathbad stared around the bridge at his crew. What should

he do? It was almost unthinkable that he should obey. But if he didn't, he was condemning everyone to death. And if he did, to almost certain slavery.

What to choose? The pressure of command crushed him. Why did it have to be him?

He tapped the communications relay again. There was only one thing he could think of to do...

Sam had felt the ship shaking under the attack, and her stomach roiled again. This constant danger and air of impending death was wearing down her nerves. No wonder the Thals were such a weird race, if they faced this kind of situation every day of their lives. She felt as though someone had taken a soldering iron to every one of her nerve endings at once.

It wasn't the same for Ayaka, who probably expected something like this every day of her life. She sat there on the bunk, staring into nothingness, probably wishing she could be at her post during the attack.

'I'm too young to die,' announced Sam, then she giggled, a low tittering that erupted into quiet, bleak laughter. Everyone ignored her, even the Doctor. He looked strained and pale. He'd had a good life, something like a thousand years, he claimed. Would that make the idea of dying easier or harder for him? He was giving up so much more than she was. Even if she survived this, she'd probably be dead by the age of seventy or so, some fifty more years. He could go on perhaps a hundred times as long.

Not for the first time, she admired his courage. To give up what amounted to immortality and spend your life fighting for causes you believed in – that was real heroism. Most of his fellow Time Lords stayed at home, hoarding their precious years and rebirths. The Doctor squandered his by helping the less fortunate. She reached out and pressed his hand. He gave her a brief smile, and then returned to his own thoughts.

And Chayn... The engineer looked scared and defiant at the same time. Like the rest of them, Sam supposed, she really didn't want to die, but probably couldn't see any alternative. She looked at the Doctor suddenly and asked, 'Do you think the *Quetzel* got away safely?'

He blinked and looked at her. 'Probably,' he conceded. 'They had nothing the Daleks wanted, and couldn't be much of a threat. The killcruisers wouldn't have bothered going after her.'

'Most likely,' Chayn said.

'Most likely,' he agreed. His tone said there were never any guarantees with the Daleks.

'I'm glad they at least had a chance to live,' Chayn decided. 'They may be a bunch of screw-ups and losers, but they're my friends.'

The Doctor managed a smile at that. 'I feel like that a lot of the time, too,' he confessed. 'But we're not dead yet.'

'We're close,' Ayaka said abruptly. 'I know this ship; the shields are failing. You can tell because the decibel count is rising.'

Like they needed to know that... Sam grimaced, trying to warm the icy rock of fear inside her. It wouldn't be much longer.

And then the communications link sounded again. Ayaka, surprised, answered it.

'The Daleks have offered a surrender again,' Cathbad reported. 'Ayaka, our shields are failing. We can't hold out much longer. If we don't surrender, they will destroy us. And if we do, then we'll be slaves for however long we live.' He lowered his voice. 'I can't decide, Ayaka. What should I do?'

Ayaka was about to speak when the Doctor held his hand over her wrist, covering the bracelet. There was a fierce light in his eyes. 'Surrender,' he said.

The Thal was shocked. 'Doctor, you know what the Daleks will do to us if we do. I can't condemn my crew to Dalek slavery.'

'I don't think it will come to that,' the Doctor replied enigmatically. 'This whole thing was a Dalek trap. They've some grand strategy in mind. I think you've got a good chance for survival.' Then his face fell, to be followed by a thin smile. 'Of course, as soon as they realise who I am, the Daleks will exterminate me. It's their standing orders. But you have to survive. I have confidence in you. Whatever the Daleks plan, you'll be able to counter.'

'Doctor...' Sam began, scared now for him.

'No,' he said abruptly. 'No arguments. If you can, escape to the TARDIS. There's an emergency system that will return the ship to Gallifrey. The Time Lords will help you get home again. They won't like it, but they'll do it.'

Sam realised that the Doctor was saying goodbye. She couldn't believe that he was so sure he'd die. He was always so optimistic, even in the worst of situations. Why not now?

Because this was the worst possible situation?

Ayaka stared at the Doctor, still unsure.

'Do it,' he ordered her roughly, then held up his hands in apology. 'Please, trust me on this. There will be a way out, if you try. Just don't give up. Listen to Sam, and Chayn. Work together, and I don't think that the Daleks will stand a chance against you.'

Ayaka came to her decision, and triggered the bracelet.

'Agree to their terms,' she ordered Cathbad. Sam could hear his sigh of relief that he didn't have to make the decision any longer. Ayaka had saved the ship – but condemned the Doctor to death.

Seconds later, the ship stopped shaking as the barrage ceased. The whine of the shields died out, too, as Cathbad ordered them dropped. The noise level dropped almost to zero as the guns ceased firing. Sam's ears were ringing and she had the start of a headache. But at least she'd be alive to suffer it.

But now what would happen?

As the Thal ship's airlock door hissed open, the Red Dalek glided into the enemy craft. Warrior Daleks streamed after it, to secure the ship and prepare it for its journey. The door into the main corridor slid open. There were three Thals waiting there, all unarmed. One of the males stepped forward nervously.

'I am Cathbad, in command,' he said. 'We have all disarmed.'

'You are no longer in command,' the Red Dalek replied. 'The Daleks own this vessel. You will prepare your crew to be confined. Any resistance will be met with retaliation.'

'That is understood,' Cathbad agreed, bowing his head.

'Good.' The Red Dalek surveyed the corridor. 'Where is Davros?'

'In one of our storage rooms,' Cathbad answered. 'He was being guarded.'

'That is now unnecessary. We shall take charge of Davros.' The Red Dalek moved off. Its warriors were spreading about the ship, moving to where they could check on key command stations. 'Your flight crew will prepare to receive new instructions,' the Red Dalek grated. 'You will follow instructions exactly or die.' It began to glide down the corridor. 'Accompany me.' The Thal did so. The Red Dalek was not concerned with the possibility of treachery. The Thals were humanoids, and, like all humanoids, weak. They had surrendered, and would keep their word.

They were stupid.

The Red Dalek halted as it suddenly saw something totally unexpected. 'The Doctor's TARDIS,' he stated, staring at the familiar blue box standing in the corridor. It swivelled his eye stalk to stare at the Thal. 'You have the Doctor aboard?'

Cathbad licked his lips and nodded nervously. 'Yes. He is a prisoner in a holding cell.'

Standing orders flickered into the Dalek's mind: Kill the Doctor... It opened a direct channel to the Black Dalek on the killcruiser and relayed the information silently. A moment later, the response came through. The Red Dalek stared at Cathbad again. 'Take me to the Doctor,' it ordered.

The silence now was very unnerving. Sam wanted to pace about the small cell, but this would be impossible without walking into one or more of the others. What was happening? The Daleks had to be on board by now. She glanced at the Doctor again. He appeared to be deep in melancholic thought, making him look more like a consumptive poet errant than ever. But there was no despair in his eyes. She couldn't fathom what he might be thinking right now, and she knew he would never tell her. She wished there was something she could do or say to make this easier for him, but she was completely out of her depth.

There was a metallic clang, and the door shuddered.

'They're here,' Chayn whispered. She was shaking slightly,

and looked across at the Doctor. He stood taller, and moved to the front of the group.

'I wish I could think of some terribly brilliant final words,' the Doctor murmured. 'But all that comes to mind is: I'm sorry, Sam.'

'It's OK,' she told him, a catch in her throat. She wasn't going to break down and cry. Not yet, anyway. But no other words came.

The door suddenly clanged open, and Sam's blood froze. In the doorway stood a red Dalek, its blaster raised and pointed directly at the Doctor.

'You are the Doctor,' it stated. 'You are the enemy of the Daleks.'

Sam saw the hatred and loathing in her friend's eyes, saw his face set in a sneering defiance. 'Yes,' he agreed, at last, a hint of resignation in his voice.

Sam tensed, and then, to her complete shock, the Dalek lowered the barrel of its gun. 'You will wait here,' it ordered. 'You will not be harmed while you stay in your cell.' The eye stalk surveyed Sam, Chayn, and Ayaka in turn. 'It is known that you travel with companions. Do these humanoids accompany you?'

'Yes,' the Doctor agreed, somewhat faintly.

'They will be safe also, provided they stay here,' the Dalek said. It added, 'A Dalek guard will be posted in the corridor to see that no harm comes to you. I shall return when the ship is secure.' It spun about and glided away. Cathbad shrugged helplessly and followed it. A grey-coloured Dalek took up station outside the open door.

Sam collapsed back on to the bunk, shaking with terror and relief. The Doctor was alive! They all were! And the Daleks were guarding them from trouble. 'You know,' she said, almost laughing, 'I think I already like these Daleks better than the Thals. They seem a lot more civilised.'

The Doctor turned to face her. To Sam's shock, he looked worse than he had before.

'What's wrong?' she asked him, confused. 'You don't seem to be very happy that the Daleks have spared your life.'

'I'm not,' he said bluntly. 'They have standing orders to kill me on sight. Since they haven't done that, obviously they've received fresh orders about me. If they're spared my life, it's because they've got something far, far worse than death planned for me.'

At that thought, all of Sam's newborn confidence and hope died in a second.

INTERLUDE
DRACONIAN SPACE

The Draconian captain sat immobile in the command chair. It was not proper to show emotion, even at a time like this. His eyes flickered as he scanned the image cast into the picture pit of his bridge.

Eight Dalek killcruisers...

And he had only five destroyers, along with his beloved ship *Hunter*... It would be no fight, merely a massacre. But fleeing the enemy was literally unthinkable. If he was to die, he was to die.

Finally, he motioned to the communications officer. 'Send a message to the Home World,' he ordered. 'We have sighted Dalek intruders and are preparing to attack.'

'Understood, Captain.'

The captain studied the picture pit again. The Daleks had clearly detected him, and were intent on intercepting his small fleet. He had expected nothing less. Honour was unknown to them, and they thought nothing of attacking a weaker foe. Well, perhaps he could at least take some of them with him.

'Tactical?' he called.

He still could not get used to having females aboard his ship, but he knew that this was prejudice, and he supposed he was still behind the times. Well, that would likely cease being a problem very shortly. His tactical officer moved to his side, her skin flushed with anticipation of the inevitable battle.

'They outclass us,' she said simply.

'I can see that,' the captain growled. 'What are our options? Aside from dying?'

'We are smaller, but more manoeuvrable,' she pointed out. Touching her hand control, she raised a schematic of the planetary system they were in. Four worlds and an asteroid field sprang up. 'We can reach the asteroid field before they can,' she pointed out. 'We can go where they cannot.'

There was a sour taste in his mouth. 'You suggest that we hide?' he asked her incredulously, all of his prejudices coming to the fore.

'No!' She glared at him, genuinely angry that he thought so little of her. 'I suggest that we prepare teams to seed the asteroids with proximity mines. The Dalek shields are good, but are they good enough to withstand numerous impacts?'

The Captain felt ashamed of his suspicions. 'A good plan,' he conceded, bowing slightly to show respect. The officer flushed with pleasure. 'Organise it.' He turned to the navigation officer. 'Alter course for the asteroid field, maximum drive. I want to know how long we'll have there before the Daleks arrive. We must make every moment count.'

There was hurried but quiet activity in response to his orders. His small fleet moved as fast as they could towards the asteroid belt, and his crews began to prepare for their mission. They would not have long, but he had every confidence in his crew. If only he had more time!

The tactical officer moved to join him again. 'All is ready,' she reported. 'The EVA teams will be standing by. As soon as we enter the field, they will begin to exit and work.'

'Excellent.' He scratched the ridges of his forehead, something he did .subconsciously when agitated. 'Do you think the Daleks will be expecting a trap?'

'Perhaps,' she acknowledged. 'What you said earlier about hiding…'

'I apologise,' he told her. 'It was wrong of me to think you meant that.'

'Thank you. But that's not what I meant.' She gestured at the picture pit, which showed the Dalek killcruisers closing in. 'The Daleks have no concept of honour. They cannot know that we would not hide from them. Perhaps if we made it look as though that was what we were doing, they would not be looking for a trap.'

Even the thought of hiding made the captain angry, but it had the merit of sense. The Daleks would believe the worst of their foes. Though it went against the grain, he nodded. 'Another fine suggestion,' he complimented her. 'If we survive this, I will make sure you will be commended.'

She inclined her head, her ears tinged yellow with pleasure. 'That is not necessary. I am only performing my job.'

'On my ship,' he informed her, 'when someone performs their job well, they are commended.' He turned from her, and concentrated on the task in hand.

The *Hunter* entered the field, and his officers began to report the release of the work crews. From the fleet, he had managed to assemble ten crews, each with three mines. That meant thirty mines. Some of them would fail, without doubt. But, perhaps, some would succeed. The captain directed the navigator to burrow into the asteroid field and find a good, metal-rich asteroid to 'hide' behind.

All the time, he studied the picture pit, watching the killcruisers draw closer.

The *Hunter* shook, and the science officer reported,

'Minor collision. Our deflector grids repulsed it without damage. It is likely to get worse, Captain.'

It did. The ship shook from the asteroid impacts every few minutes. Each time, though, the grid held up, and no damage was sustained. Then one of the smaller ships lost an antenna to a collision.

And then they were in the lee of a large asteroid, and the Hunter matched velocity and direction with it, hugging close to the rocky surface. The captain had a satellite launched, since they were now out of sight of the Daleks. He needed to be able to continue to track them.

They were still closing in.

'The Daleks will enter the field in two units,' the science officer reported from his post. 'The first three ships will all be in the vicinity of the mined asteroids. I cannot tell about the other five yet.'

'And the EVA crews?' the captain asked.

'Have finished their work,' Tactical answered. 'They are waiting for us to recover them once the battle is over.' She didn't need to say that they would not survive their air supply should the battle not favour the Draconians.

'Arm all weapons, and power up for attack,' he ordered. 'Order the fleet to follow. We shall attack first, and then they are all free to find their own targets.' He raised his voice and his arm in salute. 'For the Emperor and Empire – glory and honour!'

'Glory and honour!' the bridge crew chorused proudly.

The captain nodded, happy with his team. They were the best. If *Hunter* was going to die, they would take as many of the enemy with them as they could.

'Killcruisers entering asteroid field,' Science reported. 'They are slowing, but apparently not suspicious.'

'Good.' The captain studied the image in the pit intently. The mined asteroids were marked in green, and he could see that the first killcruisers were drawing closer... The tension that came before every battle held him immobile and entranced. Would their plan succeed? Or would the Daleks notice the trap? Would their ships' shields prove too strong for the rocks to penetrate?

'Detonation,' Tactical said softly, as one of the green lights flared.

'Magnify!' he ordered, and the picture focused in on the lead Dalek ships.

Two asteroids had detonated almost simultaneously. As he had hoped, the fragmented rocks had been blasted apart at high velocity, and many of them had slammed into the Dalek ships. 'Scan,' he called.

'They've sustained damage,' Science reported. 'The lead ship is holed, and a second appears to have lost some sensor power.'

'Good.' The captain turned to Navigation. 'Take us out of here in an arc. Intercept course on their planned trajectory. Prepare for engagement.'

The *Hunter* rose from behind the asteroid, and began the movement he'd ordered. The Dalek ships were still penetrating the asteroid field, but at a much reduced speed. One of them was firing at asteroids as they approached, obviously hoping to destroy the rocks before the mines could. That might be a problem.

'Detonate one-third of the mines,' he ordered Tactical. 'Some of the debris might get through. And it might make them think we've detonated them all.'

'Understood.'

There were nine flashes of green from the pit, and the

Daleks ceased firing.

'Some minor damage from those blasts,' Science reported. 'Not worth speaking of.'

Well, that gamble had failed. But did the Daleks believe he'd triggered all of his remaining mines? He'd find out if they started firing on asteroids again.

They didn't, and were now approaching the next block of mines. The captain permitted himself a small smile. They were going to get a nasty little surprise in a moment. The lead ship was approaching one of the larger asteroids that had been booby-trapped. When this one went, it would be spectacular.

There was another flare of green in the picture pit, followed within seconds by a larger explosion.

'Lead killcruiser has been destroyed,' Science reported unnecessarily. They had all seen it go up. The captain smiled openly now.

'Our first kill,' he predicted.

The remaining seven Dalek ships now began firing in all directions again, wasting their fire power on harmless rocks, but taking out four more of the mined asteroids.

'Detonate the remaining mines,' the captain ordered. The chances of causing more damage might be slender, but the Daleks would have no way of knowing that the mines were all gone. This time, they would assume that there were others, even after these exploded.

There was a burst of green light, and then spreading debris markers.

'More minor damage,' Science announced. 'One killcruiser seems to be crippled. Its engines are mistimed, and it's spinning.'

It was better than he'd expected – one killcruiser

destroyed and one out of the fight. Only six of them now. Still enough for the Daleks to win, but better odds. The *Hunter* was almost within striking distance now as it topped out of its arc and began to descend towards its targets.

'Fire when ready,' he ordered. 'All ships to independent action.'

And then they were in range, and the guns opened up.

The noise was intense, but satisfying. The two forward cannons raked across the closest killcruiser, which returned fire. The *Hunter* shook as the grids absorbed the energy bolts, radiating the effects away into space. He could hear them whine, knowing they were under strain. Still, he kept the Hunter on path, and the firing continued.

At last, the Dalek screens gave way, and a great gash was opened in the bows of the killcruiser. Air and Daleks gusted out of the breach.

'Target the gap,' he ordered. 'Plasma missiles.'

Twin missiles streaked from the Hunter's belly towards the gap. The Dalek fire power exploded the first at a distance. The second homed in. Defensive fire found it barely seconds before impact – too close. The resulting explosion ruptured the gash wider, and engulfed one of the storage bays.

The killcruiser erupted into a huge ball of plasma and flame that burst out almost instantly, leaving the charred wreckage floating dead in space.

'Acquire next target,' the captain ordered, allowing no time for a victory cheer. The Daleks wouldn't hold back.

He glanced at the pit again. Two of his ships were gone, floating debris marking their passing. The rest were engaging killcruisers, and fighting for their lives. They didn't ultimately stand a chance, but with the *Hunter* to aid them, the odds brightened slightly.

His craft swung about, and moved to the closest of the battles. Firing away, it closed in on the killcruiser. The other Draconian ship shuddered in the wake of Dalek fire, and then exploded. Another loss... The *Hunter* closed in, raking the killcruiser with all batteries. The ship shuddered about him as the Daleks returned fire. The grids were whining loudly now, and he knew they were taking a serious battering.

Again, his weapons managed to find a small weakness in the Dalek ship, and a fissure in its side opened up. A small barrage of plasma missiles sealed the fate of the enemy ship. The *Hunter* accelerated away from the detonation, seeking another target.

'We're alone, Captain,' Science reported. 'The Daleks have destroyed all of the fleet but us.'

And there were still four killcruisers left – not good odds at all.

Then one of the Dalek ships slammed into an asteroid. Perhaps they had been focusing so intently on the Hunter that they had not seen the asteroid in its path. Or their tactical computer had sustained damage. The collision broke the Dalek ship into two parts, both of which were engulfed in fireballs. A surprising but acceptable victory.

The remaining three ships all moved to intercept him, cutting off any possible retreat. How little the Daleks understood his people!

'To the death,' he ordered firmly. 'For the Emperor and Empire!'

The *Hunter* sprang forward, into the hail of fire the three killcruisers laid down. The grids whined at fever pitch, and his ship shuddered about him. His own fire pounded the first killcruiser, opening it for another strike.

Then the whine from the grids ceased entirely, and he knew what that meant.

The entire universe exploded about him and his crew...

PART THREE
CIVIL WAR

'War is at best barbarism… Its glory is all moonshine. It is only those who have neither fired a shot nor heard the shrieks and groans of the wounded who cry aloud for blood, more vengeance, more desolation. War is hell.'
General William Sherman, 1879

CHAPTER 7
EXPECT THE UNEXPECTED

Davros whirled to face the door as it slid open. He had been attempting to monitor what was happening in the battle, and had already concluded that the Daleks had won. Though the Thals had spared his life and attempted to secure his cooperation, he was under no illusions that the Daleks would do the same. As a result, he had expected to be exterminated immediately the door was opened, and had prepared for it, knowing precisely what kind of radiation to expect.

To his surprise, the Red Dalek in the doorway did not fire. Instead, it regarded him steadily. Davros was puzzled to note that one of the Thals had accompanied it. 'Davros,' the Red Dalek stated, 'you are being taken back for trial. You will be given minimal contact with Daleks.' It paused. 'You will be executed at the end of the trial.'

'Why this insistence on a trial for me?' he demanded. 'You already know the verdict and sentence. Why bother with this charade?'

The Red Dalek studied him. 'The trial is not yours.'

Intriguing… Davros looked at the Thal. 'Why have you spared your foes?' he asked. 'Surely the Daleks have not developed mercy?' He almost spat the word out.

'No,' the Red Dalek acknowledged. 'But we have developed wisdom.' It considered a moment, and then added, 'The Doctor and his companions have also been spared.'

Davros was almost beside himself with rage. 'The Doctor is alive?' he exclaimed. 'No! That must not be! It is he who

165

tricked me into destroying Skaro! He must be exterminated!' When the Red Dalek did not respond, an idea occurred to Davros. 'Is the trial his, then?'

'No.' The Dalek turned away, apparently indifferent. 'Consider wisely what you will say at the trial,' it advised.

'If I am not told whose trial it is to be, how can I prepare a statement?' Davros asked.

The Red Dalek's eye stalk swivelled back to regard him. 'Logical,' it acknowledged. 'The trial is of the entire Dalek species.' The door slid shut, leaving Davros to stare at its black façade.

But the Red Dalek had been very careful and selective in the information it had given him. Davros merely needed time to assimilate it – and to devise a scheme to use it to his own advantage.

To Sam's surprise, their cell door was not closed again. Several Daleks glided past in the corridor, but none paid the captives any attention whatsoever. This was not the kind of behaviour that she had expected of the universe's most ruthless killers. As she'd told the Doctor earlier, they were being far more civilised than the Thals had been. So far, they had killed none of the crew of the ship, and this clearly disturbed the Doctor.

Sam wasn't sure how she felt about anything right now. She was still in some shock from having witnessed Delani's murder. A twinge or two of guilt, too, in fact, since she had been instrumental in persuading Ayaka to spare their lives. She was starting to see how the Doctor could have felt that creating the Thals as a fighting force might have been his fault. After all, some of the guilt for Delani's death had to rest upon her own shoulders. True, Sam had not expected Ayaka to kill her commander, but that was no real excuse. She'd incited a soldier to mutiny, for what she firmly believed were good reasons. But to be accomplice to murder – even one that was arguably justifiable – left Sam feeling empty.

To be honest, she wasn't absolutely sure why. It was partly because she believed in trying to see the good in everyone. Delani had, after all, been a product of his environment. He had grown up in a society that had waged war for generations; it was only natural that he become a killer, desensitised to murder and violence. But, then, Ayaka had grown up in exactly the same environment, and she still believed in a code of morality. Not exactly the one that either Sam or the Doctor did, it was true, but her own code. One that would not allow her to kill the innocent simply because she'd been ordered to do so.

Sam didn't know what to make of the Thal woman. In some ways, she despised Ayaka, and in others she admired her.

Why was the universe always so confusing? It was really easy to believe in absolute right and wrong when all you had to do was to study the issue in the abstract. But when you were actually plunged into the thick of life, suddenly the obvious became less clear. Could she condemn Ayaka for doing what the Thal believed was right? It looked as though Ayaka was asking herself pretty much the same questions. She had not killed Delani lightly, or on impulse, but because she had genuinely believed it to be for the greater good. And, at the same time, she blamed herself for doing it. Ayaka was a complex person, and Sam was at a loss as to how to take her.

And what was to happen to them now? The Doctor had been convinced that the Daleks had intended to murder them all, but he had been wrong. Ayaka was convinced that they would all be made into slaves, but the Doctor seemed to think this might not be the case. He was certain that the Daleks were up to something. Sam could agree with that. But what? That question was clearly vexing the Doctor.

'Information,' he finally said, startling them all. Suddenly aware he was being stared at, the Doctor explained. 'We need more information. Like where we are being taken, for one thing.'

'Maybe you should just ask the Daleks,' suggested Chayn. 'They seem to be being awfully reasonable right now.'

The Doctor grinned. 'It's worth a shot,' he agreed, and then winced at his choice of words. Crossing to the open door, he waved a hand in the direction of the guard. 'Ah, excuse me,' he called. 'Could you tell me where this ship is heading?'

The Dalek stared at him. 'I do not have that information.'

'Well, that's a start,' the Doctor murmured. 'He didn't tell me to shut up or be exterminated.' Raising his voice, he asked, 'Could you find out if we're allowed to know?'

The Dalek fell silent, and the Doctor studied it. 'It's sending for directives,' he said, sounding surprised. 'We're certainly being given the royal treatment – at least by Dalek standards.'

The Dalek's eye stalk swivelled to face the Doctor again. 'You may all proceed to the monitor room,' it stated. 'Do not attempt to deviate from instructions.'

'We wouldn't dream of it,' the Doctor assured it. He beamed at his three companions. 'Come on. We may as well take advantage of their generosity. At the very least, it'll be less cramped than this cell.'

The Dalek led the way down the corridor to another room. It activated the door and ushered them in. 'The door will remain open at all times,' it stated. 'You will be observed.'

'Naturally,' the Doctor agreed. He raised an eyebrow when he saw that Cathbad was already there. 'Hello! You out on parole, too?'

Cathbad shrugged. 'The Red Dalek ordered me to wait in here and to assist you if I could.'

'That's jolly decent of it,' the Doctor answered. 'And, frankly, that scares me. Why would the Daleks want us to have access to all of this equipment? They have absolutely no reason to trust me.' He stared about the room, which was clearly a communications subcentre, even to Sam's untrained eyes. There were numerous machines that looked like radars or televisions, and several computers. The lighting in the room was dimmed to make the screens clearer.

Chayn smiled. 'Doctor, I think they've discovered something that keeps you their prisoner far more than locks and chains – curiosity.'

The Doctor grinned. 'You know, you may be correct in that.' He turned to Cathbad. 'Can you discover our destination from all of this?'

'No problem.' He bent to the work.

Sam couldn't help feeling useless again. So far, she'd been able to help the Doctor very little, beyond helping to persuade Ayaka to switch sides. All this technical stuff was way over her head. Chayn had taken a seat at one of the computers, and Ayaka at another. Sam couldn't even see a mouse to play around with, and she knew she'd never be able to get the hang of any of this. If only there were some way in which she could contribute. She gave Chayn a calculating look. How could she possibly compete with someone like that? Or like Ayaka, given her build and features? Sam was embarrassingly reminded that she was just a seventeen-year-old schoolkid, without many talents and without a sense of direction in her life. It was not a good feeling.

Cathbad looked up, finally. 'Here we are, Doctor.' He gestured to the screen. 'It's pretty logical, really. We're headed for Skaro.'

'Skaro?' The Doctor's voice was sharp. 'That's not possible. Skaro's been destroyed. I should know.'

Ayaka turned around in her seat. 'You've said that before, Doctor,' she commented. 'I kept trying to ask you about it, but I never seemed to get the chance. Why do you think Skaro's been destroyed?'

The Doctor collapsed into one of the chairs, his forehead furrowed. 'Because I engineered its destruction,' he said quietly. 'I tricked Davros into believing that a terrible weapon would give him virtually infinite power, and he loosed it on Skaro's sun. It turned Skaro's sun nova and vaporised the planet, destroying Davros's entire army.'

Ayaka and Cathbad glanced at each other in confusion. 'Doctor, that's impossible,' she stated. 'According to our instruments, Skaro is still intact. Its sun has not become a nova.'

Sam could see that the Doctor was having trouble assimilating this information. Well, she reflected, if you thought you'd vaporised a planet, it must be a shock to discover it's still alive and well. 'Maybe we're back in time before the destruction of Skaro?' she suggested.

'No,' the Doctor said slowly. 'I paid a special trip there just before I took on this body – not normally allowed, but I had a special mission to perform. The year then tallied with what I know of Skaro. Anyway, Davros believes it to have been obliterated, too. And the time coordinates in the TARDIS indicated that this is thirty years after the explosion, which accords with Davros's memories. So what's going on?'

Sam thought furiously. 'Maybe the Time Lords changed history again,' she suggested.

'Unlikely,' the Doctor replied. 'Oh, they could do it, but they're very wary of such things. Besides, they hate and fear the Daleks. At one time they wanted me to avert their creation in the first place. No, they'd never affect Skaro's timeline in any such way.'

Chayn shrugged. 'Maybe you're just a lousy shot.'

The Doctor looked very indignant at the thought. 'I knew exactly what I was doing,' he insisted with dignity. 'I programmed the Hand of Omega very precisely for the correct coordinates, and...' He stared at Cathbad's screen and then scowled. 'Those aren't the correct coordinates,' he said firmly.

Ayaka crossed to check Cathbad's data. 'Yes, they are,' she insisted.

The Doctor looked shaken. 'I don't understand,' he muttered to himself. 'It's not possible I destroyed the wrong planet...'

Sam could see he was going through some deep agony. She knew how much he was opposed to senseless violence, and that it had taken a great deal of soul-searching for him to have decided to destroy an entire planet to begin with. Now to discover that it wasn't the one he thought it was... It was starting to be more than he could bear. She placed a hand gently on his shoulder, and he pressed it there with one of his own, grateful for her support.

'Do you recall the coordinates you programmed your super-weapon for?' Cathbad asked the Doctor, starting a new pattern. The Doctor nodded, and tapped them into the computer. A moment later, a new point showed on the screen, some distance from their marked trajectory.

'Antalin,' Ayaka breathed. 'Now it's starting to make sense.'

'What is?' the Doctor demanded. 'I wish it made sense to me.'

'Thirty years ago, Antalin's sun went nova for no apparent reason,' Cathbad explained. 'The entire system was destroyed. It's about ten parsecs from Skaro. Our intelligence forces assumed that the Daleks were testing some new weapon that could detonate stars, but they never used one in combat. We always figured that they'd simply had a problem with it.'

'Antalin?' the Doctor echoed. 'But those are the correct coordinates. I checked them from the TARDIS.' He held up a hand. 'No, give me a moment.' He blinked several times, and then shook his head. 'Of course, the Daleks have the technology to pilot whole worlds by using the planet's core, but...'

'There's something very strange going on here, Doctor,' Ayaka mused thoughtfully. 'Nevertheless, according to our instruments, Skaro exists where it always did, and we are heading there at this moment.'

'Perhaps,' Sam suggested, 'you'll be able to get some answers there.'

'I hope so,' the Doctor said. 'Because Antalin was the home of an advanced civilisation at one time. The Daleks turned it into a slave world, with millions of natives forced to work the mines for the Dalek war effort.' His face was very pale. 'If that is the world I destroyed, then I'm guilty of the murder of millions of innocent beings.'

Davros was fuming quietly to himself. The Daleks had not

made the same mistakes with him as the Thals had done. They had left him strictly alone, locked in a room with guards outside. They had depowered a lot of his chair, giving him access to his life-support system, but not his weapons or computer. They were clearly taking no chances with him. He couldn't blame them; from their point of view, their actions were perfectly logical and wise. But it left him their prisoner, and that was a situation that he could not tolerate for very much longer.

The door opened, and a grey Dalek glided in. It was carrying a small power pack. The door slid shut behind it, and the Dalek approached Davros. 'I am here to replenish your resources,' it grated.

'Do so, then,' Davros said impatiently.

It moved forward, connecting the power cell to the chair's inputs. Then, as it worked, it looked up. 'There are those who still believe in you,' it stated.

'What?' Davros focused on the Dalek. 'What do you mean?'

'You are our creator,' it stated. 'It is appropriate that you should be in command of the Daleks. There are many others who believe as I do.'

Davros stared at the Dalek with interest. Was it telling the truth? Or was this some form of elaborate trap? 'I still have supporters?' he asked. 'Daleks who will listen to me?'

'And obey you,' the Dalek replied. 'We are prepared to help you.'

'Interesting…' Davros considered the matter. 'Are there many of you?'

'On this ship, only seventeen for certain,' the Dalek grated. 'On Skaro, many more. We are ready to assist you in any way that you desire.'

This was getting more promising by the minute – if this

173

Dalek was to be believed. 'And what about the Dalek Prime?' he questioned.

'The Dalek Prime should be serving you. He should not have usurped your rightful place. You are the creator.'

Davros nodded slightly, virtually the only movement he could still physically make. 'Good. I am glad that you understand. Then carry this message from me to your companions. Tell them to prepare to be ready for the hour when Davros will need them.'

'I obey.' The Dalek uncoupled the spent fuel cell. 'One of our number will contact you again shortly. We must be cautious. If the Daleks loyal to the Dalek Prime suspect anything, we shall be exterminated.'

'Yes,' Davros agreed. He watched as the Dalek left, and then resumed his deliberations. This time, however, he had a lot to think about. Could he trust what the Dalek had said? If so, then his power was far from spent…

Sam saw that Chayn and Cathbad were deep in conversation, and that Chayn was touching the Thal's hand. She smiled to herself, and glanced at the Doctor again. He was seated by himself, brooding. It wasn't good for him. She went across the room to join him, kneeling down on the floor in front of him so he couldn't avoid her.

'Cheer up,' she told him. 'It can't be as bad as all that.'

'It can be,' he replied. 'There's something very wrong here, and with the Daleks involved, anything that feels bad has to be far worse. They're up to something, and it involves Davros, the Thals and myself. The Daleks should have killed us all on sight, but didn't. Why? And now it looks as though I've destroyed an entire world for… nothing.' He shook his head. 'It doesn't make sense.'

'Maybe not yet,' Sam agreed. 'But it'll be all right, Doctor. You'll work it out, and beat the Daleks, too.'

He managed a watery smile. 'Thank you for your faith in me, Sam,' he said. 'Though it may well be misplaced. I may have been instrumental in killing millions of people, and that's something that my soul couldn't bear.'

'Doctor,' Sam said firmly, 'Stop it, for God's sake. What's wrong with you? You're not thinking straight. Whatever planet it was you blew up with this Hand thing, it was where Davros had his base. Does it really matter what the name of the planet was? Whether it was called Skaro or Fred? Davros's army was there, so they must have already killed whoever was there in the first place. All you did was to destroy Davros's forces, and you said you believed that to be worthwhile. So what's your problem?'

The Doctor's eyes lit up at this, and he abruptly placed both of his hands on her shoulders, leaned forward and kissed her on the forehead. 'Sam, Sam, Sam, Sam, Sam!' he exclaimed in relief. Her forehead burned at his touch, and she flushed. 'Destroying that planet was probably the most difficult decision I've ever had to make in my entire life. And to have done it for nothing...' he smiled at her.

Sam was confused and recharged at the same time. The Doctor surged to his feet once more. 'Right,' he said briskly. 'Let's get to work again. Cathbad, can you give me an estimate of how long we've got before we reach Skaro? Ayaka, try to get the sensory web working, and plot whatever we pass on the way in. If we're coming out this way again, it will help us to know what to look for. Chayn, tap into communications. If the Daleks send out any recognition codes to anything we pass, I want a full record of them. Sam, you keep an eye on me and make sure I stay on course.' He flopped down into one of the chairs and started to access the computer memory cores.

Sam grinned. She had done something to help him, after all. Maybe she wasn't as technical as Chayn, or as drop-dead gorgeous as Ayaka, but she still had something that they didn't.

A kiss on the forehead, for one thing!

She watched as the others bent to the tasks that the Doctor had assigned them. After a few moments, Cathbad announced, 'We're now at the outer limits of the Skaro system. Time to landing, approximately one hour.'

'I'm picking up the first of the perimeter defences,' Ayaka announced. 'Killstations.' She threw a picture up on one of the screens. Sam grimaced. The thing looked like something out of *Star Wars*: a huge, vaguely circular space platform, bristling with gun emplacements, and with ships docked at it. It was certainly something that nobody could get past in a hurry.

'I'm hacked into the communications grid,' Chayn reported. 'I'm picking up the recognition codes and downloading them.'

'Excellent,' the Doctor murmured, watching everything with darting eyes. 'It's certainly well protected. Getting back out won't be easy.'

'You think we can get back out, Doctor?' Cathbad asked.

'Anything's possible,' the Doctor replied vaguely. 'But it's nice to keep our options open.'

For the next hour, Sam watched and listened, getting more and more worried all of the time. They had passed eight of the space gun platforms, and two of the outer planets in the system were even more heavily fortified. She thought of her earlier pep talk. Now she was beginning to think that the

Doctor was being wildly optimistic to even think they stood a chance of getting back out again. The fire power they were passing could easily take out a hundred ships like theirs without a problem.

'This doesn't look like a race that's lost a war to me, Doctor,' she finally said. 'If the Movellans beat the Daleks, you'd hardly expect this kind of fortification, would you?'

'No,' agreed the Doctor. 'I'm afraid you're quite right, Sam. This is not a beaten foe by any means.' Strangely enough, he didn't sound too worried.

And then they were approaching Skaro itself. There seemed to be hundreds of ships in orbit about the planet. 'Isn't that overkill?' she asked.

'No,' the Doctor answered, rubbing his chin. 'Most of those ships are transports, not war vessels. It looks to me as though there's been a large recall of Daleks to Skaro.'

'Why would they do that?' asked Ayaka, puzzled. 'They're certainly not in trouble on their war fronts.'

'Summit meeting perhaps?' the Doctor suggested. 'This must all tie in together somehow, and I'm sure we'll discover the meaning very shortly. We'd hardly have been brought all this way and allowed such access to information, only to be left in the dark at the end.'

Chayn glanced up. 'The ship's asked for and received landing clearance,' she announced. 'We're going down.'

Sam leaned forward, eager for her first glimpse of the surface of this world she'd heard so much about - one that wasn't even supposed to be here... They descended towards a large range of mountains, eventually dropping through the low clouds. She could make out a large mountain lake, and then a large city close to the base of the mountains. It was difficult to get a proper idea of what it looked like from above, but it was quite clearly huge. It was also constructed almost entirely of polished metal.

There was a slight shudder as the ship touched down on the perimeter of the city, clearly in a large spaceport. The view screens showed dozens of other such ships around them, many of them disgorging Daleks onto sloping ramps.

The Dalek in the doorway turned to them. 'Prepare to leave the ship,' it commanded. A second Dalek glided to join them. 'Doctor, you will accompany me. The others will join the Thals in confinement.'

Sam was suddenly terrified of being left apart from the Doctor. She clutched the Doctor's hand. 'No,' she insisted.

He nodded. 'Sam comes with me,' he said gently.

'Very well,' agreed the Dalek, surprisingly accommodating. He turned to the other Dalek. 'Escort the prisoners to the holding cell in the docking bay,' it ordered.

'I obey.' The second Dalek turned to face Cathbad, Ayaka, and Chayn. 'You will accompany me.'

The Doctor caught Ayaka's worried look and gave her a reassuring smile. 'Go on,' he said encouragingly. 'I'm sure that everything will be fine. I'll see you shortly.'

'Very well, Doctor.' Ayaka led her companions out of the room and followed the Dalek down the corridor. It was clearly not worried that they would try to escape. After all, they were on Skaro, the heart of the Dalek empire. To where could the prisoners possibly attempt to flee?

'Doctor, you will come with me,' the first Dalek said.

The Doctor nodded, and he and Sam accompanied the Dalek as it glided along the ship's corridors. They exited an airlock, where the Doctor paused for a moment, waving a small instrument he'd taken from the communications room. 'No radiation,' he murmured. 'Odd. The entire planet ought to be radioactive.'

'One more little mystery,' Sam quipped, as he slid the device back into his pocket. The Dalek proceeded down the sloping ramp, and through a doorway into the city proper. Sam looked behind her before she followed it. The spaceport stretched as far as she could see. There were hundreds of ships, all with Daleks flowing back and forth. How many Daleks were there on this entire planet? And how could they possibly hope to get out of here without being killed? The situation was certainly not improving in the slightest.

Inside the city, the walls, ceiling, and floor were all polished metal. Thankfully, it wasn't too slippery. The doorways were arched, conforming to the pepper-pot shape of the Daleks. The walls were bare, except where there were controls or other mechanisms installed.

'It's a bit bleak, Doctor,' she commented.

'As I told you,' he explained, 'Daleks have no interest in anything but conquest and war. Art, decoration, poetry, music – it's all irrelevant to them.' He gave her a quick smile. 'Good thing, really. Can you imagine a Dalek trying to sing?'

The thought of their grating monotones attempting anything of the kind made Sam smile. 'Worse than the Spice Girls,' she agreed.

There were many other Daleks about, all moving purposefully along the corridors. Most were of the grey colour, Sam noted, but there were occasionally ones in red, or black, and some in blue. She nudged the Doctor and asked him about this.

'That's how you can tell status in Daleks,' he explained. 'The grey ones, like our friend here, are the warriors. They're the foot soldiers – or in this case – the roller soldiers. Very limited intelligence, good at obeying orders and chanting choruses of "Exterminate! Exterminate!" Next up are the Blue Daleks. A bit brighter, the non-coms – you know, corporals, sergeants. if you like. The Red Daleks are where you start to see the real brains. They have a certain autonomy of action, and can actually think for themselves.'

Sam was both bemused and slightly alarmed to see the Doctor warm to this subject so thoroughly. 'And the Black Daleks are in charge of that lot, and are a lot nastier and smarter. Above those are the Gold Daleks. They're the elite. And at the top is the Dalek Prime, the one who makes all the big decisions.'

'Sort of a colour-coded society,' Sam said.

'Quite. It comes of being bred in vats. The Daleks select what kind of an embryo they need and breed the right numbers up. The grey outnumber everyone, because they're the most expendable.'

They had reached a moving walkway now, similar to those Sam had ridden on in Heathrow Airport. The Dalek led them onto it, and it carried them deeper into the heart of the city. Sam couldn't help wondering what was in all the rooms and buildings they were passing, but she knew that there was no point in asking. Whatever the Daleks wanted them to know, they would be told. She just stared around, trying to take it all in.

It was entirely devoid of personality. The place needed some pictures, books, potted plants – anything to relieve the monotony of the metallic finish. Every now and then, they passed huge glass windows, and she could catch a glimpse of the exterior of the city. Tall spires, vast minaret-like shapes, towers, walkways – rollways? – of the same metallic shade as indoors, broken only by the occasional doorway or window. It was a staggering piece of workmanship, but almost totally without soul. Exactly like the Daleks themselves.

Finally, the moving walkway ended, and the Dalek gestured for them to enter what was clearly a lift. It followed, and then inserted its pad into a control surface. A moment later, the lift began to rise. Sam lost count after about forty floors, but they must have ascended at least a hundred before the elevator came to a halt and the doors opened.

They were in a large control centre. Panels lined the walls, with dozens of Daleks operating them. Sam didn't have a clue what most of them could possibly be for. One was clearly a map of Skaro, though, showing mostly land masses and very little water. Another was a three-dimensional globe of the galaxy, with coloured markers obviously showing the distribution of the various forces in all the wars the Daleks were fighting. The sheer number of these metal killing machines was terrifying.

The Doctor stopped in his tracks, and stared at one of the panels. Sam followed his gaze curiously. It was not being operated by a Dalek but by what looked like a tall humanoid. He was dressed in a white jumpsuit, and had dreadlocked hair. He gazed at the Doctor and Sam incuriously, and then returned to his work.

'Movellans,' the Doctor breathed.

'I thought you said they were the enemies of the Daleks,' Sam pointed out.

'I did. They are.' He frowned. 'They're humanoid robots. See that little tube on his belt? That's his power pack and brain. I think the Daleks must have reprogrammed him to obey them. That's the trouble with having a brain like that.

181

No allegiance.'

The Dalek they were following led them to a door at the far end of the control centre, and triggered the lock. Its eye stalk swivelled to face them. 'Enter,' it ordered, obviously planning on staying outside itself.

'Thank you, Jeeves,' the Doctor murmured. He breezed into the next room, Sam close behind him. She barely heard the door close behind her, staring as she was.

The ceiling and far wall here were a single piece of glass, or glass-like substance. She could see out across the city, and most of the way up the mountain range, until the clouds closed in. It was a staggering view, incredibly impressive.

'Doctor,' said a Dalek voice. 'Welcome.'

Sam and the Doctor turned to face their host. It was a Dalek, but not like any she had seen before. This one was slightly larger than the others, with a bulbous head. It was a burnished gold colour, and had about a dozen lights about the expanded dome instead of the average Dalek's two.

'The Dalek Prime,' the Doctor murmured.

CHAPTER 8
PLOTS AND COUNTERPLOTS

Davros followed his captors down the ramp from the Thal vessel and towards the waiting city. His sensors showed him what he was seeing, and he stopped in astonishment.

'You will proceed into the city,' the Red Dalek ordered.

'Wait,' Davros said, scanning all that he could see. 'Where am I? What world is this?'

'You are on Skaro,' the Red Dalek replied.

'No!' Davros exclaimed. 'That is not possible! I destroyed Skaro.' He whirled to face the Red Dalek. 'You are lying!'

'No,' the Dalek answered. 'This is Skaro. You are in error.'

Davros realised that he would get no further arguing with the creature. He powered his chair and moved forward again, trying to assimilate this information. The Dalek believed it was on Skaro, which was absurd. Skaro was dead – this was some other world. Perhaps the Daleks had simply renamed it Skaro after they had occupied it. 'Skaro' after all, was simply the word for 'home' in the old Kaled tongue. It would be typical of the rigid-minded Daleks to do that. And the lesser ranks, not being bred for their intellectual prowess, simply assumed that this world was the original Skaro, having known no other.

Davros pondered his children. They were stagnant and self-delusional. He could see why some were seeing him as their messiah, their hope for a new and more glorious... well, Skaro, if they insisted.

And he would make certain they would get it. With Davros

as their leader, how could the cause possibly fail?

Ayaka surveyed the room, where the Thal troops had spread out to rest. There was very little else they could do, after all. There was only the one exit, which was closed and guarded. Shelves around the walls were meant as beds, showing that this had to be one of the slave quarters for the humanoids the Daleks employed around the spaceport. Daleks enjoyed humiliating and brutalising other life forms.

There were sixty-two troopers and crew left alive. Several had died in the attack, but the Daleks had spared everyone else. Four of the troopers required medication, and the Daleks had allowed Ayaka access to the medical supplies without a fuss. That in itself was almost unheard of in her experience. Daleks usually let injured slaves die without treatment. They could always be replaced.

So the Doctor was right – there was some reason the Daleks wanted them alive, and relatively well. Ayaka had no clue as to what that might be, but she knew that her first task was to thwart it. Whatever the Daleks wanted, she must counter.

Ayaka went over to Cathbad and Chayn, slumped on a bench. 'This is not a good situation,' she said.

Chayn grunted. 'Agreed,' she answered. 'We're in a jail cell on the Dalek home world, surrounded by one of the greatest war fleets in existence and millions of Daleks. It kind of throws a damper on my life. What there is left of it, anyway.'

Ayaka nodded. 'Therefore we must escape.'

Cathbad gave a bitter laugh, and gestured at himself. 'All I have is my clothing,' he pointed out. The Daleks had confiscated their weapons along with their battle armour. 'It is all that any of us have left. We cannot attack Daleks with cloth.'

'Perhaps not,' agreed Ayaka, looking at Chayn in her far looser clothing. 'But the Daleks did not search you. Do you have any resources on you?'

'Me?' Chayn asked innocently. Then she grinned and pulled up her tunic. 'Don't get the wrong idea,' she told Cathbad. Ayaka saw that Chayn had several small packages taped to her bare skin. 'Careful when you free them,' she said. 'I don't want to lose my epidermal layer, too.'

Ayaka and Cathbad gently removed the packages, and Chayn replaced her tunic. 'I figured they might come in handy,' she explained. She gestured at Ayaka. 'You can barely hide yourself in that outfit, so I knew it was up to me. Prudery has its advantages at times.'

The packages contained several sets of microtools. Ayaka could hardly believe their good fortune, or the foresight of this alien engineer. 'That was extremely clever of you,' she commented.

'That's me all over,' Chayn answered. 'Still, I'm glad the Daleks didn't want to do a strip-search.'

'You don't have anything else hidden, do you?' Cathbad asked in amazement.

Chayn grinned. 'Ask me that when we're alone.' Ayaka chuckled as Cathbad blushed ferociously. 'So, fearless leader,' she asked Ayaka. 'What's the plan?'

Ayaka studied the door with interest. 'All of the control panels are on the outside. We don't have a cutting torch in your tools, so we can't gain access from this side.'

'Sorry I couldn't hide one,' Chayn replied. 'But this was all I had access to while we were free.'

'It was not a complaint,' Ayaka said hastily, lest she be misunderstood. 'We can still gain access when the door opens. A small microprobe inserted under the door will be able to work through the circuitry to the panel. Then we will gain access to the control systems.'

Cathbad frowned. 'Are you sure that the door will open?' he asked.

'Yes. The Daleks are carefully preserving our lives. They will therefore logically supply us with food and water within the next several hours. Once they do, we can begin work.' Ayaka surveyed her dispirited troops. 'Once we are free, we will return to our ship.'

'And what about the Doctor and Sam?' asked Chayn. 'We just ignore them?'

'There is nothing that we can do to help them,' Ayaka said simply. 'They are at an unknown location in the city. We dare not attempt to penetrate further. We would be bound to be detected and exterminated.' She shook her head. 'I'm afraid the Doctor and Sam will have to fend for themselves.' She had a responsibility to her troops that overrode any obligations to the Doctor. She was sure that he would understand.

But she wasn't sure that she could forgive herself for making that decision. That was the problem with trying to wage a war with moral considerations. Sometimes you had to sacrifice one belief for another.

'So,' the Doctor asked in a conversational tone, 'is this the bit where you exterminate us personally, or is it where you explain your masterplan and gloat a lot?'

Sam wondered if it was terribly wise of the Doctor to bait the Dalek Prime like that, but the Dalek Prime took it with surprising mildness. Sam had been expecting the Dalek leader to be a homicidal machine slobbering oil and spouting propaganda and death. Instead, the creature seemed to be calm, controlled and thoughtful. Which was definitely far scarier. It was even phrasing its speech much closer to that of humans. That was scary, too.

'I have no intention of killing you, Doctor. Or,' he added, the eyestalk moving to take in Sam, 'your companion.'

The Doctor raised an eyebrow. 'That's a bit of a change from your usual policy, isn't it?' he asked. 'You know – shoot first, interrogate the remains later?'

'Yes,' agreed the Dalek Prime. 'However, circumstances have changed. The next time we meet, I shall probably exterminate you.'

'Oh, good,' the Doctor replied. 'I was starting to get worried that you'd discovered religion, or something, and wanted to convince me you had reformed.'

'Nothing of the kind, Doctor,' the Dalek Prime answered. 'Do you desire refreshment?'

The Doctor blinked again. 'Better not,' he decided. 'Somehow the notion of sitting down to tea and crumpets with you does awfully strange things to my mind. Couldn't we just get down to your explaining what is going on?'

'As you wish.' The Dalek Prime moved forward, revealing two tall stools behind him. 'Sit down. You will be more comfortable.'

'This is very worrying,' the Doctor muttered to Sam as they accepted the invitation. 'The next thing you know, he'll be playing musak.' Once they were seated, though, he looked to their host. 'I have a lot of questions, starting with the obvious one. How come this planet still exists?'

'You allude to the Hand of Omega?' the Dalek Prime asked.

'Yes. When Davros used it, I was under the distinct impression it had annihilated Skaro.'

The Dalek Prime paused for a second. Sam had the distinct

feeling that the Doctor had somehow surprised him.

'There was no mention of your role in the records.'

'The records?' The Doctor nodded to himself. 'So I was correct in my assumption, then? That you learnt about the Hand of Omega during your invasion of earth?'

Sam nudged him in the ribs. 'Invasion?' she asked.

'Yes, Sam,' the Doctor replied. 'Actually, the Daleks have invaded earth several times, mostly long after your era. In fact, they conquered earth in the 22nd century. They managed to batter down the human race severely at that time, and occupied a large slice of the globe. While they were in charge of London, they raided the Ministry of Defence vaults and discovered that the Hand of Omega had been on Earth in 1963.'

'Correct,' the Dalek Prime confirmed. 'As a matter of precaution, we scanned the records for anything relating to Daleks. It was possible that the humans had developed some stealth weapons to use against us. We found no such weapons, but there were entries relating to two previous human contacts with the Daleks.'

'The Styles business and the Hand of Omega,' said the Doctor. His eyes narrowed. 'And what did your researches uncover?'

'That Davros was on earth and utilised the Hand of Omega to destroy Skaro,' the Dalek Prime answered. 'There was no mention of your involvement.'

The Doctor leaned over to whisper to Sam, 'That was the work of my last incarnation. He wiped most references to me from the computer records. He was a paranoid chap at times, but then often with good reason.'

The Dalek Prime paused. 'The information that Davros was still alive caused some concern,' it admitted.

'But not as much as the news that he was going to destroy Skaro, I'll wager,' the Doctor guessed. 'I'm starting to see what you must have done next. You waited on the information to see what would happen to your invasion. When that was foiled, you then used your nascent time-travel abilities to attempt to change the results of that failure, creating a parallel timeline. That also failed. That failure made you more cautious about attempting to interfere with time, while alerting you to the fact that such alteration was theoretically possible.'

'Correct,' the Dalek Prime admitted. 'It became clear that we could not save Skaro by travelling back to earth year 1963 and stopping Davros. Our unit was therefore sent back to ensure that his plan succeeded, but without his realising it.'

'Ah-ha,' the Doctor said, snapping his fingers. 'But to ensure the ultimate failure of his plan, you led him to believe that Antalin was actually Skaro.'

'Affirmative,' the Dalek Prime agreed. 'When we discovered that Davros would be resurrected, a search was conducted for his remains. They were discovered buried deep within the old Kaled bunker in suspended animation. This was unexpected.'

'I imagine it was, since you tried to bump him off and claim the imperial throne for yourself.' The Doctor shook his head. 'Uneasy lies the head that wears a crown.'

'We knew that Davros would believe that he was on Skaro when he awakened,' the Dalek explained. 'His memories were altered, and Antalin was prepared to match his implanted memories.'

'Close enough to Skaro to match in many details,' the Doctor mused. 'And the inhabitants of Antalin?'

'It was necessary to render the surface sterile and radioactive,' the Dalek Prime answered.

'In other words, you murdered the lot of them.' The Doctor glared angrily at his foe, and then turned to Sam. 'Still think they're more civilised than the Thals?'

Sam just stared at the creature they were facing. 'They wiped out an entire civilisation just to trick Davros?'

'Yes,' the Doctor answered sombrely. 'And when I arrived, it fooled me, too.' He put his head in his hands, and muttered to himself. 'That wretched randomiser I'd put in. I never checked... but it felt so familiar...' He shook his head. 'You know, I recently told Davros that he fooled himself by wishful thinking. Could I really have done the same myself? I never asked why, if that world was Skaro, the Daleks had simply abandoned it. I simply took it for granted that they had. But then the unexpected happened, didn't it?' he asked the Dalek Prime. 'The Movellans arrived and tried to take possession of Davros to help fight a better war against you.'

'Incorrect,' the other answered. It stared at the Doctor, obviously challenging him.

'Incorrect?' he repeated, puzzled. 'But which part?'

'All of it,' the Dalek Prime responded.

The Doctor considered this reply for a moment, and then slapped his forehead with his palm. 'What are you asking me to believe?' He clenched his fists. 'That the Daleks needed Davros to believe he'd been awakened because he was needed? That they appealed to his ego, as their creator, showing him a situation where he and only he could save them? They were at war with the Movellans, and caught in a deadly impasse. This disaster made perfect sense to Davros, and he exploited it for his own ends. But you're telling me now... that it wasn't true?' His voice tailed off, and when he spoke again, his voice barely more than a whisper, Sam thought he sounded for all the world like a lost little child. 'That there *was* no war?'

'I am not asking you to believe. I merely impart knowledge.'

'You want me to believe, or you wouldn't be telling me.' The Doctor stared into the Dalek Prime's eyepiece. The Dalek said nothing, as the Doctor continued. 'The Movellans are a robotic race, defined by logic, but astonishingly weak in many areas. I never asked myself, who built the Movellans?' He shook his head. 'The Daleks?'

Again, the Dalek Prime said nothing. 'So following your argument…' The Doctor began to pace around. 'The Movellans are the Dalek concept of what a humanoid is like. And the Movellan out there in the control room hasn't been reprogrammed – he's simply obeying his orders. The Daleks created a false emergency simply to make Davros believe that they had wakened him because they needed him. They manipulated him totally, and I unwittingly helped them in their plan. But then Davros was taken off to Earth for trial…' He sighed. 'By the humans that the Daleks brought to Skaro in the first place.' He gazed at the Dalek Prime. 'It's certainly a staggeringly ingenious scheme. You ensured that Davros would be captured and taken to Earth. Then you arranged for him to be sprung from prison and given access to the time-travel technology he needed to go back in time to the 1960s and obtain the Hand of Omega.'

The Dalek Prime took up the story. Sam frowned. This was getting like *Jackanory*. 'But Davros refused to follow the plan. We manufactured the false information that the Movellans had won their non-existent war with us, thinking that this would prompt him to seek the ultimate weapon.

Instead, he began constructing his own race of Daleks.'

'At Tranquil Repose, yes,' said the Doctor, thinking back. 'So you helped shut down that operation,' the Doctor continued, 'and threatened to return him to Skaro for trial. He escaped – so conveniently – again, and then he elected to go for the Hand. He massed all of his Dalek army on Skaro or whatever planet it was – and then I tricked him into using the Hand, wiping out his forces.' He shook his head in astonishment. 'Complex... brilliant... nasty, vicious and unprincipled. But true?'

Again, the Dalek Prime simply stared at him.

The Doctor shook his head. 'All simply to stop Davros from destroying your home world. I never realised you were so attached to it.'

'You still do not understand fully, Doctor,' the Dalek Prime informed him. 'It was only partially to safeguard Skaro that the plan was evolved, to preserve our war factories and manufacturing industries that are here. Losing them would hamper our plans. But there is more to the deception than simply the salvation of Skaro.' He started to move to the huge glass window. 'Come with me, Doctor.'

Though she hadn't been asked – the Dalek no doubt considered her to be insignificant – Sam went along as well. They all gazed out across the Dalek city. Despite her feeling of revulsion for the Daleks, Sam had to admit that it was a very impressive place. Hundreds of Daleks were moving about the pathways, and many in hoverbouts filled the air.

'Here is the heart of the Dalek empire,' the Dalek Prime stated. 'You can see a number of Daleks at work. But which of them are loyal only to me?'

'So that's it,' the Doctor said. He turned to Sam, a grim smile on his lips. 'Now we get to the real reason for this whole elaborate charade. Power politics.'

'I don't understand, Doctor,' Sam admitted. Her brain was throbbing under the influx of information.

'It's very simple, Sam. Before the resurrection of Davros, the Dalek Prime was the sole undisputed leader of the Daleks. But once Davros was reawakened, their creator had returned. Some Daleks obviously feel that they should still be loyal to their creator. Which means that the Dalek Prime here isn't undisputed leader any longer. And that's one thing that the Daleks can't stand. They need a single claw to guide them.'

Sam caught on. 'Like the old joke about the Second Coming putting the Pope out of a job.'

'Quite. Davros is back, and the Dalek Prime has to deal with it.' His eyes narrowed. 'But how will this help your cause?' he asked the Dalek. 'Flushing out the traitors?'

'Partially,' the Dalek Prime agreed. 'Certain Daleks loyal to Davros have been allowed access to him. They have suggested he make a play for power.'

'Which you will then crush,' the Doctor said.

'No,' the Dalek Prime answered. 'The attempted revolution will be allowed to take place. Those who deviate from my law will be exposed and annihilated. I allowed Davros to go through with his foolish plan to utilise the Hand of Omega so that all Daleks would see that his madness could have led to their destruction. They must see that he is unstable and unworthy to lead them.'

'And what if they don't?' the Doctor asked quietly. 'What if they still decide that they prefer Davros to you? You're gambling on this revolution failing so that you can eliminate the rebels and purify your race for you. But what if it succeeds?'

'That is why I have spared your life, Doctor,' the Dalek Prime replied. 'I have run an extensive computer simulation of the forthcoming rebellion. There is a thirty-nine-per-cent chance that Davros will succeed.'

The Doctor shrugged. 'The odds are still in your favour.'

'Yes. But I cannot rely on winning. Therefore I need another weapon. You.'

The Doctor glared down at the Dalek Prime. 'I will never work for you,' he said coldly. 'There is nothing that you can offer or threaten that would make me do your dirty work for you.' His eyes widened. 'Is that why you spared the Thals? To use them as leverage against me?'

'Correct, Doctor.' The eye stalk stared unwaveringly at him. 'Their lives are hostage to your behaviour. But I do not think it will come to that. What I require of you, I believe you will willingly give.'

'No.' The Doctor almost shouted the word, and shook his head.

'You will. If Davros's revolution succeeds, Doctor,' the Dalek Prime replied, 'you are to kill Davros before he can regain control of the Daleks.' There was a slight pause. 'Surely you will agree that this is a logical request that you can comply with? You have been willing to kill Davros in the past.'

The Doctor considered the point for a moment. 'Yes, I have considered it as an option,' he agreed. 'But for my reasons, not yours. I'm no hired assassin.'

'Then kill him for your own reasons,' the Dalek Prime intoned. 'It is of no consequence to me. My only concern is that Davros should not live to make use of his victory.'

The Doctor hesitated. 'Give me a minute to consider.'

'You may take as long as you wish,' the Dalek Prime

answered. 'I will check on progress and return shortly. Speak with your companion, and give me your decision when I return.' He started to move away, and then its head swivelled to look back at them. 'If you agree, I will order your release and the return of the TARDIS to you. You will be allowed to leave Skaro unharmed.'

'And if I refuse?'

'You will not refuse,' the Dalek Prime said with finality. He glided out of the room, and the door closed behind him.

The Doctor threw himself down on to a ledge beside the window, staring out across the city below. Sam joined him, wondering what to say to him, knowing he must be in turmoil. He gestured out of the window. 'The first time I came to Skaro, I saw a similar view to this,' he confided in her. 'Only then it was of Thals approaching the Dalek city. I was forced to make a decision then, too – should I help a race of people I barely knew, even though so doing would put my granddaughter and myself in greater jeopardy?' He smiled at her. 'Fortunately, I had with me two people from your world. They refused to consider the danger a factor, and believed firmly that they had to help. I learnt a lot from them.' Abruptly, he asked, 'What would you do in my shoes, Sam?'

'Flop about a lot,' she answered. 'Mine are a lot smaller.' She managed a thin smile. 'Doctor, is Davros really the menace to the universe that you've made out?'

'Undoubtedly.'

'Well, you said you'd considered it before,' she pointed out. 'If you were willing to do it then, why not now?'

'Because then it was my decision,' he replied. 'If I agree to do it for the Dalek Prime, I'm a Dalek agent.'

'But you're going to agree anyway, aren't you?' she realised.

'I have to,' he answered. 'Because there are a lot of other factors involved here. The Daleks would undoubtedly start executing you, Chayn, and the Thals until they forced me to agree. I can't put Davros's twisted existence above yours and theirs.'

An age seemed to pass. The door slid open, and the Dalek Prime moved into the room. 'Events are unfolding as anticipated,' he reported. 'Have you reached a decision yet?'

'Yes,' the Doctor replied, his voice devoid of emotion. 'I've decided to accept your offer. Set us free, and I promise I will kill Davros if his revolution succeeds.'

'Good. I knew you would be reasonable, Doctor.' The Dalek Prime turned away again. 'As soon as Davros strikes, I will have you and your companion escorted back to the TARDIS. Until then, rest. I will send in any refreshments that you may need.'

'And the Thals,' the Doctor pressed. 'They must be freed, too.'

'No, Doctor,' the Dalek Prime answered. 'I still have use for them. They will remain on Skaro. The bargain applies only to the two of you. That is not negotiable.' It left the room again.

'Not negotiable?' the Doctor echoed. 'If it thinks I'm leaving them here, it really doesn't know me very well.' He gave Sam a grin. 'It looks like it's up to us to save the day, as usual.'

'I'm game,' Sam agreed. 'We'll take them all on. And we'll win.'

'I hope so,' the Doctor agreed. 'I hope so.'

CHAPTER 9
TRIAL AND ERRORS

Davros brooded. From the contacts he had made already, it appeared that there was a severe split in the Dalek race. He had been informed that many were ready to fight for his cause, to reinstate him as their undisputed leader. It felt good to know that, even after so long, he still had followers who acknowledged his right to rule.

But were there enough of them to win in the inevitable battle with the Dalek Prime? And how high up did his support go? One of the Black Daleks had been to see him, claiming to be on his side. But was that a ruse to test him, or the truth? None of the Gold Daleks seemed to back him, which made sense. They were in virtual command now, and their powers would be minimal if Davros took over. The problem was that they were the brightest and best of the Dalek Prime's supporters. A few intellects of their calibre would have been a great help to Davros's cause.

Still, he was prepared to act with whatever forces he possessed. Even if he couldn't beat the Dalek Prime in a straight fight, there was the possibility of capturing a number of killcruisers and fleeing the Skaro system to begin again somewhere new.

The Skaro system? Was he starting to believe the absurd stories he had been told about some gigantic plot by the Dalek Prime to discredit and destroy him? Davros knew this had to be a lie. Skaro was dead, destroyed by his own hand – and Omega's. The Dalek Prime was simply spreading propaganda that only the credulous Daleks could possibly believe. Davros knew from his own memories that the world he had shattered was his own. Nothing anyone told him would ever convince him otherwise.

The important things now were timing and targets. When would be the best time to strike? And where should he have his forces move? The spaceport was essential; he needed a method of retreat, and also the certainty that the Dalek Prime couldn't bring in further supporters. The Black Dalek had been assigned to take this target when the command was given. The control room for the city, too, was a vital target.

The door opened, and a Spider Dalek entered. These were one of his stranger designs, but effective, and he was pleased to see that they were still in existence. Many of the Spiders were in his camp, he was pleased to see. This one strode across the room to join him.

'The Dalek Prime has announced that the trial will begin in four time units,' it informed him. 'The sentence of death against you has already been recorded, and will be administered once the trial is over.'

Davros considered this news. Clearly, the revolution would have to begin shortly. 'Alert our allies,' he informed the Spider. 'The start of the trial will mark the commencement of the plan. But no one is to strike until the trial concludes. If the Dalek Prime wishes this farce to be played out on a public stage, then I think we should allow him his final pleasure. We shall play it out for all the Daleks to see! Let them choose who they will follow. The future is ours! I shall perfect the Dalek race, and we will go on to become the dominant species of the entire universe!' His voice had risen to a grating crescendo. He lowered it.

'However, do you know how the Dalek Prime intends to execute me?'

'Matter dispersal,' the Spider Dalek informed him.

'A tidy solution,' Davros agreed slowly. 'So, then, there is one further service you may perform for me.'

'As you command.'

'You will fight against me,' Davros informed it. 'You must convince the Dalek Prime that you are on his side. And, should his forces prevail, then you will be present at my execution...'

Ayaka had her ear to the door, listening for any signs of motion. Chayn sat hunched against the wall beside the door, looking casual and inconspicuous. The Daleks were quite likely to be monitoring the room, though they seemed to have missed the retrieval of the toolkits. Perhaps they simply believed her to be engaging in some sort of humanoid ritual. In her fist she held an activated microprobe.

'They're coming,' Ayaka murmured, and moved away from the door to join Cathbad and a small group of other Thals, all carefully chatting about nothing. A moment later, the door slid open. A Dalek entered, pushing a cart laden with cubic metallic bottles and trays of reconstituted food. As it did so, Chayn slipped the probe into the gap and released it. It immediately wormed its way out of sight in the door's mechanism. Then she scuttled away from the door before regaining her feet.

'Food and drink,' the Dalek informed them, releasing the cart. 'You will make it last until the morning.' It backed out of the room, and the door closed behind it.

Ayaka moved to the cart, where Chayn and Cathbad joined her. 'Make sure that everyone gets something to eat and drink,'

Ayaka ordered Cathbad. 'If we are to make an escape attempt, it may be quite some while before we'll eat again.'

'I'd feel better about that if the Daleks had provided us with a bathroom,' Chayn grumbled. 'I can see that they've not much use for one themselves, but we do.'

'They're not particularly bothered about humanoid comfort,' Ayaka replied. 'The probe is on its way?'

'Yes.' Chayn grinned. 'It's nosing about right now, looking for the circuits we need. I reckon it won't take me long to get the door working when we want it to. Then I'll have to tap into their monitoring system to check that the corridor outside is clear.'

'Good.' Ayaka looked pleased. 'I am sure we shall succeed.'

'I admire your optimism,' Chayn answered. She picked up a tub of the 'food'. 'Yuck. What is this?'

'It's... nutrition,' Ayaka answered. 'The Daleks –'

'– aren't particularly bothered about humanoid taste buds,' Chayn finished. 'I know, I know.' She grimaced, and considered going hungry.

Davros was prepared when the door to his cell opened again. One of the Black Daleks entered. Not the one on his side, he knew – Davros had ordered his partisans to generate a low-tone pulse for his detectors, so that he could tell who they were. Once the fighting began, his troops would then be able to recognise one another.

'You will accompany me,' the Black Dalek commanded. Davros could detect four more Daleks waiting outside – his escort.

'This farcical trial is about to begin?' he asked, obeying the order and moving forward.

'The trial is prepared,' the Black Dalek confirmed. 'You are ordered to attend.'

'I see no need for a trial,' Davros complained, though he was glad for the delay it would offer his partisans in getting ready, and for a public forum to express his views. 'Since the verdict has already been reached, this is a waste of time.'

The Black Dalek regarded him impassively. 'The trial is necessary,' it informed him. 'You must condemn yourself – as we know you shall.'

Arrogance! Well, that was hardly its fault, since he had programmed it into their matrix. And, in this case, that arrogance would work against them. As they moved through the corridors, Davros said to the Black Dalek, 'I should not be placed on trial. I am your creator. Without me, you would be nothing. You should be praising me and following me.'

'You are an irrational, inferior humanoid-derivative,' the Black Dalek replied. 'You are to be exterminated, not followed.'

'I created you,' Davros told it.

'Incorrect,' the Dalek stated. 'I was created by the neutron war. You merely accelerated the process. The Daleks would have arisen anyway in the fullness of time. The universe was ready for the rise of the Daleks. It was inevitable.'

'Is that what the Dalek Prime tells you?' Davros sneered. 'Such arrogance! Without me to guide your creation, the Daleks would have been as weak and pitiful as the humanoid race from which they sprang. It was my genius that created the travel machines you utilise. My genius that made you what you are. Without me, you would all be mewling balls of slime, without technology or a future. The Thals would have destroyed you had I not made you strong. You owe me everything.'

'You will have the opportunity to speak at your trial,' the Black Dalek informed him.

Davros chuckled to himself – the Black Dalek was, of course, unable to refute logic it refused to accept. Perhaps this trial might have its amusing aspects, after all…

Sam had tired of staring out of the window, and returned to the doorway to think. Despite the fact that the Dalek Prime had promised to set them free, she couldn't help feeling that the danger wasn't over yet. There was something about the Daleks that she simply didn't trust. 'Do you really think they're going to let us go?' she asked the Doctor.

'Hmm?' He blinked and focused on her. 'Oh, yes, I'm sure of it. The Dalek Prime is crossing his I's and dotting his T's.'

'Shouldn't that be the other way around?' she asked him, with a mischievous grin.

'The Daleks have their own logic about everything.' He stood up abruptly. 'But we've certainly not been told the whole truth. There's a lot that's still hidden from me.' He gestured at an instrument panel beside the door. 'How about a little eavesdropping?' he suggested. 'Perhaps we'll get to overhear something we're not supposed to.' He moved to the panel and started to fiddle with it.

Sam stood on tiptoe and examined it over his shoulder. There seemed to be a monitor screen and several controls. 'What is that thing? In-home phone?'

'No, the Daleks communicate with one another using radio waves over a distance. This is a security monitor. The Daleks keep slaves in the city, and they like to be able to watch them.' He gave her a quick smile. 'They're understandably worried about revolts and attempted escapes. But if I can figure out the codes for this thing, we can use it to watch the Daleks instead.' The screen came on and he frowned. 'That's interesting.'

'What is?' she asked. 'Found the cable channels?'

'No. I didn't turn it on, so the Daleks must have done.' He tapped his lips with his right index finger. 'This must be something they want us to see.'

'Probably a party political broadcast, then.'

The Doctor grinned. 'I think you've got it,' he told her. 'Look.'

The screen showed an immense room. It had to be six hundred feet long, and at least three hundred wide and tall. There were layers of glideways about the walls, all of them filled with Daleks. Sam gasped, as she realised that there were several thousand of them within that one room. They were all assembled, staring at the centre of the room.

Here was a built-up section, with the Dalek Prime on an elevated platform. Behind him were ranked a dozen Gold Daleks. Around them, a score of Black Daleks. Red and Blue Daleks were ranged behind them, reaching back to the walls.

Facing the Dalek Prime was another raised platform, and several smaller ones. On the raised platform sat Davros, immobile, watching and waiting. Several Daleks were grouped about him, obviously guarding him.

'Which one's Rumpole?' Sam asked.

'It's the trial all right,' the Doctor confirmed. 'And the Dalek Prime wants us to see at least a part of it.' He shook his head. 'Davros thinks he's the one on trial, the poor fool. He doesn't realise that it's the Dalek race being purged here.'

'Do you really think he stands a chance of winning the case?' Sam asked. 'Are there really that many Daleks who support him?'

'It's hard to say,' the Doctor answered. 'But if the Dalek Prime is worried, then I'd say the battle's likely to be close to fifty-fifty. Whatever the outcome, there's both a good and bad aspect to it. Good, in that it'll take whoever wins quite some time to build their strength back up. That will give the rest of the galaxy a breather. Bad, because once the winner *is* built up, the Daleks will have a single focus, and that will be conquest.'

'Unless they kill each other off,' Sam suggested.

The Doctor sighed. 'I'm afraid not. It's a curse sometimes, having seen the future.'

Sam glared at him. 'If you've seen the future, then you know who's won!' she exclaimed. 'Why are you acting so coy?'

'Sam, Sam, Sam, Sam, Sam...! Because I only know that the Daleks will survive,' he replied. 'I don't know who they will be following.' He held up a hand. 'Hush. I think it's starting.'

Davros surveyed the room with contempt. The proceedings were certainly being relayed all across the city – and, no doubt, the planet and the Empire itself. This was a public spectacle, obviously designed by the Dalek Prime as a method of showing the Daleks just who was in charge. Well, time would soon show the answer to that! This trial wouldn't be as cut and dried as the Dalek Prime seemed to imagine. Davros was clearly supposed to be intimidated by all of this – instead he simply wondered how many here were secretly on his side.

The Dalek Prime was suddenly picked out by a spotlight, one that made him look even larger than he really was. Again, Davros sneered to himself – even his casing was a simple redesign of Davros's own carriage. He'd also seen Special Weapons Daleks about, another of his own innovations. Clearly, the Dalek Prime was unoriginal, snatching what he could of Davros's and laying claim to it. Little wonder, then, that he was insisting that they were on the original Skaro. He didn't dare admit that Davros had done something he couldn't undo.

'Daleks,' the Dalek Prime grated, his amplified voice echoing about the room. 'We are assembled to accuse Davros of betraying our race. He has attempted to steal our heritage, destroy our ancestral home, and usurp the power of the Daleks for his own purposes. He has not learnt from his follies. He must be annihilated to prevent further contamination of our species.' Its eye stalk spun about to face Davros, and a second spotlight picked out the accused. 'What do you have to say to the charges?'

'First, that you have no right to charge me with anything,' Davros replied. 'I created you all. Without me, there would be no Daleks, no destiny for our race – and no asinine trial being held. Without me, you would not be here to accuse me so foolishly.' He stared about the room, but it was impossible to assess the impact he was having.

'Secondly,' he continued, 'as your creator, I should logically be the one to lead you. I alone know what is best for the Daleks. I alone know how to shape and manipulate our joint destinies. You have claimed authority to speak for the Daleks. But on what grounds do you base this claim? I will not acknowledge the authority of anyone without good reason. You are a Dalek, like all of the other Daleks here, and should have no power over the rest. You, like them, should logically recognise your one, true leader – myself.'

The Doctor raised an eyebrow. 'I think he's getting a trifle too messianic here,' he murmured. 'It's not going to go down too well.'

'Plus,' Sam added, 'he's basically telling them all that they're a lot of skivvies who should be grateful to slave for him. Not a smart tactic.'

'Davros has always favoured arrogance over intelligence.' The Doctor gestured to the screen. 'Rebuttal time, I think.'

The Dalek Prime spoke again. 'Your statements are irrelevant,' he announced. 'You did not create the Daleks – our creation was a fortuitous consequence of war. We were destined to become the race we are today. Instead of allowing destiny to run its course, you interfered. That was the first time that you attempted to usurp the power of the Daleks. It was not the last. These travel machines we use were created by the scientists of the Kaled race. You took credit for their work to lend support to your claim of supremacy.

'The first Daleks understood your futile madness when they elected to destroy you. I am the last survivor of those first Daleks, which is why I am the Dalek Prime. This is why I speak for the Daleks, and hold authority. I am the ancestor of the billions of Daleks alive today. I have guided the race throughout our history, and brought us to the position of strength we hold today. This entire galaxy is poised to collapse before us. This is my achievement and my claim to rule.

'Your madness has brought us time and again to the brink of destruction. Yet you still claim that we should follow you. Following you would lead to the destruction of the Dalek species.'

Davros moved slightly, and sighed. 'So, you claim to be the one to rule the Daleks solely because of your longevity?' he demanded. 'And that gives you supreme power? A foolish notion, indeed!'

The Dalek Prime repeated, 'You are accused of attempts to steal power over the Daleks, and of attempting to destroy Skaro. Respond to these charges only.'

Davros realised that he already had the Dalek Prime on the defensive, refusing to discuss his authority. 'The charges are ridiculous,' he replied. 'I am only seeking what should be mine by right of being your creator. And the destruction of Skaro was accomplished by the creature known as the Doctor – whom you are protecting. Do you deny that he is here, in this city, at this very moment?'

'Irrelevant,' the Dalek Prime responded. 'The Doctor is not on trial here.'

'And why not?' Davros cried. 'From the very start of the Dalek race, the Doctor has attempted time and time again to destroy you all! He is the one who destroyed Skaro, not I. He is the one who should be here on trial before the Daleks, to pay for his crimes. Why is he not?'

'The Doctor's time will come,' the Dalek Prime answered. 'Now it is your time.'

'That's his defence?' Sam asked. 'That everything he's accused of is your fault?'

'I don't think he's making a defence,' the Doctor replied. 'Davros is completely out of touch with reality. It's never, ever occurred to him that anything he's ever done is wrong. Not creating the Daleks to be merciless killers, not betraying his own race, not attempted genocide. Davros has no morals at all. The only thing that matters to him is achieving his goal.' He gave Sam a sober look. 'He's worse than the Daleks; at least they were created the way they are. Davros has no such excuse. Many of the Kaleds were noble, if misguided people. Davros was always a monster,

207

long before he became one in appearance. Still, I wonder why the Dalek Prime didn't want me down there to add testimony to the trial.'

Sam gave him an incredulous glance. 'Come off it! If you testified against Davros, the Daleks would probably not only free him, but give him a medal. And think how many itchy trigger fingers are down there. If they caught sight of you...'

The Doctor nodded. 'Practical as always. Thank you, Sam.'

The Dalek Prime turned from Davros to the Gold Dalek beside him. 'Prepare the evidence,' he commanded.

'I obey.' The Gold Dalek's arm moved, interfacing with a computer panel before it. There was a short pause, and then the central portion of the room above the trial area lit up with a holographic display showing earth from space. 'During the course of our invasion of the planet its humanoid occupants term "earth", a search of all captured documentation was implemented. A recording was discovered that demonstrated Dalek presence on the same planet some two hundred years earlier. The relevant portion of this recording follows.' It evidently gave the computer a command, because the picture switched to show the face of an attractive woman in her mid-thirties.

'This is Professor Rachel Jensen, recording for Military Intelligence. Subject: the Coal Hill incident. Summary: an alien invader, Davros, and his force of Daleks, led a force into London with the purpose of retrieving and utilising an alien artefact known as the Hand of Omega. When deployed, the artefact destroyed Davros's home world of Skaro. Detailed report as follows...' The recording ended.

The Gold Dalek continued. 'Earth records indicated that the Hand of Omega was a device manufactured by the Time

Lords of Gallifrey. It was placed on earth for unknown reasons. Davros believed that it would give him the power to conquer time, and took a killcruiser back in time to retrieve the Hand of Omega. He obtained the device and triggered it. He did so despite warnings that the Hand would not perform the actions he believed that it would. He ran no tests on the device, but fired it directly at the heart of what he believed was Skaro's sun. This caused a supernova effect, destroying the star and its planetary system.'

The Dalek Prime was spotlighted once again. 'The only reason Skaro still exists is because of my planning. Discovering Davros's aims and the end result of his insanity, the Daleks constructed a decoy world that Davros believed to be Skaro. It was this world that he destroyed.'

'Constructed?' echoed Sam. 'I thought he said it was Antalin?'

'Just what *is* going on – who's fooling who?' mused the Doctor. 'The Daleks are always devious, but this... is the Prime claiming all this to strengthen his defence against Davros?'

'But what about Antalin's sun?' wailed Sam, her head hurting.

'Surely they can't move whole stars...' the Doctor shook his head. 'I just don't know.'

'Nor, I bet, do the Daleks,' said Sam. 'You said the Daleks get most of their information from their inbuilt computers. And I'll bet that the Dalek Prime decides what goes into them – he's not likely to include their greatest disasters, is he?'

The Dalek Prime was continuing his attack. 'If the Daleks had followed Davros as he claims they should, then the

Dalek race would now be utterly annihilated. His own deviant force of renegade Daleks were so destroyed, leaving him defenceless. If Davros were to lead the Daleks, his egotism and insanity would result in our total destruction.' He stared at Davros. 'Do you deny causing the destruction of the world you believed to be Skaro?'

'It *was* Skaro,' Davros insisted. 'I know this. But its destruction was caused by the Doctor, and not by me. He reprogrammed the Hand of Omega and tricked me into using it.'

'Tricked you,' the Dalek Prime repeated. 'You admit that the Doctor out-thought you and manipulated you. He defeated you. He has not defeated me. He, too, believed Skaro to have been destroyed. You have condemned yourself by your own testimony. You have failed in your quest for power, and you have almost destroyed the Daleks in your insane desires.'

'Perhaps,' Davros answered, 'that is because I am willing to take risks. You sit here, safe and secure, on this planet of yours – whatever you believe it to be – and send out your forces to do your will. I, on the other hand, take personal charge of everything I do. I do not command others to take those risks for me. True, the Hand of Omega turned out to be a trap. But if it had not, then imagine what power would have been ours! The Daleks would have been the lords of all of time and space! We could have achieved our aims in years, instead of millennia! We could be masters of the galaxy – of the universe!'

'Delusions,' the Gold Dalek stated. 'None of these things happened. Your foolish insistence on taking unwarranted risks created grave danger for the Dalek race. You are a threat to Dalek survival. Why did you not test the Hand of

Omega first on earth's sun instead of targeting the Dalek star?'

'Such a test would have wasted time,' Davros replied.

'So you elected to risk destroying the Dalek species instead of exercising reasonable caution,' the Dalek Prime pointed out. 'You aimed for the position of ultimate power and failed. In the same way, you have tried to take over control of the Dalek empire – and failed. If you had achieved the power you desired, only the Daleks you had created would have shared in it. None of the Daleks here on Skaro would have been a part of your plan. You would have utilised your power to annihilate us.'

'All Daleks who do not acknowledge me as their creator and master should die!' Davros exclaimed. 'Without me, you are nothing!'

'Without you,' the Gold Dalek interjected, 'we are the masters of space. Our armies are unstoppable. We are achieving victory on many worlds. Once you are gone, the Dalek race will continue as a unified race. We shall obliterate all inferior species.'

'Enough,' the Dalek Prime decided. 'The trial is over. You have admitted your desire to rule the Daleks, even though you have destroyed all Daleks loyal to you. You have admitted that the Doctor has outwitted and defeated you. You have admitted that you caused the destruction of the world you insist was Skaro.' The Dalek Prime surveyed the assembled Daleks. 'Are there any who would speak on behalf of Davros at this time?'

'Oh, right,' Sam sneered. 'Like anyone would back him up right now. Talk about kangaroo courts!'

'It's just a ploy,' the Doctor agreed. 'To make Davros look

worse, as if he has no support. But watch. There'll be trouble soon, you'll see.'

Davros had expected the silence. Any Dalek foolish enough to speak up now would deserve the extermination it would get. Still he sat reassured – the low-frequency signal had begun. His supporters were preparing to move. Soon, very soon...

The Dalek Prime slowly surveyed the room. 'None,' he finally summarised. 'Davros stands alone. His insanity is clear to all. The decision is obvious.' He turned to face Davros. 'The trial is over,' it announced. 'From your own words, you stand condemned. You cannot be allowed to live. You are to be taken for annihilation. The Dalek race will be out of your control for ever.' He turned to give the order to the Gold Dalek.

'No!' A Black Dalek moved forward, its gun raised. 'Davros must live!' Electronic flame spewed out, and the Dalek Prime's casing exploded in a gush of fire.

A dozen Daleks fired immediately on the Black Dalek. It, too, erupted in a ball of fire.

The hall fell into pandemonium.

INTERLUDE
HESPERUS

Mechon 179 went about its tasks in a passionless, unhurried fashion. Humans liked gardens, and Mechon 179's assignment was to keep the garden here on Hesperus in perfect order, ready for when the humans would arrive. It carefully weeded and watered, tending the growing plants, pruning trees and bushes and matching the end results with the optimal model stored within its data banks. The garden was looking acceptable.

It had been looking acceptable for two hundred and seventy-five years.

Mechon 179 was not programmed for curiosity, so it did not think that this was an overly long period to wait for its human masters. Nor did any of the other Mechonoids on Hesperus. Their assignment had been simply to prepare the planet for the humans who would arrive to colonise it. The slight delay in their arrival signified nothing to the Mechonoids. They were programmed to prepare the planet and await their human masters; this they would do until the humans arrived to give them new programming.

Meanwhile, the Mechonoids continued with their assigned tasks and Mechon 179 tended its garden carefully. It had no pride in its work, nor did it consider the garden a thing of beauty. It had been programmed without emotions to confuse it. It simply found the garden within the acceptable parameters of its programming.

The day was like all other days. When the sun rose,

Mechon 179 went out into the garden to check that all was well. It would patrol the garden, eliminating pests, cutting any grass stalks that were above the optimal two inches tall, and removing any kind of native weed that might spoil the look of the roses. When the sun went down, Mechon 179 would return to its indoor duties of keeping the dwelling units in prime order, ready for their eventual occupants. The fact that it had been doing substantially similar work for more than two hundred years didn't bother it; Mechon 179 was not programmed for boredom, either.

Mechon 179 trundled its rotund form down the garden paths, patrolling vigilantly for any slight deviation from the accepted norm. Any that were found were dealt with instantly. There was a slight insect infestation on the geraniums. It administered a mild spray from its stock via a thin rod it extruded from its midsection, where all of its tools were housed, and then made a note to check the progress of the repellent the following day. It then moved on down the pathway.

Then, Central Computer issued a general alert. Such a thing had never happened before.

It informed all Mechon units that a spacecraft had been detected approaching the planet Hesperus. For a moment, Mechon 179 computed the possibility of this being the arrival of the humans at last. It was neither eager nor disturbed by the thought; it was simply a possibility. Central Computer quashed the possibility a second later.

"The arriving ship does not respond with the correct command codes,' it informed the thousand or so Mechonoids working in the otherwise empty city. 'It must be considered a non-human vessel.' After another moment, it added, 'Though the ship is receiving our signals, it has not responded at all. It must therefore be considered inimical. All Mechon Units must prepare for possible alien contamination.'

Mechon 179, like all others, immediately acknowledged this new order. Gardening was finished for the day; it was time to prepare for a possible invasion. There was a chance that the arriving creatures simply didn't understand Machine Code, of course. If that was the case, then Central Computer would find some other way to communicate with them. The aliens must be told to leave; the Mechons were preparing this world for humans, and nobody else would be allowed to remain without correct authorization from humans.

If they refused to leave peacefully, they would be ejected or else negated.

Mechon 179 rumbled into the house, feeling no alarm, apprehension or concern. It emptied its storage units of the various chemicals that it employed in the garden. Fly spray would not be useful in a police action. It was, of course, impossible to be certain what would be useful until contact had been made with the aliens. Still, there were several devices that would be helpful in a variety of situations.

Mechon 179 upgraded the laser cutter it used for pruning, powering it up to a steel-cutting intensity. That was a sensible precaution. It also refuelled its flame-thrower; not for dead branches this time, but for potentially hostile creatures.

Then it waited for further instructions.

Central Computer would not bother the Mechonoids with pointless updates, and Mechon 179 felt no curiosity about what was happening. Whatever was needed, it would be told.

'The aliens have landed and are preparing to disembark their ship,' Central Computer reported. Mechon units 719 to 741 have been despatched to effect communication."

215

Mechon 179 had been given no instructions, so it simply waited patiently.

'The aliens have been identified as Daleks,' Central Computer announced a moment later. 'They are known to be hostile to humans and must therefore be removed from this planet. All Mechon units must guard the city and prepare for attack.'

Mechon 179 knew what Daleks were from its memory banks. If it hadn't, it could simply have tapped into Central Computer and downloaded the relevant data. As it was, there was no need. All Mechonoids knew about Daleks, and the standard order was to dispose of them. To Mechon 179, this was no different from spraying the plants to eradicate bugs. It was simply a problem to be resolved.

In the absence of direct orders from Central Computer, Mechon 179 considered the matter. The Daleks were all confined at the moment to the area around their ship. Staying here in its assigned house would not be an efficient use of resources. It opened the domicile door automatically, and then moved down the street toward the reported landing area.

Dozens of other Mechonoids had made the same, logical decision, and were emerging from other dwelling units. Together, they moved through the streets. Mechon 179 had its laser cutter and flame-thrower ready in case they should be needed. All of the other Mechonoids had their own weapons held ready.

There was an explosion close to the landing site. Switching to infra-red, Mechon 179 saw the blast clearly. 'The Dalek intruders have destroyed Mechon units 719 to 741,' Central Computer reported dispassionately. 'All available Mechon units are to engage the intruders.'

Since Mechon 179 was already heading in the right direction, it didn't need to amend its behaviour. It continued to move ahead, watching for Daleks. The loss of 22 units was unfortunate, but they could be replicated fairly easily.

Then it saw the Daleks. There were eight of them, moving along the street. Their guns were firing at targets on the way. Mechon units close to them were returning their fire. Mechon 179 noted that the Daleks could take direct hits without serious damage. It took the combined firepower of four Mechonoids to break through whatever armour the Daleks wore. One Dalek exploded, joining more than a dozen burning Mechonoids.

'Mechons 179, 803 and 212,' came a signal from the Mechon 84 unit to the left of 179. 'We must combine our fire on one intruder.'

Mechon 179 sent an acknowledgement to unit 84, which then selected a target. Mechon 179 instantly fired its laser at the selected Dalek. Similar beams from the other three Mechon units raked the target also. The Dalek fired back, even as its casing heated up under the combined fire. Unit 803 experienced a systems failure as a result, and exploded at virtually the same nanosecond as the Dalek target.

'Mechon 612,' 84 sent. 'Join with us.' The next Mechon unit replaced the burning 803 and unit 84 selected their next target.

The battle continued. More Daleks had emerged from their ship, including unusual Spider Daleks that scurried along, their own guns blazing. Accompanying them were human-looking machines that Mechon 179 recognised as Movellans. It was not puzzled as to why these creatures had joined with the Daleks; it was simply a fact to be accepted. And they were considerably simpler to destroy. Two Mechons together could obliterate a single Movellan. Hardest to hit were the Spider Daleks, which were more manoeuvrable than the usual Daleks. But they were not as heavily armoured, either, and could be destroyed more easily.

Mechon 179 simply kept firing its laser at assigned targets. Mechon 84 exploded, having been hit by a blast from a Movellan trooper. Mechon 179 took over directing the fighting of their small group. Whenever a Mechon unit was destroyed, it simply co-opted the closest available unit to assist.

The war raged for eighty-seven minutes. Several hundred Daleks were destroyed, along with eight hundred and seventeen Mechon units. Mechon 179 was not concerned, except that it meant that finding replacement units for the foursome was becoming harder. The Daleks were slowing, but not stopping, their own assault. All about, burning and burnt-out shells littered the city. Some of the buildings were on fire, too. It would be quite a task to clean up.

'Daleks are making their way into core areas,' reported Central Computer. 'All Units must protect me from attack.'

Mechon 179 understood and acknowledged. 'We must move forward,' it informed the three units with it. 'These Daleks must be passed to allow us to aid the Central Computer.' Its laser was now severely low on power, so it switched to the flame thrower. This proved to be remarkably effective on Movellan units. They tended to catch fire and then detonate. The Spider Daleks found the flames harder to dodge than the more focused laser blasts, too. However, the regular Dalek units simply ignored the flames unless they came from several concentrated sources at once.

Mechon 179 moved slowly forward, firing continually. Its

fuel reserves were down 54 per cent already; it would lose the use of its flame thrower in eight point two minutes. At which time, it would have to improvise some other weapon. It was nothing to consider at this moment.

Beside it, Mechon 17 exploded, caught in the crossfire from two Daleks. Mechon 179 attempted to find a replacement unit, but there were none close enough to offer aid.

Then Mechon 906 was hit and disabled. Its drive unit ceased. A second blast from two Movellans opened it up completely, and it was finished. Mechon 179 fired, and enveloped both Movellans in flame. Both would be destroyed.

A Spider Dalek scuttled forward before 179 could realign its flame-thrower. The blaster on the Spider spat, and Mechon 179's sensors reported a serious rupture in its integument. Critical systems had been damaged, and total systems failure was expected momentarily.

Mechon 179 sent a final message to Central Computer, to inform it that another Mechon unit would have to be assigned to check on the insect infestation on the geraniums tomorrow.

Then its systems crashed.

PART 4
TOTAL WAR

'Cry "Havoc!" and let slip the dogs of war.'
William Shakespeare, *Julius Caesar*

CHAPTER 10
ESCAPE

Sam stared at the viewscreen in shock and horror, watching the Dalek Prime explode. She had been expecting almost anything, she thought, but never that. 'Talk about a miscalculation,' she gasped.

'Oh, I don't know,' the Doctor answered. 'Didn't you spot something a bit *too* mechanical about his actions?'

'You know me well, Doctor.'

Sam whirled to see the Dalek Prime glide into the room. 'What?'

'Bait,' The Doctor explained. 'A fake.'

'I anticipated an attempt on my life,' the Dalek Prime explained. 'All was prepared.'

'So I saw,' the Doctor answered. 'And now?'

'And now the civil war begins,' the Dalek replied. 'You must leave now, Doctor, before I can no longer protect you.'

'Well, nothing lasts for ever,' the Doctor murmured. 'I can't say it's been a pleasure. Come along, Sam.'

'That's it?' she asked him. 'We just go?'

'Yes,' he replied. 'We just go.' A Red Dalek moved into the room. 'Ah, our escort, I see.' He turned back to the Dalek Prime. 'I trust you won't be upset, but I sincerely hope you manage to wipe one another out.'

'We shall see, Doctor.' The Dalek Prime spun about to face the other way. 'I have a war to win.' It moved from the room, in the direction of the control room.

'This way,' the Red Dalek commanded. It led them down a

short corridor to a different lift. Sam took one last look at the screen before following.

War had, indeed, begun.

The Black Dalek had exploded under intense fire. As it did so, Davros was surrounded by several other Daleks, each of them transmitting the recognition code. They formed a living shield about him as others in the room turned on one another.

It was utter chaos. Dalek fired on Dalek, the air crackling with the discharge of energy weapons. Davros caught only wild glimpses around as his escort sought to move him from his exposed position. A Dalek on the ramps exploded, falling to the floor below in a raging fireball. Three Daleks fired on a Black Dalek, damaging it, and then finished it with a second burst. A group of Daleks took on a second group, flashes detonating all around. The holographic projector collapsed in on itself.

The Gold Daleks formed a phalanx, firing about them. They didn't appear to be distinguishing friend from foe, annihilating anyone who was in their way. They were simply attempting to retreat from the room, probably to head up the battle.

'The Dalek Prime is dead,' one of the Black Daleks informed Davros.

'Idiot,' Davros snapped. 'That wasn't the Dalek Prime. It was a robot. There was no protoplasm inside it. The Dalek Prime expected our revolution.' For the first time, Davros began to wonder if he was out-thinking the Dalek Prime after all. 'Concentrate our forces. We must take the spaceport first, and then the control centre.'

'All has been prepared,' the Black Dalek assured him.

'Victory will be yours.'

Yes! This prophecy was surely correct.

Sam looked around apprehensively as the lift doors opened. She had expected to see Daleks battling one another in the corridor, but there was nothing. 'This is a very peaceful war,' she muttered.

'Right now, both sides are going to be concentrating on the most important targets,' the Doctor answered.

'Which are?' Sam asked. 'If it's all the same to you, I'd sooner avoid any major areas of conflict.'

The Doctor shrugged. 'The spaceport is bound to be one of them,' he confessed.

'Terrific.' Sam glanced around. 'I just wish we had something to defend ourselves with. Something to hold the Daleks off.'

'We have our brains,' the Doctor comforted her as they hurried along.

'Great. I'm defenceless.' But she managed a weak smile.

'Hurry,' the Red Dalek instructed them. 'We must reach the spaceport before the rebels attack it in force.'

The Doctor glanced at the corridor they were in and then said, 'Sorry. I've a prior engagement.' He whipped his sonic screwdriver from his pocket and held it against the Dalek's dome as he triggered it.

The Red Dalek let out an electronic scream, and spun about on the spot several times before coming to a rest, its eye stalk pointing straight up.

'Is it dead?' Sam asked.

'Yes.' The Doctor sounded almost regretful. 'Ultrasound. It destroyed its brain almost instantly.'

'So we *can* defend ourselves!' Sam exclaimed.

'Very short-range,' the Doctor informed her. 'I have to hold it against the casing for it to work.'

'Oh.' Sam glanced around. 'So why are we here?'

'It's where Ayaka and the Thals were imprisoned,' the Doctor answered. 'We have to get them free.'

A door opened further down the corridor, and Sam looked around for somewhere to hide. It had to be Daleks, and they were now unprotected...

Instead, she saw a familiar dark-haired head. 'Chayn!' Sam exclaimed.

'Doctor! Sam! Over here!' Chayn called urgently.

Sam needed no further urging. She even beat the Doctor to the safety of the room, where she collapsed in relief. She noted that the Thals were all together, and clearly ready for action.

The Doctor smiled. 'Somehow, I didn't think you were waiting around to be rescued,' he commented.

'Not us,' Chayn agreed, grinning. 'Ayaka thinks we can make it back to the ship and get out of here.'

'It's quite possible,' the Doctor agreed. 'But there's a civil war going on.' He brought them up to date quickly. 'While the two factions will be fighting one another, we're fair game for either side.'

'Then we need our weapons first,' Ayaka said firmly. 'Chayn, how's that microprobe of yours doing?'

Chayn checked her instruments. 'It's located the storage room, and it's working on the lock,' she answered. 'By the time we get there, it'll be ready.'

'Good.' Ayaka looked grim. 'We don't have time for armour,' she decided, clearly not too happy about that. She addressed her troops. 'Just grab whatever you can. We have to fight our way to the ship before the spaceport is sealed off. It's bound to be a target for both sides.'

Sam frowned at Chayn. 'Ayaka's been forgiven?' she asked.

'Necessity,' the engineer answered. 'Cathbad's not cut out for this, and she is. They're all forgetting she's supposed to be a prisoner for the time being.'

'Terrific. Well, I suppose they can court-martial her afterwards. If there is an afterwards.'

Chayn glanced down at her hand control again. 'Right, the door mechanism's been triggered. Let's move.'

Ayaka led the charge down the corridor. As they headed for the opening door, three Daleks glided from a side corridor, heading across. Their eye stalks swivelled to take in the escaping prisoners, and their bodies swung about to target them. Ayaka threw herself under the door as it was partially open, and two others made it. The next three were all hit by the Dalek discharge, glowing and screaming as they died. The Doctor pushed Sam to the floor, covering her with his own body.

Sam was touched by his concern and scared by his stupidity. He was so much more important alive than she was! She struggled to get out from under him, and managed to see the Daleks fire again. She tensed herself for death, but the atomic flames enveloped charging Thals instead. Charred bodies fell to the floor as the Daleks spun to fire again.

There was a flash of light from the side chamber, and the lead Dalek exploded. The other two started to turn, but never completed the move. The second one had its dome blasted apart, and the third became a pillar of fire. Ayaka dashed from the room, ready for further battle, her companions behind her. All were armed with their rifles.

'Move!' Ayaka barked. The living Thals piled into the storage room, grabbing whatever weapons they could and rushing out to back Ayaka up. Sam would have followed, but the Doctor held her back.

'You don't know how to use them,' he said gently. 'Leave it to the experts.'

'I feel so useless,' Sam complained.

'Blowing your own feet off wouldn't help the war effort,' he told her. 'The Thals know what they're doing. They've been doing this sort of thing for generations.'

What am I even thinking of? thought Sam, dazedly. I'm not a killer. I don't *want* to kill. Jesus, I just want to stay alive. She sat next to Chayn, who, she saw, was also unarmed – but at least contributing her engineering expertise. She gave Sam a grin.

'My probe's in the control mechanisms,' she said. 'I've ordered it to half-close any doors between here and the spaceport. We can duck under them. Daleks can't.'

'Good thinking,' the Doctor commented, as he fell in with the forward rush.

Cathbad joined them, a rifle in his hand, and two bandoliers of grenades over his shoulders. 'I'll watch out for you,' he promised. Sam wasn't sure whether he was referring to them all, or just to Chayn.

Ayaka led the way ahead, ducking under the paralysed doors. Any Dalek trapped between the malfunctioning doors was shot instantly. They left a trail of wreckage behind them.

'How much further?' Cathbad asked Chayn.

She examined her readouts. 'Four more doors, and we're at the spaceport. I haven't been able to affect their systems at all.'

'And the fighting's bound to be more intense there,' the Doctor added. Cathbad just nodded.

The four doors were passed swiftly, and then Ayaka rolled through the last one into the port area. Almost immediately, explosions lit the room. The Thals dived through the gap, their guns firing continuously. Sam struggled through in the midst of an incredible din. Explosions threatened to knock her from her feet and blind her. The Doctor jerked her under cover of a mass of boxes.

She caught only brief glimpses of what was happening. They were in the large room before the boarding corridors began for the various docked ships. Two factions of Daleks were clearly battling it out for command of the area. One bunch seemed to be beside the various tunnels, the other was ahead of the Thals, aiming outwards. Sam saw Daleks hit and exploding, spinning and firing, burning... Several had their shells holed, oozing green slime down their metallic coats and onto the floor.

It was an inferno, and the Thals only added to it. They targeted both the Daleks in front of them and the ones guarding the boarding ramps, firing frantically – and accurately. In response, both groups of Daleks detailed individuals to fire back. But they didn't pause in their own fighting. Everything degenerated into a three-way fire fight of screaming intensity.

Sam kept her own head down, wishing she could keep out some of the tremendous noise. A Thal close by rose to fire her rifle. Instead, she was caught in Dalek crossfire. Her body glowed, and she screamed as her cells exploded. Her hair sizzling, she fell back, virtually at Sam's feet. Sam stared at the corpse, knowing she didn't have the luxury either to panic or to feel sorry for the destroyed beauty. Instead, ignoring the Doctor's advice, she pulled the woman's rifle from the smoking body and clutched it to herself.

Cathbad leapt up and fired three times, before ducking back. The air above his head crackled, and he grinned. 'Missed me,' he mocked.

'Which loading ramp is ours?' Ayaka called from her own defensive position to Chayn. The engineer checked her comp.

'That one!' she yelled back above the blasts, pointing to the second on the left.

Ayaka nodded, and called orders to the Thals that Sam couldn't hear. Her ears and head were ringing from the continual gunfire. Being in this inferno was horrendous, but she knew that it was undoubtedly worse elsewhere in the city.

The Dalek Prime surveyed his instruments. As expected, Davros's forces had gone for the spaceport first. Typical – he was preparing for his own escape. That had been anticipated. The Dalek Prime turned to the Gold Dalek closest. 'Order all ships to be locked to their cradles,' he instructed. 'Davros is attempting to secure a line of retreat that must not be given. He must die here.'

'I obey.' The Gold Dalek turned and went to the relevant control panel.

The Dalek Prime stared out across the control room. The map of the city now showed that fighting had broken out in eighteen locations. Davros's forces were pressing inwards. There would certainly be an attack on the control complex. But the Dalek Prime had foreseen such a move...

Forces loyal to Davros pressed on through the city, towards the command complex. If this could be taken, then the city could be locked down, and the other side isolated and wiped out in stages. Eight lift shafts led up to the tower where the command centre stood. Daleks loyal to the Dalek Prime guarded the approaches, but Davros's troops contained several Special Weapons Daleks. These led the way, firing their hideously destructive explosive bolts as they moved.

Tangled remains were all that were left of the Dalek Prime's troops as the lifts were reached. The Black Dalek in charge of this assault ordered, 'Special Weapons Daleks into each lift. Be prepared for resistance.'

They moved into the lifts, their guns pointing towards the door, ready to open fire when they reached the required level. The Black Dalek watched as the indicators showed the lifts rising…

Above, the Dalek Prime watched the lift indicators showing their ascent. 'Stand by,' he ordered, as his own forces moved towards the lift shafts. Several adapted Daleks were among their number. As the lifts rose higher, the Dalek Prime finally ordered, 'Terminate.'

The special Daleks moved forward. Instead of pads, their arms possessed only computer interfaces. They joined with the control computers and released the safeties on all of the shafts.

The rising lifts lost power and dropped like rocks.

The Black Dalek below felt the ground vibrate. It had seen the indicators showing a loss of power, and realised that all of the shafts had been terminated. The Special Weapons Daleks had most probably been destroyed in the sixty-floor drop.

'Phase two,' it ordered.

The hoverbouts crashed through the huge glass windows in the observation deck, skidding to a halt on the metallic floor. Immediately depowered, they were abandoned as the three Daleks in each disembarked, and moved across the room. One triggered the door to the corridor beyond, and instantly exploded in the gunfire. Its companions fired through the flames and smoke of its immolation.

The battle for the control room had begun.

Sam could hardly follow the course of the battle. For one thing, she spent most of it with her head down, her eyes averted and her ears covered. She wasn't a soldier, she'd always despised war and knew she wouldn't stand a chance even if she tried to fight. But she was comforted by the fact that Chayn and the Doctor were with her, and neither of them were fighting either.

The Thals, on the other hand, were on the attack. Sam could see warriors running, firing, diving and, from time to time, dying. The room was a bedlam of insane commotion, filled with noise, smoke, fire, and confusion. Despite the Thal force, the two opposing Dalek factions were still fighting among themselves, struggling to claim the spaceport. Daleks were exploding all over the place, but it seemed that there were always more to shove aside the blazing wreckages and continue the battle.

One section of the wall exploded under the impact of fire from a Special Weapons Dalek. Sam had no idea which side it was on, of course, but she saw it being buried under a barrage of Spider Daleks. These used their pointed legs as weapons, piercing the Special Weapons Daleks' casings and causing shorts and systems failures. The whole bunch of them went up in a fiery blast.

The Doctor grabbed her arm and hauled her to her feet. 'Come on!' he yelled.

The Thals had managed to cut a swathe through the fighting, a pathway they were holding against incredible odds. The Doctor, Sam and Chayn fled down the line of fighters as the Daleks blasted away. There was a scream from behind them, but Sam knew better than to turn to look. She kept low, clutching the rifle she'd taken as though it were a magic talisman, as if it would somehow protect her even though she didn't fire it.

Then they were up the ramp, and heading for the airlock above them. The problem was that the ramp was even more exposed than the floor, and Dalek sniping shots increased. The air sizzled around them from the discharges, and more Thals fell.

Sam threw herself through the airlock door, going down in a tangle with two Thal warriors. Several more came through behind them, and then Cathbad slammed his hand on the control panel. The door slid shut behind them, and the cacophony from the battle died down considerably. Sam's ears rang from the noise, and her head ached. She was emotionally and physically drained, and just wanted to lie where she had fallen. Her friends' hands wouldn't allow that, however, and insisted on her rising.

'Come on,' the Doctor encouraged her. 'We don't want you in the way.'

She followed him on automatic pilot, as he and Chayn threaded through the ship. The Thals were carefully leading the way, checking side doors and corridors for any Daleks sealed in with them. From time to time she heard the sound of gunfire, and twice thin, echoing cries. They reached the control room, where Ayaka had shoved two smouldering

233

Dalek casings aside to start powering up the drive.

'Can we lift off?' the Doctor asked her.

Ayaka flashed a look at Argini, one of the engineering crew.

'It looks like it,' he replied, studying the boards. 'We've still got power, and the docking clamps are pretty loose. Of course, once we're in the air, all guarantees are void.'

'That's all I'm asking right now,' Ayaka replied. Several other Thals had begun to settle into the other controls. Sam hung back with the Doctor and Chayn. Cathbad hurried in and settled into the navigator's seat. 'Bring us up to power,' Ayaka ordered. 'Release the clamps as soon as you can.'

Chayn was fiddling with the viewscreens, and managed to get a shot of the entrance ramp. 'Uh-oh,' she muttered. 'Better hurry up. I don't like the look of this.'

Sam studied the screen, and saw that several Daleks were moving up the ramp. Two of them had what looked like laser cutters instead of blasters. They were obviously going to try to cut through the airlock door to attack the escapees.

Chayn looked at Sam, her face mirroring the worry on Sam's. 'If they make a hole in the airlock door, we won't be able to enter space,' Chayn confirmed. 'We've got to lift off before they can break in.'

Sam could do nothing but pray they would have enough time.

The Black Dalek turned to Davros as they hurried together away from the trial room. 'The battle for the spaceport continues,' it reported. 'However, the Dalek Prime has ordered the lock-down of all Dalek killcruisers. Even if we control the spaceport, the ships are useless to us.'

'You are wrong,' argued Davros. 'We can turn their

weapons on the city even if they are securely docked. But we need a line of retreat…' He thought quickly. 'The Thal cruiser that brought me here would not be sealed down.'

'No,' agreed the Black Dalek. 'But the Thals have escaped and are now occupying it. They are preparing to take off.'

'Stop them!' Davros ordered. 'I need that ship!'

'The Dalek Prime's forces are attempting to breach the hull,' the Black Dalek reported. 'I have given the order for an attack by our Daleks.'

'Good.' Davros would feel safer once the ship was captured. It was vital that he have an escape route, in case his plans didn't work out.

Two Daleks came around the corner, and raised their guns. Davros's forces annihilated them before they could fire.

Davros asked impatiently, 'And the battle for the control room?'

'Our troops are preparing to strike,' the Black Dalek answered.

The Dalek Prime studied the information as it came in. The assault via the lifts had been broken, but surely Davros would have anticipated that. It was such an obvious move. Therefore, there had to be a second assault. Several of the Black Daleks had defected to Davros's side, and they all knew the layouts of the city perfectly. So there had to be another way to approach the control room.

And then the Dalek Prime realised the weak spot – his own room overlooking the city. A wall of glass, easily accessed by hoverbouts – and the rebels certainly possessed those. To the Gold Dalek, he ordered, 'Prepare for an assault from my quarters. Bring all available warriors to cover this side of the building.'

'I obey!'

The Dalek Prime felt certain that this was the direction from which the assault would come. Now it was covered, he turned to pay attention to the rest of the battle. The Thals had escaped their cell, and boarded their ship. They were, logically, planning to flee Skaro in it. There had been no report from the Red Dalek escorting the Doctor to his TARDIS, so it wasn't very difficult to assume that the Doctor had something to do with the Thal escape. He was no doubt with them as they took back their ship. The Dalek Prime ordered an assault to regain the ship.

Davros was retreating, as was to be expected. Though he had boasted that he led his troops, this was a lie, as usual. Davros was very concerned with preserving what little was left of his own skin. His forces needed the spaceport in case of retreat. Davros always prepared for defeat, even when he was convinced of his own infallible ability to win. He was insane, but no fool. The Dalek Prime could not afford to allow Davros the opportunity to escape. This civil war had to end here and now, one way or the other. The Dalek race must be unified and pure again. If Davros were to flee, everything the Dalek Prime had planned for would be for nothing. It would all have to be fought over again.

Whatever happened, Davros must die.

The Dalek Prime began to move his assault force into position to intercept the retreating Davros.

'We're almost up to power,' Argini reported. 'Beginning release of docking clamps.'

'Hurry,' Chayn urged him, studying the screens. The Daleks had begun to cut at the airlock door. 'They'll be through shortly.'

Sam curled up beside Chayn, eyes focused on the screen.

As a result, she was the first to see what was happening. 'A counter-attack!' she exclaimed. 'The other Daleks are moving in!'

Davros's Daleks moved through the shattered docking bay, firing at anything that didn't give the correct identifying signal. Several Spiders scurried across the room, dodging blasts aimed in their direction, then pausing to return fire. They had finally made it to the ramp where the Thal ship was still docked.

At the top of the ramp, a party of Daleks was attempting to breach the airlock door. If they succeeded, it would prevent the ship from lifting off, but would render it useless until repairs could be made. It was clear, though, that the Thals were already inside and powering up their ship. Allowing the craft to lift off would render it useless to Davros, too.

'Destroy them,' the Red Dalek in command ordered. Its forces began the assault on the loyalist Daleks, aiming primarily at those cutting through the doors – who started to return fire. In seconds, the ramp was ablaze with wrecked Daleks.

The Red Dalek watched as three of the Spiders managed to get to the Thal ship, digging into the exterior with their legs, and watching, as ordered, not joining in the fight. They would be the last line of attack if all else failed.

And then the Thal ship came to life, subspace engines screaming as the docking clamps were released. The generators powered up instantly, their roar drowning out the sound of gunfire in the room.

'Take us up!' Ayaka yelled, and Argini slammed home the controls.

Freed from the restraints, the Thal ship whirled up into the sky, away from the city below. In the last seconds, Sam had seen the backwash from the drive annihilate the Daleks fighting on the ramp. Then the city fell away below them so fast that Sam was nearly airsick.

'No ground fire,' Cathbad called. 'The city's defences are trained inwards, not upwards. We're escaping.'

On the screens, the city shrank, and then the mountains, too, vanished into the curve of Skaro as the Thal craft rose higher, shooting through the tenuous cloud layer.

'We've made it!' Chayn called out ecstatically.

'Hardly,' Ayaka answered, settling into the command seat. 'We've only passed the first barrier. We're off Skaro, but still deep in the heart of their empire.' She shook her head. 'We're going to be very lucky if we get out of this alive.'

CHAPTER 11
THE ODYSSEUS STRATAGEM

The Doctor gave Sam a reassuring smile and patted her hand. 'I think you can probably let go of that gun now,' he said gently. 'There's not a lot to shoot at in here.'

Sam let it fall to the ground with a clatter. 'Why can't we just load everybody into the TARDIS and take off? That way, we'll avoid all the Dalek defences.'

'It's not the time for the TARDIS quite yet,' the Doctor answered. He seemed to be deep in thought.

'Approaching the first line of satellite defences,' Cathbad reported, calling up a schematic. It showed several hundred small satellites in orbit about Skaro, each of them bristling with fire power.

'I'm on it,' Chayn answered from the communications board. 'I'm recalling the Dalek command codes and transmitting the appropriate ones. Hopefully, they'll recognise us as friends and let us through.'

'If the Daleks don't change their codes regularly,' Ayaka answered. 'I've got every spare person on cannon duty.'

'How many is that?' the Doctor asked quietly.

'Twenty-five,' Ayaka replied. 'Everyone outside of this room who's still alive.'

Sam realised that over half of the captive Thals had not survived to escape. She felt almost numb to their deaths, and it worried her that she was becoming too conditioned to slaughter. 'Shock,' she told herself. 'Please let it be shock.'

As the ship approached the satellite ring, the tension became almost unbearable. Cathbad was studying the devices from his own panel. 'They're all powered up,' he reported. 'I don't know if it's because of us or because of the situation down on the planet.'

'I'm not getting any acknowledgment codes,' Chayn reported, her voice strained. 'Shouldn't they be answering by now?'

'All gun crews,' Ayaka said into the microphone on her seat. 'Prepare to open fire on my command.'

Closer… closer… Sam's stomach seemed to be in knots now, and she stared hard at the closest screen.

'Codes being transmitted!' Chayn cried happily. 'They're responding.'

'Weapons are turning away,' Cathbad announced. 'They've accepted us.'

'Keep watching!' Ayaka ordered sharply. 'This could still be a trick.' On the screen, their position continued to show as they approached the orbital of the satellites…

…And then passed through it unscathed. The satellites had their attention focused elsewhere. The codes, it appeared, were still valid.

The tension in the room drained slightly, but this was still not the final hazard to be faced. There were still the floating space platforms on the edges of Skaro's system.

'Ten minutes to platforms,' Cathbad announced. 'Traffic is light in this section of space.'

'Everyone's somewhat occupied fighting on the surface,' the Doctor said. 'We're insignificant at the moment.'

Ayaka nodded, her attention mainly on the readouts. 'Keep us on course,' she ordered. 'And monitor the platforms. As soon as we're in range, start transmitting the recognition codes. This is going to be a lot harder. The satellites were simply robots; there will be Daleks on the platforms, and if they get suspicious, they may want visual confirmation.' She glanced at the two wrecked Daleks in the control room. 'And they aren't likely to be reassured by what they would see.'

Sam sighed, and glanced at the Doctor. He seemed to have retreated into himself, a faint frown on his forehead. 'Doctor,' she said gently, 'is something wrong?'

'Yes,' he answered, abstractly.

'What?'

He shrugged. 'I don't know – yet.'

Sam didn't know what to say so she kept quiet, watching the crawl of their progress on the screen.

As the Dalek Prime had anticipated, Davros's forces broke into the short corridor from his quarters, anticipating a swift victory. Instead, they were met with heavy fire from the Gold Dalek's forces. Explosions and discharges filled the air as both sides clashed. In the control room, the Dalek Prime felt only satisfaction, knowing that he was still out-thinking his greatest foe.

Davros would not win this conflict. Such a thing was unthinkable.

'The assault on the control room has faltered,' the Black Dalek reported. 'The Dalek Prime anticipated the raid, He has established a blockade.'

'It is to be expected,' Davros answered. 'We can still surmount the problem. Have a force attack the power generation station. All power to the control room must be cut off. Then have a second force plant explosives in the ruined lift shafts. When they are in place, detonate them.' Davros chuckled to himself. 'If we cannot get up to the control room, then we shall bring the control room down to us...'

* * *

Sam turned her attention back to the smaller screen beside her again. It was still showing the exterior view of the ship looking aft. There was no ramp to see now, of course, but there was something else that bothered her. Leaning forward, she tapped Chayn on the shoulder. When the engineer turned round, Sam pointed to the screen. 'Look,' she said. 'Here.'

Chayn studied where Sam was pointing and then stiffened. The hull had what looked like a shadow cast across it in one section – where there should be nothing to cast a shadow. 'Trouble,' Chayn agreed. 'Ayaka! It looks like something's managed a small hull-breach. It's not in a sensitive area, so we're not losing air, but it wasn't there a few minutes ago.'

Ayaka caught on immediately. She studied the same picture on her own console, then tapped the microphone. 'Team eight – leave your cannon and investigate the breach in section D.'

There was no reply.

'Trouble,' Sam guessed. It wasn't the deduction of a genius.

The door to the bridge opened, and a Spider Dalek leapt inside, bringing its gun round to fire.

Chayn didn't even think. The rifle she held came up and fired. The recoil almost blew her across the room. She wasn't a terrific shot, but the Spider Dalek was virtually too close to miss. The top third of it exploded backward, sending it crashing back into the corridor. Ayaka sealed the door instantly.

The Doctor offered no congratulations. He turned grimly to Ayaka. 'I'd like to think that was the only one that sneaked aboard, but I wouldn't want to bet on it.'

'Nor I,' she agreed. She managed to raise another team, and had them sweep the ship. They all waited in silence. Two more Spiders were discovered and terminated, and then no more appeared. 'We seem to be clean again,' she reported.

'Just in time for the next crisis,' Cathbad observed. 'We're approaching the space platforms.'

Once again, the codes were transmitted. They were within range of only two of these platforms, but each was far more dangerous than the satellites they had already passed. These were under direct Dalek control, and these Daleks might want a more tangible response than simply codes.

The seconds seemed to crawl by as the distance closed. 'No response yet,' Chayn breathed, her eyes rapt on her instruments. The Doctor slipped into a seat beside her, studying the panel too.

Sam saw that they were now almost entering the orbit of the first platform. Was this going to work?

'They're demanding visual contact,' Chayn reported, a catch in her voice.

Oh, great...

'Spin the ship,' the Doctor ordered abruptly. 'Let them see the hull breach. Then retransmit the acknowledgment codes.'

'Do it,' Ayaka ordered, and Argini bent to the controls.

Chayn looked worried. 'You're trying to make them think our visuals are damaged,' she realised. 'Do you think they'll believe it.'

'I hope so,' the Doctor replied. 'Let me know if they change their request.' He turned to Cathbad. 'Are we being targeted?'

'Very definitely.' Cathbad gestured to his panel. 'Almost everything they've got will be coming at us if they don't fall for this.'

'Then start praying that they fall,' the Doctor suggested.

Sam's stomach seemed to have given up attempting to

combat the tension. She just felt sick, and almost resigned. If the Daleks did open fire, at least it would mean an end to this continual strain on her shattered nerves. How much longer could they go on living?

'They've sent the recognition codes,' Chayn said, with a sigh of relief. 'You did it, Doctor!'

As Sam watched, their track crawled past the platform orbit on the screen.

'We're not safe yet,' Ayaka cautioned. 'They could be trying to make us feel secure before they blast us.'

'They're realigning their weaponry,' Cathbad reported. 'They've stopped targeting us. We seem to be free and clear.'

'I'll believe that when we *are* free and clear,' Ayaka responded. 'Everyone, stay alert until we can go to full drive. The second we clear this system, engage light speed.'

'No!' the Doctor exclaimed, jumping to his feet. 'Don't even think about that!'

Ayaka gave him a puzzled look, one that was on everyone's face. 'Why not? Whatever is the matter, Doctor?'

'Trouble,' he replied, striding up and down a short section of the deck feverishly. 'Wouldn't you say that we've got off very lightly?'

'Lightly?' Ayaka scowled. 'Doctor, almost two-thirds of my force died in this escape attempt. That's hardly what I'd call light casualties.'

'An escape attempt from the Dalek home world, where their greatest power is concentrated?' the Doctor countered. 'We should never have been able to escape.'

'What are you talking about?' asked Chayn. 'We outsmarted the Daleks, that's all.'

'Did we?' he asked. 'Did we?' He pointed to the communications panel. 'On the way to Skaro, they allowed us to monitor the approach. Luckily, they didn't realise we could detect their signals and record them for our own use. Then they kept everyone alive and put you all in a cell close to the ship, and your weapons in a room conveniently close to you. Then they didn't manage to kill us all as we fled. Now they believed my claim that we're too damaged to show them a picture of our bridge. A trifle coincidental, wouldn't you say?'

'What are you getting at, Doctor?' Ayaka demanded, turning her seat to face him.

'Sam, I've been an absolute idiot,' he said, ignoring Ayaka for the moment. 'I take great pride in being the Daleks' greatest enemy, but I sometimes forget that I'm not their only one, and that not every plan they come up with revolves around me.'

Sam shrugged. 'I'm sure we'll let you off this time,' she assured him. 'But I've got no idea what you're talking about.'

'Think, Sam, think!' he urged her. 'Why did the Dalek Prime let you and me go?'

'Because he wants you to destroy Davros if Davros wins the civil war,' Sam answered.

'Exactly,' the Doctor agreed with satisfaction. 'That's his plan. But –' He threw out his hands dramatically. 'How did he know I was on the Thal ship? My wanderings are terribly unpredictable, even by myself. There's no way that the Dalek Prime could have expected to see us on the Thal ship, Sam. His forces would have noticed the TARDIS after they boarded the ship, and then known I was aboard. But not before.'

'So?' Sam still couldn't see what he was driving at. 'They took advantage of you, obviously.'

'Obviously,' agreed the Doctor. 'That's the point. They took advantage of me. The Dalek Prime admitted that he hadn't known I was even involved with the Hand of Omega, let alone being on the *Quetzel*. But they already had a plan in operation before I arrived. Davros's survival pod had a homing beacon on it that was triggered once the pod was opened. Davros clearly wouldn't have set that up. If he'd wanted rescuing, the beacon would have been activated while he was floating in space. And he certainly didn't expect his own Daleks to rescue him. They were all dead and gone. So it had to have been the Dalek Prime's Daleks who placed the homing beacon. Which means that they had already found Davros before the *Quetzel* did.'

Chayn scowled. 'And threw him back? If they wanted to put him on trial, then why not do it there and then?'

'Exactly,' the Doctor said. 'If they had already found Davros, they could have taken him back to Skaro then. Why didn't they? Why did they wait until someone else found him?'

Sam was starting to catch on. 'Bait,' she said. 'They used him as bait to draw someone in. But how did they know the Thals would fall for it?'

'I don't think they did,' the Doctor answered. 'If they'd been looking for a Thal ship specifically, they could have tried to capture one anywhere along the battle front. On the contrary, they seem to have been angling for a ship like the *Quetzel* – a lone ship, often on its own, off the beaten path. It was sheer luck that Delani was after Davros at the same time. The Daleks took whatever they had, carefully keeping the crew alive, back to their planet. And then allowed us all to escape.'

Ayaka nodded slowly. 'You're starting to make an awful lot of sense, Doctor,' she agreed. 'It would explain a great deal that has been puzzling me. The obvious question is, why did they let us escape?'

'Hang on,' Sam said. 'They must have planted something aboard the ship, just like in Davros's pod!'

'I agree,' said the Doctor. 'The Daleks have planted something aboard this ship that they want you to take with you.'

'But my forces have searched the ship and found nothing,' Ayaka objected.

'On the contrary, they found Daleks. They killed them, but they were here.' The Doctor frowned. 'What were they up to?'

'Guarding the ship,' Cathbad suggested. 'Obviously.'

'Then they didn't do a very good job of it,' the Doctor objected. 'No, they were here for some other purpose. Cathbad, can you scan the inside of the ship for any kind of anomalies?'

'It would help if I knew that I was looking for,' he answered.

'If we knew, then you wouldn't need to look.' The Doctor patted his shoulder. 'Look for anything that doesn't match the readouts from earlier. I've no idea what could be significant at this stage.'

Sam moved closer to the Doctor. 'Then we're not out of the woods yet?' she asked.

'Not by a long shot,' he replied. 'On the contrary, I suspect we're deeper in them than ever.'

'Terrific.' Feeling utterly dejected, Sam slumped to the floor, waiting for tears that refused to come.

The fighting in the spaceport was starting to die down. With the departure of the Thal vessel, the port's strategic importance was reduced. Only in one small section did Davros's troops keep attacking. They were working their way onto a docked killcruiser which was being defended by a small loyalist force.

The Black Dalek urged its warriors on. Davros had demanded the capture of this particular ship, and the Black Dalek grasped its significance. The fighting intensified, as Daleks on both sides were hit and exploded. Shattered Dalek shells littered the area as the attack was pressed home.

The final move was accomplished when a Strider moved into the fray. Normally it would have been far too large to enter the city, but the docking bays were deliberately huge, and it had managed to stalk through the gap in the wall that had been blown out earlier. Its belly guns fired down at the defenders, annihilating them in short order.

'Seize the ship,' the Black Dalek ordered. 'Ensure that no enemy forces are left aboard.' It moved to the command deck, and began activating the onboard weaponry.

From the foredeck, it had a clear view of the city, including the tower that housed the main control room. In a few moments, it would be able to target the tower and take out the heart of the enemy resistance.

Success was within their grasp!

Inside the control room, the Dalek Prime was still scanning the reports of the fighting. Davros had lost the second assault on the control room, but he was unlikely to give up. Without this area, he could hardly take the city, and without the city, he could never hold the Dalek empire. He was bound to try again; the question was where he would strike?

'Power-generation station is under attack,' the Gold Dalek reported. 'Heavy fighting is under way.'

There. If the power to the control room was cut off, then the Dalek Prime's hold on it would be useless. The internal generators would hold up several hours, but they weren't meant to last for longer. Still, given the importance of the power station, the Dalek Prime already had large forces assigned there. This was a significant, but hardly unexpected, battle.

Davros was planning other attacks, of that the Dalek Prime was certain. How would he strike next? He scanned the information from the city's internal sensors, and could see that some of Davros's forces were moving back towards the broken lift shafts. Was it possible that he intended to have Spiders attempt to climb the shafts? But there was no sign of Spiders in the team. What, then? If the shafts weren't to be climbed, why target them?

And then he realised. The shafts were located from the top to the bottom of the building. If an explosive device was placed in each one, then detonated, it might well undermine the stability of the structure. As far as Davros was concerned, taking out the control centre was an acceptable alternative to capturing it.

'Bring forces to defend the lift shafts,' the Dalek Prime ordered. 'Davros is attempting to mine them. This must be stopped.'

The Gold Dalek moved. 'I obey,' it acknowledged.

The Dalek Prime continued to monitor events. His own counterstrike was moving into place to take on Davros's core of defenders. If they could be taken out and Davros recaptured, then the fighting would soon begin to wind down. Davros had been a great help, without intending it. He must have insisted his forces all send a low-frequency signal to identify themselves. Now they had discovered this signal, the Dalek Prime's warriors could identify them too. Each supporter of Davros had been branded, and they could all be hunted down and exterminated. The Dalek race would be cleansed of its imperfections.

Provided Davros's plans didn't take effect before the Dalek Prime's did. But, even if Davros should win this battle and take the planet, the war would not be over. The Dalek Prime examined the track of the departing Thal vessel. Two further plans were even now under way, and there was no way for Davros to affect them. The Doctor was free, and alerted to Davros's survival. The Dalek Prime knew that the Doctor understood the menace that Davros represented, and knew that he would do his utmost to destroy Davros.

And, of course, in case the Doctor failed, there was still the original plan to fall back on...

Cathbad rubbed his neck, scowling as he bent over his instruments. Sam smiled as Chayn went over to him and began to massage his shoulders gently. It was good to see that she was continuing to transfer her attentions away from the Doctor. Cathbad seemed to appreciate the shift, too.

'It's no good, Doctor,' he finally announced.

'Oh, I don't know,' the Doctor replied, his eyes twinkling. 'It looks rather nice to me.'

Cathbad reluctantly asked Chayn to stop. 'I don't mean that,' he replied. 'I mean my search. I really can't find anything.'

'There's nothing different about the ship at all?' the Doctor asked, bouncing over to his station and gently easing Chayn aside. 'There has to be something.'

'Honestly, Doctor,' Cathbad informed him, 'the only thing I've noticed is that the ship's a bit sluggish at the helm.'

'What?' The Doctor stared at the controls. 'What do you mean?'

Cathbad shrugged. 'It's just that we're not manœuvring as well as we normally do. It's probably due to the damage caused by the Spider Daleks. We seemed to be about five per cent underpowered.'

The Doctor bent over the console, and his fingers started to ripple across the panels. 'That's odd. I wonder why that should be.' He tapped in more commands and then gave a tentative smile. 'Somebody must be very out of shape. Even though two-thirds of the crew is missing, the ship seems to have gained an extra five per cent in mass.'

'What?' Ayaka moved to join them at the station. 'How can that be?'

'I'm not absolutely sure yet,' the Doctor admitted. 'But I think we've discovered what the Daleks have been up to. While you were in their cell, they added a little something extra to your ship.'

'A bomb,' Cathbad suggested. 'A planet-wrecker, perhaps, aimed at detonating on our home world and annihilating us.'

'I'd believe that if the Daleks could have known you were coming.' The Doctor shook his head. 'Remember, they were expecting a tramp steamer like the *Quetzel*, which wouldn't be heading home for months or years. It's something else.'

'Doctor,' Ayaka said, 'I do not understand. How could the Daleks increase our mass by five per cent without altering the ship in some fashion? Yet the internal scanners show nothing amiss.'

Chayn laughed. 'The Daleks would have to be really stupid if they didn't fix your scanner readings,' she pointed out. 'I'd be willing to bet that your sensors don't have a hope of finding what the Daleks have done. We'd have to do a walk-through of the entire ship.'

'Given the forces I have left,' Ayaka answered, 'that could

251

take quite some time.' She glanced at the Doctor. 'Do you believe that there is a time limit?'

'I don't know,' he admitted. 'But I'd be very reluctant to go to light speed if I were you. The Daleks could very well have tied their whatever-it-is into the drive unit. Let's just chug along for a while until we can find it, shall we?'

'Very well,' agreed Ayaka. 'But it would be nice if we had a faster way to scan my ship.'

'We do,' he assured her. 'Sam, Chayn, you'd better come with me.' He gave Chayn a wide grin. 'You're going to love this next bit. Trust me!'

Davros's Daleks continued to move their bombs into position by the lift shafts. They had forced open one set of doors. The shattered wreckage of the lift and the Special Weapons Dalek were mostly small pieces speckled with gunk. The first device was placed in position, and the lift shaft sealed. Attention moved on to the second.

Electronic fire broke out as loyalist Daleks broke through a wall they had been undermining. Several of Davros's Daleks exploded. The others whirled about to fight back. The Blue Dalek in command of the detail ignored the fighting and primed the first bomb. Two more Daleks exploded beside it, as the loyalists started to close in.

Making a hasty decision, the Blue Dalek aborted the countdown and detonated all of the bombs immediately.

The building shook, and alarms sounded throughout the control room. The Dalek Prime's eye stalk whirled to survey the readouts. The floor continued to shake as the information flooded in. 'Explosive devices have been detonated,' the Dalek Prime stated. 'One shaft had collapsed, weakening the building. Part of the ground floor has been atomised. The structure has been compromised.'

'We still stand,' the Gold Dalek pointed out.

'Yes,' agreed the Dalek Prime. 'But the building is weakened. It is important that we consolidate power. Order the forces in the generator station to attack Davros's forces directly. They must be annihilated immediately. The power to this room must not be severed.' The Gold Dalek whirled about to carry out its orders. The floor trembled as it moved.

'Prepare to evacuate the control room,' the Dalek Prime ordered. 'Hoverbouts must be brought to this level to offload all workers. Any further damage here will bring the building crashing down. It is vital that this be prevented until power can be re-routed to one of the secondary control centres.'

In the killcruiser, the Red Dalek had the power systems up and working. It was realigning all of the weaponry to concentrate on the command building. A few moments earlier, it had witnessed an explosion that had torn out part of the lower floor and sent a gout of fire into the air. Bombs had clearly been triggered there, damaging the integrity of the structure. A few well-placed shots could bring the tower crashing down in ruins.

In moments, it would be in a position to do precisely that.

A Black Dalek moved cautiously across the control room to the Dalek Prime. 'One of Davros's units have taken command of killcruiser 809,' it reported. 'The weapons are all being targeted on this building.'

'It was only to be expected,' the Dalek Prime replied. 'A logical move.' His eye stalk swivelled to one of the controllers. 'Detonate 809,' it ordered.

'I obey.' The Dalek interfaced with the computer and sent its signal.

The Red Dalek started the command sequence to fire all of the killcruiser's weaponry when a light flashed on the main panel. It stared at it for a second, and then realised what it was. It attempted to fire a barrage in the next second, as –

The docking bay was rocked by the explosion that tore the killcruiser apart, scattering blazing wreckage about the port. A ball of fire climbed to the sky, falling back and consuming spent fuel and any Daleks left undestroyed in the explosion.

Davros felt the building rock from this blast. 'What was that?' he demanded.

'The Dalek Prime has sabotaged the killcruisers,' the Black Dalek reported. 'The captured ship was destroyed before it could fire on the tower.'

'We must destroy the tower!' Davros exclaimed. 'The Dalek Prime is there, along with the heart of his surveillance network. Once that is down, the loyalists will be split. Only then can we hope to defeat them! Order all forces to focus their attacks on the tower.'

'The unit at the power station is under assault,' the Black Dalek announced. 'They are unable to pull back.'

'Then tell them to fight and die there!' Davros cried. 'We need more troops to attack the tower.'

'All available units are being brought in,' the Black Dalek informed him. 'The battle will continue.' It paused. 'Our margin for success has been reduced.'

'Reduced, perhaps,' Davros growled. 'But not destroyed. We shall win through! It is my destiny to lead the Daleks to the complete conquest of the entire galaxy! I shall succeed!'

Chayn stared about her in awe. 'This is your spaceship?' she asked.

'And home,' the Doctor added, beaming with pride. 'Do you like it?'

'Like it?' She turned to stare about the room. 'It's astonishing! How could I not like it?' She took in the central console, with the linkage up into the high ceiling. That was clearly where the craft was controlled. To one side were racks and racks of books; clearly the Doctor enjoyed reading. There were dozens, perhaps hundreds, of clocks clustered along one wall, and filing cabinets containing who-knew-what. Down the side opposite the library section was a row of columns that seemed very antique and out of place. It was an astonishing ship.

Sam leaned closer and added, 'This is just the control room. If you've a couple of years to spare, you might want to look at the rest of the ship.'

'It's too much to take in,' Chayn answered. She moved to the console, staring at the antique-looking controls. 'Very stylish,' she said with approval. 'And clearly a lot more sophisticated than it appears.'

'Yes,' agreed the Doctor. 'But machinery always seems more personable if it has a little whimsy, don't you feel?'

'Definitely,' Chayn agreed, somewhat breathlessly. 'So, what do we do in here?'

'Scan the Thal ship,' the Doctor replied, powering up the console. 'The Daleks couldn't have affected my machinery; it's far too sophisticated for them to muck about with. Besides which, they can't get into the TARDIS.'

'Except you dismantled the lock,' Sam pointed out.

'Anyone could push that door open. I told you it was a bad idea.'

'I'll fix it,' the Doctor promised. He had started to power up the machinery, and Chayn watched in fascination. She was a pretty decent engineer, but she didn't have a clue as to what most of the equipment in this TARDIS was for. 'Starting the scan... now.' He pressed home a lever that sighed. 'It should just take a moment or two.' He gave Chayn another delighted smile. 'I thought you'd like the old girl,' he said happily.

'The old girl is wonderful,' Chayn informed him. 'I'd love to take her apart to see how she functions.'

'Not you, too,' Sam complained. 'It's bad enough when the Doctor does it.'

There was a soft chime from the console, and the Doctor glanced down. 'Ah...' He suddenly looked rather worried.

'What? You've found it?' Sam asked, concerned.

'Yes,' he agreed slowly. He glanced at Chayn. 'The TARDIS interior is made possible because the Time Lords have mastered transdimensional engineering. Fitting big things into tiny packages. The Daleks can do something similar – a lot cruder, taking a lot more power and with inherent instabilities. But they can do it. And they *have* done it. They've hidden something inside this ship's storage bay, camouflaged by routine equipment.'

'But what is it?' Chayn asked. 'A bomb?'

'No.' The Doctor looked terribly serious. 'Worse than that. It's the Odysseus Stratagem.' When he realised that they were both staring at him uncomprehendingly, he explained, 'The Trojan Horse. The Daleks have hidden a complete factory ship inside this craft. Potentially an entire army of Daleks. That's what we're taking back to Thal space!'

CHAPTER 12
CHECKMATE

Sam stared at the Doctor. 'That doesn't sound good' was all she could say.

'It isn't,' he informed her. He shook his head. 'It's a brilliant idea, I'll have to say that. Have one of your enemies unwittingly transport away from Skaro a factory capable of turning out a Dalek army. Once it reaches its target, it begins operations and starts churning out fresh Daleks to begin their wars all over again when everyone assumes that they're dead. Brilliant, and very, very nasty.'

'So what are we going to do about it?' Chayn asked.

'Get rid of it,' the Doctor said simply. 'Toss it overboard.'

'Doctor,' Sam pointed out, 'it weighs too much to chuck it out of an airlock.'

'Well, that's one idea,' he admitted. 'I had thought that rigging the TARDIS up to dump it into the space-time vortex might be a trifle more effective, to be honest.' He gave Chayn a wide grin. 'I'd appreciate some help.'

'Of course, Doctor,' the engineer agreed. 'I'd be delighted.'

'Good. Oh, Sam.' The Doctor turned to her. 'You'd better go and tell Ayaka that under no circumstances is she to jump to light speed. That'll trigger the awakening of the capsule. And dropping out of light speed at the other end of the journey finishes the job. As long as we're running slow, we're reasonably safe.'

'Reasonably?' Sam repeated.

He shrugged. 'It's the Daleks we're dealing with here, Sam.

They have a tendency to booby-trap everything as a matter of course. I'm sure we'll discover a few surprises as we work.'

'Wonderful,' Sam muttered. Leaving them to begin their work, she trotted to the doors. Then she hurried down the corridor towards the bridge.

The battle for the power room was winding down. The Gold Dalek's forces were slowly containing and annihilating Davros's fighters. The surrounding corridors were ablaze with Dalek shells and incendiary devices. Sections of the walls had been destroyed, and rubble was littered everywhere. Scanning for the low-frequency recognition signal of Davros's troops, the Gold Dalek detected the final three. It had its forces encircle the rebels, and then destroyed them in coruscating electronic fire.

'The power room has been secured,' it reported back to the Dalek Prime. 'The corridors have been cleansed. No interruption of power has occurred.'

In the control room, the Dalek Prime received this news with satisfaction. Davros's forces in both the power complex and the spaceport had now been exterminated. All through the city, battles were still raging, but Davros's forces were slowly, yet certainly, being decimated. Only one reasonably large grouping was now left – the one escorting Davros. They were presumably seeking some safe retreat. But there was no safe retreat for Davros.

The war was almost over, and Davros was about to lose.

And then...

Davros was fuming quietly to himself. His third attack force had now been wiped out. They had all failed him, the spaceport, the control room, and the power room were all still under the control of the Dalek Prime. All that was left to him was the force of a hundred or so Daleks surrounding him. He scanned the city for further signals from those Daleks loyal to him. Perhaps another hundred, as opposed to several thousand loyal to the Dalek Prime.

Fighting had been intense, and everywhere they went was scattered with wreckage and burnt-out casings. Thousands of Daleks had so far died in this battle. Davros felt no concern about that. It was what the Daleks were designed for, battle and death. They had achieved their purpose. But all of their deaths meant nothing if he was still not in power. There still had to be a way to salvage the situation. There had to be.

As they moved through an apparently deserted section of the city, past more ruins, doors all about the square suddenly slid open to reveal Daleks waiting for them. The doors through which they had entered crashed shut.

It had been a trap, after all! Davros's Daleks opened fire immediately, and the loyalists returned the stream of death.

The final battle, Davros realised, had just begun.

When Sam had delivered her message, Ayaka nodded. 'It is as the Doctor feared. The Daleks had hoped to make us their unwitting allies.' She gave Sam a compassionate stare. 'Tell the Doctor that if he cannot remove the Dalek construction, I will detonate the ship. Is it possible for his machine to take my crew to safety?'

'Of course,' Sam answered. 'We wouldn't even be crowded.'

'Good. Then Cathbad and I will prepare in case that

eventuality is necessary.' Ayaka turned back to her work.

Sam left the bridge and headed back to the TARDIS. It was funny, really, but she had changed her mind completely about Ayaka. She thought of the Thal as a kind of homicidal older sister, really.

Back in the TARDIS, she saw that there were now long connecting cables trailing from the console towards the main doors. 'Looking for a jump-start?' she joked.

'Actually, yes,' Chayn said from the floor, where she was spot-soldering connections to increase the length. 'That's exactly what the Doctor's planning on doing. He wants to connect the TARDIS to the Dalek factory ship and then use the TARDIS to push the Daleks into the vortex.'

'And then what?' Sam asked. All this technical stuff was way over her head.

'I don't know,' Chayn admitted. 'From the way that the Doctor describes the vortex, it's a sort of maelstrom of destructive energies. Ships like the TARDIS can navigate there well enough, but the stresses will do all sorts of unpleasant things to the factory ship. The Doctor didn't have time to explain it all.'

'Well, I hope it rips it apart,' Sam said with satisfaction. 'I can't think of any better candidates for being ripped apart than the Daleks.'

Chayn grinned. 'You've changed your tune a bit,' she observed. 'You were the anti-war one here when all this started.'

'I know.' Sam collapsed on the floor beside Chayn. She realised that she was still holding onto the stupid rifle. 'It's so easy to say that war's wrong and should be stopped when you're not the one at war. It's just not that simple, is it?'

'No,' agreed Chayn. 'It isn't. Oh, sometimes it is. Sometimes you can tell the good guys and the bad guys apart. The big problem is that war tends to make everyone equal. And usually at a very low level. You start out thinking that the other side is evil, and that they're baby-killers and rapists and scum, and that you'll never sink that low yourself. Then you find that they've fire-bombed one of your cities, and the only retaliation is to fire-bomb one of theirs.' Chayn stared at Sam, her eyes haunted. 'My father told me before he died that he wished he'd done something else – anything else – rather than fight for a living. He couldn't forget all of the people he'd hurt and killed.' She gave a short, barking laugh. 'The ironic thing was that he never realised that my mother and I were two of his victims, too.'

Their musings were interrupted by the Doctor bustling out of the TARDIS, smiling. 'Ready, Chayn?'

'Ready,' she agreed. Taking the leads from him, she soldered them to her own rig. 'Right, that should do it.'

'Let's see, shall we?' The Doctor hurried over to the console.

The two cables snaked under the mushroom panel and into the innards of the TARDIS. He began to flick switches, carefully studying one of the screens. Chayn had her own eyes glued to a second. Feeling useless once again, Sam hung back slightly, watching them.

'Powering up,' the Doctor murmured, watching the grid rise. 'Ready to transfer energy to the vortex shift...'

A sudden thought struck Sam. 'Doctor?' she said hesitantly. 'The Dalek Prime knew you were likely to be back aboard this ship, didn't he?'

The Doctor's hands paused in mid-motion. 'Yes,' he agreed slowly.

'And he must know roughly what the TARDIS is capable of, surely?'

The Doctor's eyes opened wide. 'He'd be a fool not to.' Grimacing, he abandoned what he was doing and started a diagnostic running. 'Aha! Sam, you're a genius! There's a little subroutine in the factory ship for just this eventuality. If I try to tap it into the vortex, the power will feed back and blast this room there instead. Sneaky...'

'Can you get around it?' Chayn asked.

'Yes,' the Doctor assured her. 'But if Sam hadn't been even more suspicious than I am, we'd have been in serious trouble.' He fiddled with the equipment again, punching in new codes. 'There we go, that will subvert the subroutine, so it feeds off itself.' He grinned. 'And another quick check to make sure there are no more little surprises waiting for us.' He shook his head. 'That was the last trick. So...' He bent over the controls again, and shoved home the final levers.

The time rotor gave its familiar howl, but the TARDIS didn't move. Instead, the cables began to glow, as power flowed from the console and down to the Dalek stowaway.

'It's working,' Chayn reported. 'Power couplings are holding firm.'

'And there it goes,' the Doctor said, with a smug expression. 'The factory ship is entering the vortex now. The Thal ship is clean.' He cut the power, and the rotor fell silent. 'Let's reel these in, shall we?' He started to pull on the wiring.

'That's it?' Sam asked. 'Flick a few switches, and the Daleks are defeated? The factory ship's destroyed?'

'Yes and no,' he answered, jerking on the wires, as Sam and Chayn helped. 'Yes, the Daleks are defeated. For the time being. And no, the factory ship's not destroyed exactly. I rather think it's just been flung back through interstitial time and space.'

Chayn stared at him in horror. 'Then we've just sent it somewhere else! We've not solved the problem at all!'

'Chayn, in another time, and another place... I think I already have,' said the Doctor. 'Believe me. Please.'

Chayn almost collapsed. 'I do,' she admitted.

The battle raged all about Davros. He fumed, angry weaponless and impotent. His circuitry had been disabled by the Dalek Prime's scientists when he had arrived on Skaro. All he could do was to watch and curse as his followers were exterminated one by one.

The Dalek Prime's squad moved in. Daleks on both sides were being destroyed all around the battle zone, but the loyalists were still pouring in. Now that Davros's other thrusts had been defeated, more troops could be spared for this last offensive.

Davros winced as the battered Black Dalek beside him finally took several direct hits at once and then exploded. Other Daleks died, and the enveloping circle closed in. Finally, only Davros was left alive. Three Gold and two Black Daleks had him surrounded, their guns at the ready. Davros realised that he had finally been defeated. His power play had come to nothing.

'Do as you will,' he challenged them. 'Exterminate me! Seal your own sterile future! Without me, you are nothing!'

'You are not to be exterminated,' one of the Gold Daleks declared. 'You will accompany us. Your madness has run its course. The Dalek race has been purged of your insanity. We who are left are of one mind. You will see this, and then die.' It moved, allowing him an opening through which to proceed. With no other option, Davros moved as he was bidden.

The Dalek Prime was waiting for him in the matter-transfer chamber. His eye stalk surveyed him coldly. 'You have lost, Davros,' he stated. 'Your folly has taken part of the Dalek race with you. But we who survive are stronger for it. All that remains is to finally destroy you.'

'Destroy me, and you destroy your own future,' Davros warned him. 'Without me, you have no hope. I can give you vision! I can give you purpose! I can show you your destiny!'

'No,' the Dalek Prime answered. 'Your purpose is insanity. Your destiny is death. The Daleks will go on without you.'

'I created you!' Davros insisted. 'You owe me everything that you are.'

'No,' the Dalek Prime contradicted him. 'You helped create us. We have changed. We have improved. We have become a different species. I have experimented on myself. I have altered the genetic code that you laid down. I am no longer what I once was. I am the future for the Daleks. You are not.' It turned to face one of the Spider Daleks. 'Prepare the chamber.'

'I obey.' The creature's manipulator legs began to activate the controls. Close by was the bulk of the transmat equipment. Before Davros, now open, was the matter-transfer tube. Davros stared at the Spider Dalek. Was this his hidden ally? He could not tell, he could only hope. Perhaps the game was not yet over…

'In moments,' the Dalek Prime informed him, 'your atoms will be taken apart and scattered through space, in a ring about our sun. You will not survive matter dispersal. This is your end, Davros – and the way ahead for the Dalek race!'

* * *

The Thal ship had leapt to light speed now, unencumbered by the Dalek factory ship inside its belly. Relief was written on everyone's face, and Sam knew hers was probably the most relieved of all. It was finally over.

'Well,' the Doctor said to her quietly, 'I think it's probably time for us to be on our way, don't you?'

Sam sighed, and then nodded. It might have been nice to stick around for a few more days, just enjoying the company of the Thals. Without constantly having to fight for their lives, Sam suspected that they would turn out to be all right. But the Doctor was ever restless and footloose, and he was already wanting to be off.

'Must you go so soon?' asked Chayn. She looked rather disappointed. 'I'd been hoping I could get another look at the TARDIS's systems. They're quite intriguing.'

'I know,' the Doctor agreed. 'But I'm not sure that the Time Lords would approve of my letting you be privy to some of their most jealously guarded secrets.' His lips twitched. 'Of course, you could always come with us...' he suggested.

Sam felt a flare of jealousy again, which she fought to suppress. Chayn was a nice person, and she really didn't have any designs on the Doctor... Did she?

Chayn looked very seriously tempted. Then she glanced at Cathbad, who sat in his seat, trying very hard not to look at her or say anything. But even Sam could see the strain on his face. 'No, thanks,' Chayn finally said.

The Doctor gave her a quick kiss on the cheek. He smiled at Cathbad, who was looking tremendously relieved.

Two could play at that game... Sam leaned over and kissed Cathbad's cheek. 'Treat her nicely,' she said.

'I've never met a girl like Chayn.'

'You've never met a non-blonde before, Cathbad!' said

Chayn, eavesdropping.

'I shall,' he promised, and Sam knew that he meant it.

The Doctor turned to Ayaka. 'And what will happen to you?' he asked.

'I have to surrender myself for trial,' she said simply.

'You don't have to do that,' the Doctor said. 'You could come with us. See the universe. Get away from it all.'

Sam had rather been expecting him to make that offer. 'Yes,' she added. 'Ayaka... can't you just walk away?'

Ayaka smiled sadly. 'I wish I could,' she said. 'But I can't just decide that it's too dangerous for me and walk away. There are people who rely on me. And I owe it to those who died, like Dyoni... like half my crew. And, if I don't stand up and say that what Delani did was wrong, perhaps they'll try it again. I have to take my chance. I must try to denounce this madness.' She paused. 'And I shall see my daughter again. That's something I've learnt from Chayn. If I'm fighting for her future, the least I can do is be a part of it.'

The Doctor nodded. 'I'm proud of you, Ayaka. Whatever happens to you, you'll face it with dignity and courage.'

'And with friends,' Cathbad added. 'You saved our lives. I could never have guided us this far. I will stand with you at your court martial.'

'We all will,' Argini added. 'The whole crew. If they condemn you to death, they will have to condemn us all.'

'Strength in unity,' the Doctor suggested. 'It's worked for a long time and on many planets.' He smiled again. 'I have no doubt that you'll win, Ayaka. With such support, how could you lose?'

'Come with us,' Ayaka urged. 'The two of you. We've so much to do, and you could be such a great help. We've stopped the Daleks this time, but they're still out there. Still fighting. Help us to finish their menace for ever.'

'They're not stopped,' the Doctor said gently. 'At best, they've lost this one gambit.' He sighed. 'And staying in one place to see a job through to the end really isn't my style. That's for people with commitments to a place, a race, a vision.' He actually looked wistful for a moment, as if they had something that he wished he might find. 'Well, I hate long goodbyes.' He whirled on his heels, grabbed Sam's hand and jerked her out of the room. She just had time to wave before she was out of sight.

'So, it's all over?' Sam asked.

'Hardly over,' he replied. 'Barely begun, in some ways. The Daleks have taken a beating, but it's not permanent. They'll be back.'

Sam really didn't want to think about what that might mean right now. 'Will Ayaka be all right?'

'I hope so Sam, I hope so.'

'And what about Davros?'

'I really don't know,' the Doctor confessed. They had reached the TARDIS and he pushed open the door for her. 'I really must fix this lock,' he added. Then he looked at her. 'I believe the Dalek Prime will win. Davros has some support, but it most likely won't be enough. He's most likely been caught and executed by now.' He suddenly stopped dead in his tracks, and the colour drained from his face. 'What an idiot I am!'

'Huh?' Sam stared at him as he suddenly dashed into the console room. 'What's wrong?' she yelled, haring after him. He scared her when he went into these moods.

He was working on the controls, and spoke feverishly as he did so. 'The Dalek Prime let us go to act as his second line of attack against Davros.'

'So?'

'What if he beat Davros?'

Sam couldn't follow what he was getting at. 'Then he wins,' she said, puzzled. 'And he's happy.'

'And what use does he have for a second line of attack?'

Finally, Sam saw what he was talking about. She felt as if she'd been slapped hard across the face. 'You think the Dalek Prime's done something to get rid of us if he doesn't need us?' she realised.

'Got it in one,' he agreed. He slammed his hand down on the control panel. 'And there it is…' He dropped to the floor and pulled down an access panel on the underside of the console.

Sam peered over his shoulder. There was a small metallic globe there, pulsing slightly with an inner golden light. 'That's not supposed to be there, is it?'

'No,' he agreed. 'It's a fusion bomb.'

'Please tell me you remembered to reconnect the State of Grace circuitry,' she begged him.

'I wish I had, Sam,' he admitted. 'But I didn't. If that goes off, it will take out the TARDIS. And it's bound to go off just as soon as the Dalek Prime knows he has no further use for us. Once he's eliminated Davros.'

The Dalek Prime watched with considerable satisfaction as the matter-transfer unit came on-line. 'The battle is over and won, Davros,' he announced. 'Your time is finished.'

'You need me!' Davros insisted. 'I can be of help to you! I can improve the Dalek race!'

'You are of help to me by dying,' the Dalek Prime answered. 'And the Dalek race can improve itself. You are not needed.' To the watching Gold Daleks, he ordered: 'Place him in the unit.'

'No!' Davros snarled, as he was pushed back towards the tube. 'You cannot destroy me! I will not allow it!' As the tube hissed shut, he screamed, 'You cannot be rid of me this easily!'

The Dalek Prime said, 'We can.' To the Spider Dalek, he commanded, 'Dispersal pattern – engage.'

Davros was still saying something inaudibly as the tube lit up. The power grid glowed, and the figure gradually lost its cohesion and resolution, tiny particles of matter seeming to spatter against the glass until, finally, the power died down and the tube was empty.

'Dispersal complete,' the Spider Dalek reported. 'Davros is destroyed.'

'Good,' the Dalek Prime said. 'Purge the system memory.' It was always technically feasible that Davros's body and prints could be rebuilt using the memory core of the computer. There was no need to take chances.

The Spider Dalek obeyed. 'Memory core has been purged,' it reported, and pulled the block from the machine. It set this on a small pedestal, and backed off. Then it fired once. The core exploded, falling in small, smoking ruins.

No data could have survived that. The Dalek Prime was satisfied. Davros was finished, at last, and the war was over. Only one final act remained. He turned to the Gold Dalek. 'Trigger the bomb in the TARDIS,' it commanded.

'I obey!'

The Doctor was locked in concentration as he powered up the TARDIS systems and then engaged the time rotor. With its usual cacophonous howl, the TARDIS faded from the deck of the Thal craft, entering the space-time vortex.

'That's bought us a few extra minutes, perhaps,' he said dubiously. 'But the Daleks can signal across time, and they'll expect me to be in flight. This next part's very tricky...' He began to reset the controls.

'What are you doing, Doctor?' Sam asked quietly. While she didn't want to disturb his concentration, she also didn't want to be left in the dark. If she was going to die, she'd prefer to stare it in the face.

'Dematerialise the TARDIS from around the bomb,' he said, 'leaving it alone in the vortex. Then it won't matter if it's triggered. But that's a very delicate manoeuvre...' Sweat was trickling down his brow as he worked, and Sam could see the strain on his face. She stayed silent, breathing shallowly, and away from the console so as not to disturb him. He dashed around to a different panel, tapping in commands. Finally, he hesitated, hand over the dematerialisation lever. 'Well, here goes...' he muttered.

'Is this safe?' Sam asked him.

'No,' he replied. 'But it's safer than leaving the bomb where it is.' He rammed home the lever.

The TARDIS shuddered and howled about them both, as it tried to shake itself free. Several systems crackled and spat fire, and the lights dimmed noticeably owing to the power drain. Sam's eyes were riveted on the pulsing bomb. Was she just imagining it, or were the pulsations speeding up?

There was a tremendous explosion, tearing at the fabric of the vortex, whirlpooling around the boundaries of space and time.

The TARDIS gave one final, dramatic shake before settling

down once more. Sam scarcely dared hope, but she looked at the Doctor for confirmation.

He nodded, smiling. 'It's over,' he confirmed. 'We disposed of the bomb just in time. The signal must have been sent at almost the same second.'

'Then this is really it?' she asked. 'No more traps? No more tricks?'

'It's over,' he confirmed, and then looked worried again. 'Except the factory ship was a double threat,' he realised. 'And perhaps the bomb was, too. The Dalek Prime always likes to have a back-up option...' He stared at the controls again. 'No more bombs, so if there's another trap, it's something else this time.'

Wasn't this ever going to end? Sam realised she'd been asking herself that question almost continually for what seemed like hours. Every time she hoped and prayed it was over, the Daleks refused to let go. They were like pit bulls with atomic weapons, locking onto you with a death-grip and never letting up.

'Are you sure there's another trap?' she demanded.

'No,' he confessed. 'But I'm afraid it's very likely. Only... what is it?' He had the ship running a diagnostic, she could see.

Sam wasn't sure what they should be looking for, but she recalled his instructions to Cathbad – anything that wasn't there before. She glanced around the console room. It was so cluttered that it was difficult to judge if there was anything new there. If there were a new clock in the music room, how could she tell? Desperately hoping that whatever it might be was something really obvious, she scanned the room again and again.

If there was another trap... Anyway, did it have to be in

here? Wasn't it possible that it was hidden somewhere else in the TARDIS, waiting to leap out at them when they were totally off-guard? Then she realized that simply wasn't the Daleks' style. They believed in crude force with the minimum of subtlety. So if there was another trap, it would be in the console room and would be set to go off shortly after the bomb failed.

And then she saw it. There were two ornate brass lecterns over by the book cases, where there had only been one earlier. They looked like a matching pair of wing-spread eagles. The one on the left seemed to be somehow subtly wrong. It was as if it wasn't quite real, but only if you stared directly at it. Sam tapped the Doctor's arm and pointed.

He caught on immediately. 'Good girl,' he murmured, and scanned the extra lectern.

'Another bomb?' she asked, equally quietly. Somehow raising her voice near an explosive device didn't seem appropriate, as if loud noises might cause it to explode early.

'No,' he answered, slightly puzzled. 'It's reading more like a chameleon circuit... Odd...'

As Sam stared at the brass eagle, it seemed to shift. Its lines flowed, and it was as if something were unfolding itself. The air seemed to pucker, and then a familiar shape began to form. An eyestick, an arm and a gun raised to fire... The Dalek was morphing back from its disguise as the lectern.

The Doctor pushed her aside, diving the opposite way himself, as the Dalek fired.

The blast missed Sam by no more than a foot. The air sparked above her from the energy discharge, and her hair tingled from the static electricity. Staying on her hands and knees, she shot for cover behind the chair. The Doctor had plunged into hiding behind the columns. Sam peeked out, and saw that the Dalek was trying to decide which of them to go for first. It obviously decided that the Doctor was the more dangerous of the two, as it glided off after him.

Sam's heart was pounding crazily. A Dalek, here in the TARDIS! Why had the Doctor insisted on fiddling with the stupid lock!

On the floor, close to the console, Sam saw the Doctor's sonic screwdriver, and she had a momentary flash of hope. If only it was still set to that frequency that scrambled the Daleks' brains!

'Stay alive, Doctor,' she mumbled, and then dived across the floor toward the console. Her back itched, and she half-expected to feel a lethal blast cut her down as she moved. But she made it, grabbing the screwdriver and rolling into the cover of the console. The Dalek didn't seem to have even noticed her as it moved into the columned walkway.

Sam's nerves were frayed, but she had very little option here. Perhaps the Doctor could get somehow suprise the Dalek and pull another miraculous trick from his non-existent hat, but she didn't want to wait and see. She had to act as if this was up to her.

She was terrified and furious at the same time. She knew what a Dalek could do, and would do, without compunction. At the same time, she had always seen the TARDIS as a safe haven, somewhere where the insanity of her travels with the Doctor could be left at the doors. She could be comfortable there.

And the Dalek had ruined that security. She darted around. Was any of the furniture real? No, the Doctor's device had picked up only one... hadn't it?

Sam understood, clearly now, the Doctor's fear and loathing of the Daleks. Look how they were affecting her –

here she was, all in favour of saving the whales, talking problems away, and using one's brain, now grimly determined to fry the brains of a sentient being. She realised she couldn't condemn the Thals' attitudes quite as strongly now. The Daleks were evil incarnate. You had to fight back.

She crouched behind the console, staring at the columns. There was a flash of motion, and she realised that the Dalek was working its way down towards the alien altar at the far end. Maybe that was where the Doctor was hiding. Preparing a trap, perhaps?

Well, this was no time to sit around. Clutching the sonic screwdriver tightly, she shot out of hiding, heading for the end of the walkway. Maybe she could ambush the Dalek before it was aware of her...

Then she saw the Doctor. He was flattened against the final column, a tense expression on his face as he listened to the approach of the Dalek. He was obviously hoping to catch it by surprise. Sam stopped breathing, watching tensely as the Dalek drew closer to the pillar where the Doctor was hiding.

And then something made it suspicious. It moved out, whirling with surprising speed to try and catch the Doctor out. The gun was ready.

Sam knew that the Doctor didn't stand a chance, even as he dived for the cover of the altar. She screamed wordlessly to try and distract the Dalek, and rushed toward it.

The Dalek whirled and fired at her as she dived for her life. Once again, the electronic bolt barely missed her, heating the air about her. She hit the floor and winced from the impact. The blaster focused on her again as she struggled to bring the sonic screwdriver up.

Only she no longer held it. The jarring fall had shaken it

from her unsteady grip, and it had gone sliding across the floor. It was now behind the Dalek, totally out of reach. For a split second, she stared into the barrel that held her death.

And then the Doctor leapt from hiding, scooping up the screwdriver and slapping it against the Dalek's dome.

The gun sputtered, the arm jerked, and the eyestick stood straight up. The Doctor did not move the sonic screwdriver from the Dalek casing for a long time. Finally he switched it off, his face ashen, slowly backing away.

Sam looked at him as she scrambled to her feet, then collapsed, emotionally and physically drained.

The Doctor hurried to her. 'Are you all right?' he asked.

'Nothing a few years in a sanitarium won't cure,' she groaned. 'I'm battered, bruised, shocked and in dire need of a bath.' Then she smiled. 'Other than that, I'm perfectly fine, thank you.'

'Good.' He helped her to her feet. 'You just sit down and I'll make you a nice cup of tea to steady your nerves. I'm going to repair the lock before I do anything else.'

Sam gestured to the frozen Dalek. 'What about Fred there?"

The Doctor thought. 'Presumably it was monitoring our existence for the Dalek Prime. When it's sensors reported we weren't blown to bits, presumably it was told to do the job instead.'

Sam shook her head, dismally. 'I meant, what do we do with it now?'

He smiled. 'We'll clean up later,' he decided.

'Do you think it'd make a good planter?' she asked. 'Knock off the top and plant some tiger lilies...' She realized she was rambling.

Sam didn't protest as he scooped her up and carried her

to the chair. The Doctor busied himself making the tea, while Sam just soaked up the silence.

'Is it over this time?' she asked anxiously. She didn't think she could go through any more right now.

'Yes,' the Doctor assured her. 'It's over. For now.' He frowned slightly. 'But the Daleks won't simply give up, you know. If you stay with me, I think I can guarantee you a return match some day.'

'There's something to look forward to,' she muttered. She accepted the cup of Darjeeling he poured her and settled back to relax. 'But I'll worry about that tomorrow.'

'Yes,' the Doctor agreed. 'Tomorrow.'

EPILOGUE: SKARO

The Dalek Prime studied the time-tracking equipment in the secondary control room. Repairs to the primary had already begun. Work crews were moving shattered Daleks, and patching the more dangerous problems. It would take quite some time for the city to return to normal. But at least it could return to normal.

The Gold Dalek next to him adjusted the tracking. 'The TARDIS has survived the attack,' it reported. 'The experimental Infiltration Unit we reactivated inside the TARDIS has also been disabled.'

'Noted.' The Dalek Prime considered. 'The Doctor is very resourceful. He has escaped us this time, but our paths will cross again.' This was a minor setback to his plans, nothing more. Even the loss of the factory from the Thal ship had turned out to be unimportant. That particular contingency had not, in the end, been needed. Davros was dead, and his entire faction purged from the Dalek race.

It was time to move on. Though the war had cost the Daleks much, they had survived, and would soon be stronger than ever. They were all of one mind – the Dalek Prime's mind – and one purpose.

'We will rebuild,' he stated. 'We will grow stronger. And then we will strike. The galaxy will be ours. Such is the destiny of the Daleks. Nothing will stand before us!

'Nothing!'